MONEY IN THE MORGUE

THE INSPECTOR ALLEYN MYSTERIES

A Man Lay Dead
Enter a Murderer
The Nursing Home Murder
Death in Ecstasy
Vintage Murder
Artists in Crime
Death in a White Tie
Overture to Death
Death at the Bar
Surfeit of Lampreys
Death and the Dancing Footman
Colour Scheme
Died in the Wool
Final Curtain
Swing, Brother, Swing
Opening Night
Spinsters in Jeopardy
Scales of Justice
Off With His Head
Singing in the Shrouds
False Scent
Hand in Glove
Dead Water
Death at the Dolphin
Clutch of Constables
When in Rome
Tied up in Tinsel
Black As He's Painted
Last Ditch
Grave Mistake
Photo-Finish
Light Thickens
Death on the Air and Other Stories

NGAIO MARSH
& STELLA DUFFY

Money
in the
Morgue

THE NEW INSPECTOR ALLEYN MYSTERY

COLLINS
CRIME
CLUB

COLLINS CRIME CLUB
An imprint of HarperCollins*Publishers* Ltd
1 London Bridge Street,
London SE1 9GF

www.harpercollins.co.uk

Published by Collins Crime Club 2018

A catalogue record for this book is available from the British Library

ISBN: 978-0-00-820710-6 (HB)
ISBN: 978-0-00-820711-3 (TPB)

Set in Sabon LT Std by Palimpsest Book Production Limited, Falkirk, Stirlingshire

Printed and bound in the UK by CPI Group (UK) Ltd, Croydon CR0 4YY

MIX
Paper from
responsible sources
FSC™ C007454

CAST OF CHARACTERS

Mr Glossop	*A payroll delivery clerk*
Matron Ashdown	*The Matron of Mount Seager Hospital*
Sister Comfort	*A Sister at Mount Seager Hospital*
Father O'Sullivan	*The local vicar*
Sarah Warne	*The hospital Transport Driver*
Sydney Brown	*The grandson of old Mr Brown*
Rosamund Farquharson	*A hospital clerk*
Private Bob Pawcett	*A convalescent soldier*
Corporal Cuthbert Brayling	*A convalescent soldier*
Private Maurice Sanders	*A convalescent soldier*
Dr Luke Hughes	*Doctor at Mount Seager Hospital*
Roderick Alleyn	*Chief Detective Inspector, CID*
Old Mr Brown	*A dying man*
Will Kelly	*The night porter*
Sergeant Bix	*A Sergeant in the New Zealand Army*
Duncan Blaikie	*A local farmer*

Various patients—convalescent soldiers and civilians
Several night nurses, nurse aides and VADs

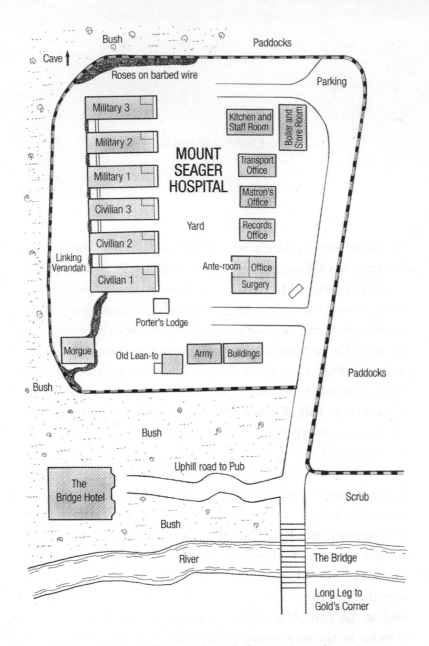

Mount Seager Hospital and the surrounding area

CHAPTER ONE

At about eight o'clock on a disarmingly still midsummer evening, Mr Glossop telephoned from the Transport Office at Mount Seager Hospital to his headquarters twenty miles away across the plains. He made angry jabs with his blunt forefinger at the dial—and to its faint responsive tinkling an invisible curtain rose upon a series of events that were to be confined within the dark hours of that short summer night, bounded between dusk and dawn. So closely did these events follow the arbitrary design of a play that the temptation to represent Mr Glossop as an overture cannot be withstood.

The hospital, now almost settling down for the night, had assumed an air of enclosed and hushed activity. Lights appeared behind open windows and from the yard that ran between the hospital offices and the wards one could see the figures of nurses on night duty moving quietly about their business. Mingled with the click of the telephone dial was the sound of distant tranquil voices and, from the far end of the yard, the very occasional strains of music from a radio in the new army buildings.

The window of the Records Office stood open. Through

it one looked across the yard to Wards 2 and 3, now renamed Civilian 2 and Civilian 3 since the military had taken over Wards 4–6 and remade them as Military 1, 2, and 3. Those in Military 3 were still very ill, those in Military 1, their quarantine and spirits up, were well into the restlessly bored stage of their recuperation. Each ward had a covered porch, and a short verandah at the rear linking it to the next ward. Before each verandah stood a rich barrier of climbing roses. The brief New Zealand twilight was not quite at an end but already the spendthrift fragrance of the roses approached its nightly zenith. The setting, in spite of itself, was romantic. Mr Glossop, however, was not conscious of romance. He was cross and anxious and when he spoke into the telephone his voice held overtones of resentment.

'Glossop speaking,' he said. 'I'm still at Mount Seager Hospital. If I've said it once I've said it a hundred times, they ought to do something about that van.' He paused. A Lilliputian voice reaching him from a small town twenty miles away quacked industriously in the receiver. 'I know, I know,' said Mr Glossop resentfully, 'and it's my digestion that's had to take it. Here I am with the pay-box till Gawd knows when and I don't like it. I said I don't like it. It's OK, go and tell him. Go and tell the whole bloody Board. I want to know what I'm meant to do now.'

A footfall, firm and crisp, sounded on the asphalt yard. In a moment the stream of light from the office door was intercepted. The old wooden steps gave the slightest creak and in the doorway stood a short compact woman dressed in white with a veil on her head and a scarlet cape about her shoulders. Mr Glossop made restless movements with his legs and changed the colour of his voice. He smiled in

2

a deprecating manner at the newcomer and he addressed himself to the telephone. 'That's right,' he said with false heartiness. 'Still we mustn't grumble. Er—Matron suggests I get a tow down with the morning bus . . . Transport Driver . . . No, it's—it's,' Mr Glossop swallowed, 'it's a lady,' he said. The Lilliputian voice spoke at some length. 'Well, we hope so,' said Mr Glossop with a nervous laugh.

'You will be quite safe, Mr Glossop,' the woman in the doorway said. 'Miss Warne is an experienced driver.'

Mr Glossop nodded and smirked. 'An experienced driver,' he echoed, 'Matron says, an experienced driver.'

The telephone uttered a metallic enquiry. 'How about the pay-box?' it asked sharply.

Mr Glossop lowered his voice. 'I've paid out, here,' he said cautiously. 'Nowhere else. I should have been at the end of the rounds by now. Tonight, I'll watch it,' he added fretfully.

'Tell him,' the Matron said tranquilly, 'that I shall lock it in my safe.' She came into the office and sat at one of the two desks. She was a stocky woman with watchful eyes and a compassionate mouth.

Mr Glossop finished his conversation in a hurry, hung up the receiver and got to his feet. His tremendous circumference rose above the edge of the table and was rotated to face the Matron. He passed his hand over his face, glanced at it and pulled out a handkerchief. 'Warm,' he said.

'Very,' said the Matron. 'Nurse!'

'Yes, Matron?' A very small figure in a blue uniform and white cap rose from behind the second desk where she had been studiously avoiding overhearing Mr Glossop's telephone call.

3

'Hasn't Miss Farquharson got back yet?'

'No, Matron.'

'Then I'm afraid you must stay on duty until either she or Miss Warne returns. I wish to speak to Miss Farquharson when she comes in.'

'Yes, Matron,' said the small nurse in a very small voice.

'I'm extremely annoyed with her. And now I want you to telephone Mr Brown's grandson. Mr Sydney Brown. The number's on the desk there. Mr Brown has asked for him again. He could come out on the next bus but it would be quicker if he used his own car, and possibly safer as there's every chance we'll have a storm to break this weather before the evening's out. Tell him, as plainly as you can, that his grandfather is adamant he sees him, and time is not on his side. I really do think young Mr Brown ought to have visited before now.'

'Yes, Matron.'

'Somebody very sick?' asked Mr Glossop, opening his eyes wide and drawing down the corners of his mouth.

'Possibly dying. It must be said, we have expected this for weeks and the gentleman seems to rally every time. It cannot go on though, and it's very important to the old man that he sees his grandson,' said the Matron crisply before turning back to the nurse and adding, 'Father O'Sullivan is cycling over from visiting a local parishioner to sit with old Mr Brown, make sure he finds me as soon as he arrives, will you? He arranged this visit a few days ago, but I'd like to update him on the old gentleman's condition first. Now come along with me, Mr Glossop, we'd better lock up that money of yours. Is there much?'

'It's all in the box,' he said, and lifted a great japanned case from the floor. 'Should have been empty by now, you know. Four more staffs are paid off after I leave here. As it is—'

'Mount Seager Hospital speaking,' said the little nurse into the telephone. 'I have another message for Mr Sydney Brown, please.'

'Just on a thousand,' said Mr Glossop behind his hand.

'God bless my soul, of course I understood you were carrying payrolls for several locations, but that is an enormous responsibility,' rejoined the Matron.

'Exactly what I'm always telling Central Office,' Mr Glossop replied, glad to have the Matron's understanding.

They went out to the steps. The little nurse's voice followed them: 'Yes, I'm afraid so. Not long, Matron says . . . Yes, he's asked for you again.'

'Just along here,' said the Matron.

Mr Glossop followed her down the yard that formed a wide lane, flanked on one side by offices, each with its distinguishing notice, and on the other by the wards set at intervals in sun-scorched plots, their utility gloriously interspersed by the roses which so recklessly floundered over the barb wire fences in front of the connecting verandahs. From the covered porch of each ward came a glow of diffused light. The asphalt lane was striped with warmth. The usual tang of mountain air was missing in the sultry evening and the subdued reek of hospital disinfectants seemed particularly strong to Glossop's sensitive nose.

As they drew level with Military 1, the porch door slammed open and in a moment a heavy figure in nurses' uniform flounced into the yard. A chorus of raucous voices yelled in unison: 'And *don't* let it occur again.'

The nurse advanced upon Mr Glossop and the Matron. Her face was in shadow, but her glasses caught a gleam of reflected light. A badge of office which she wore on the bosom of her uniform was agitated and her veil quivered. She took two or three short steps and stopped, clasping her hands behind her back. In the ward the raucous voices continued in a falsetto chorus: 'Temperatures normal! Pulses normal! Bowels moved! *Aren't* we lucky?'

'Matron!' said the stout nurse in an agitated whisper. 'May I speak to you?'

'Yes, Sister Comfort, what is it?'

'Those men—in there—it's disgraceful. This entire notion of allowing them leeway now that they're recuperating—'

'Is a well-proven method for speeding up recovery. Rest and silence, Sister Comfort, is the old-fashioned way, the men benefit tremendously when we give them something to think about that is neither their illness nor their return to the war. Distraction is a nurse's best ally. However, I do agree there's far too much noise,' the Matron nodded. 'Will you excuse us, Mr Glossop?'

Mr Glossop moved away.

'Now, Sister,' said Matron.

'It's disgraceful,' Sister Comfort repeated in a grumbling voice. 'I've never been treated like it in my life before. The impertinence!'

'What are they up to?'

'*Temperatures normal! Pulses normal! Bowels moved! Aren't we lucky?*'

'Just because I happened to pass the remark when I'd been round the ward,' Sister Comfort said breathlessly. 'They turn everything I say into ribaldry. There's no other word. I can't speak without them calling after me like parrots. And another thing, three of them are still out.'

'Which three, Sister?'

6

'Sanders, Pawcett and Brayling, of course. They had leave to go as far as the bench at the main gate.' Sister Comfort's voice trailed away on a note of nervousness. There was a brief silence broken only by the Matron.

'I thought I had made it quite clear,' Matron said, 'that they were all to be in bed by seven. Distraction by day, rest by night, you know the rules.'

'But, I can't help it. They *won't* obey orders,' complained Sister Comfort.

'They're getting better,' Matron said, 'and they're bored.'

'But how can I keep order? Almost ninety soldiers and hardly any trained nurses. The VADs are not to be trusted. I know, Matron. I've seen what goes on. It's disgusting.'

'*Nurse! Come over here and hold my hand*,' sang the patients.

'*There!*' cried Sister Comfort. 'And the girls go and do it. I've seen them. And not only that—that Farquharson girl in the Records Office—'

'*Nursey, Nursey, going to get worsey.*'

'*Come and hold my hand.*'

'Where is Sergeant Bix?' asked the Matron.

'Several of the men are due to be discharged this weekend coming and he has a huge amount of paperwork to get through before he can let them go. He's not much use anyway, Matron, in my opinion, far too warm with the men. They're the worst lot of patients we've ever had. Never in my life have I been spoken to—'

'*I'll report you to Matron*,' said an isolated falsetto. '*Call yourselves gentlemen? Well!*'

'Did you hear that?' Sister Comfort demanded. '*Did you hear it?*'

'I heard,' said Matron grimly. The chorus was renewed.

7

She folded her hands lightly at her waist and with an air of composure walked through the porch doors into the ward. The chorus faded away in three seconds. The isolated voice bawled a final line and died out in a note of exquisite embarrassment. Mr Glossop, who had hung off and on in the doorway to Matron's office, approached Sister Comfort.

'She's knocked them,' he said. 'She's a corker, isn't she?' He waited for a reply and getting none added with an air of roguishness: 'It's a wonder she hasn't made some lucky chap very happy, isn't it?'

With a brusque movement Sister Comfort twisted her head so that the light from Matron's office fell across her face. Mr Glossop took a step backwards and then checked as if in surprise at himself.

'What is the matter?' asked Sister Comfort harshly.

'Nothing, I'm sure,' Mr Glossop stammered. 'Nothing at all. You looked a little pale, that's all.'

'I'm tired out. The work in that ward's enough to kill you. It's the lack of discipline. They want military police.'

'Matron's fixed them for you,' said Mr Glossop, and recovering from whatever effect he had experienced he added in his fat and unctuous voice: 'Yes, she's a beautiful woman, you know. Not appreciated.'

'I appreciate her,' said Sister Comfort loudly. 'We're very friendly, you know. Of course, in public we have to be formal—Matron and Sister and all that—but away from here she's quite different. Quite different.'

'You're privileged,' Mr Glossop murmured and cleared his throat.

'Well, I think I am,' Sister Comfort agreed, more amiably. The Matron returned and with a brisk nod to Mr Glossop led the way into her office. After they had left her, Sister Comfort stood stock-still in the yard, her head bent down as if she listened attentively to some distant, almost inaudible sound. Presently, however, she turned into Military I but went no further than the porch; standing there in a dark corner and looking out obliquely across the yard at the Records Office. A few moments later a VAD scurried out of the ward. She experienced what she afterwards described as one hell of a jolt when she saw Sister Comfort's long heavy-jowled face staring at her out of the shadow.

'Doing the odd spot of snooping, that's what she was up to, the old stinker,' said the VAD. 'She's got a mind like a sink. And anyway,' the VAD added complacently, 'my fiancé's in the air force.'

CHAPTER TWO

Matron took a key from her pocket and opened the safe.

Mr Glossop hesitated and she looked to him, 'Yes?'

'Are you quite sure you don't have a single spare tyre out here, Matron?'

'As I told you earlier, Mr Glossop, on both occasions that you asked, we do not. There are two spare tyres for the transport bus, that's all. You know as well as I do that the bus is far bigger than your van, the tyres simply won't fit. We've all had to make sacrifices for the war, up-to-the-minute repairs and plenty of extras in stock being just two of them.'

'If you say so,' he grumbled.

She looked at Glossop's pay-box, sizing it up with a practised eye. 'I'm afraid that great case of yours is too big,' she said. 'Try.'

Mr Glossop approached the japanned box to the safe. It was at least three inches too long.

'Oh, Lord!' he said. 'Things have been like that with me all day.'

'We shall have to find something else, that's all.'

'It'll be all right. I won't let it out of my sight, Matron. You bet I won't.'

'It'll be out of your sight when you're asleep, Mr Glossop.'

'I won't—'

Matron shook her head. 'No. I can't take the responsibility. We'll give you a shake-down in the anteroom to the Surgery. I don't expect you'll be disturbed, but we can't have the door locked, our medicines are stored in there and I can't guarantee something won't be needed in the night. The money's done up in separate lots, isn't it?'

'It is, yes. I've got it down to a system. Standardized rates of pay, you know. I could lay my hand on anybody's pay with my eyes shut. Each lot in a separate envelope. My system.'

'In that case,' said Matron briskly, 'a large canvas bag will do nicely.'

She took one, folded neatly, from the back of the safe. 'There you are. I'll get you to put it in that and you'd better watch me lock it up.'

With an air of sulky resignation, Mr Glossop emptied one after another of the many compartments in his japanned box, snapping rubber bands round each group of envelopes before he stowed them in the bag. The Matron watched him, controlling any impatience that may have been aroused by the slow coarse movements of his hands. In the last and largest compartment lay a wad of pound notes held down by a metal clip.

'I haven't made these up yet,' Mr Glossop said. 'Ran out of envelopes.'

'You'd better count them, hadn't you?'

'There's a hundred, Matron, and five pounds in coins.' He wetted his thumb disagreeably and flipped the notes over.

11

'Dirty things,' said the Matron unexpectedly.

'They look lovely to me,' Mr Glossop rejoined and gave a stuttering laugh.

He fastened the notes, dropped them in the bag and shovelled the coins after them. Matron tied the neck of the bag with a piece of string from her desk. 'Wait a moment,' she said. 'There's a stick of sealing-wax in the top right-hand drawer. Will you give it to me?'

'You *are* particular,' sighed Mr Glossop.

'I prefer to be business-like. Have you a match?'

He gave her his box of matches and whistled between his teeth while she melted the sealing-wax and sealed the knot. 'There!' she said. 'Now put it in the safe, if you please.'

Mr Glossop with difficulty compressed himself into a squatting posture before the safe. The light from the office lamp glistened upon his tight greasy curls and along the rolls of fat at the back of his neck and the bulging surface of his shoulders and arms. As he pushed the bag into the lower half of the safe he might have been a votary of some monetary god. Grunting slightly he slammed the door. Matron, with sharp bird-like movements, locked the safe and returned the key to her pocket. Mr Glossop struggled to his feet. 'Now we needn't worry ourselves,' said Matron.

As she turned to leave, the little nurse from the Records Office appeared in the doorway. 'Yes?' Matron said. 'Do you want me?'

'Father O'Sullivan has come, Matron.'

Beyond the nurse stood a priest with a nakedly pink face and combed-back silver hair. He carried a small case and appeared impatient to see the Matron.

'Excuse me, Mr Glossop, this is quite urgent, you know.

I'll send someone to fetch you to the Surgery anteroom,' Matron said, and folding her hands at her waist walked out into the yard leaving Mr Glossop wiping his brow at the exertion he had just endured. He heard their voices die away as they moved off in the direction of Mr Brown's private room.

'. . . not long . . .'

'. . . Ah . . . such a time . . . Is he . . .?'

'. . . Very. Failing rapidly, but then he does keep rallying. It can't possibly go on, of course. I'm not one to believe in miracles, although with the storm . . .'

The telephone in the Records Office pealed and the little nurse hurried back to answer it. To Mr Glossop her voice sounded like an echo: '. . . Mr Brown's condition is very low,' she was saying. 'Yes, I'm afraid so . . . failing rapidly.'

Mr Glossop gazed vacantly across the yard at Military 1. His attention was arrested by something white that shifted in the porch entrance. He moved a little closer and then, since he was of a curious disposition and extremely short-sighted, several paces closer still. He was profoundly disconcerted to find himself staring up into Sister Comfort's rimless spectacles.

'Beg pardon, I'm sure,' he stammered. 'I didn't know—getting dark, isn't it? My mistake!'

'Not at all,' said Sister Comfort. 'I could see *you* quite clearly. Good night.'

She stalked off, down the steps and along the yard, no doubt to harangue yet another benighted soldier, and Mr Glossop turned away with elephantine airiness.

'Now what the hell,' he wondered, 'is that old cow up to?'

*

While Matron took Father O'Sullivan to minister to Mr Brown, Mr Glossop spent the next twenty minutes fidgeting and worrying in her office. He sat first in the chair opposite Matron's desk, a lower chair than the one behind her desk, ideal for chastising foolhardy young nurses and miscreant soldiers, he assumed. He loosened his tie still further and rolled up the sleeves of his creased shirt. 'Too damn hot by half,' he thought, hoping Matron was right and the storm that had been threatening for days would finally make its way over the mountains tonight, clearing the air. 'Not too wet though,' he added to his wishes, 'that damn bridge is worrisome enough, without the river rising as well.' The chair creaking beneath his weight, he struggled to his feet and paced several times around Matron's office. With effort, he bent down and tried the handle on the safe, reassuring himself that it was secure. He looked outside again, across to the row of wards and along the collection of offices hoping that Matron might be on her way back. He wanted someone to sort him out with that cot for the night, he wanted to get some sleep, and above all, he wanted to be on his way with his stack of cash, far too much money to be sitting way the hell out here, locked safe or no.

Wiping his brow and muttering dire imprecations against the weather, the Central Office, the roads and the general state of the nation in wartime, he sat down again, this time in Matron's own chair. Her desk was covered in papers and he absent-mindedly flicked through them, misplacing the carefully-ordered typed pages of accounts and the handwritten notes.

He shook himself when he realized what he'd done, he'd hate to get in Matron's bad books and he replaced the sheets carefully one on top of the other, grumbling to himself, 'If I don't get away from here at the crack of dawn there'll be hell to pay, four more rounds to do. Four more and all of them to be paid before Christmas Day with the shops closing up soon enough and turkeys and stuffing and whatnot to cross off the lists. Hell to pay. None of it down to me, not a bit. I told them that old banger had no more in her. If I said it once, I said it a dozen times. I need a new van and hang the expense. Well, now they know the cost.'

Matron checked her watch as she returned to her office. A lovely silver watch, held on an elegant bar, it was given to her by a young man she'd known long ago. He had shyly offered it up just before he left for the last war, the one they had promised would end them all. They had been wrong and the young man had not returned. Not a day passed that she didn't think of him, and not in a foolish way either, she admitted to herself, standing at the door to her office looking at the dozing irritant that was Mr Glossop, seated in her own chair. With a start, she noticed the papers on her desk had been moved, she crossed to the desk and, making no attempt to keep quiet for the sleeping interloper, she gathered the papers together, settling them once more with a satisfying thump.

'Well, there we are,' Glossop woke with a start, pretending he had only closed his eyes for a short while. 'And how's it with—you know, the fellow who's—'

'Dying?'

'Yes, yes, that's the—and the priest chap?'

'Father O'Sullivan is with him now.'

'Oh I see,' Mr Glossop said disapprovingly, 'All the Catholic doings, smells and bells and that carry on, is it?'

15

'Not at all, Father O'Sullivan is an Anglican priest,' Matron replied, attempting to squash his interest with the look that had her young nurses quaking and, to her chagrin, appeared to further encourage Mr Glossop.

'Right you are, Matron, I'm sure you'll tell me when I'm over-stepping bounds. I like a woman who knows her own business.'

Matron decided to ignore him. 'It's just gone eight-thirty, Mr Brown's grandson is coming in on the nine o'clock transport. I hope he makes it in time. You'll have to excuse me now, Mr Glossop, I've work to do.'

Glossop looked at the desk in front of him and realized that the papers he'd been fiddling with had been tidied out of his reach and that he himself was in Matron's seat.

'Yes, yes of course. You don't want a spot of company? Someone to help you go through all those figures? Tricky stuff, numbers, and I've a good eye for accuracy, that's why they gave me the job, of course. You've got to have a trusted man on the pay round.'

'Thank you, but no,' she cut him off. 'If you head next door to the Records Office, the young nurse there will take care of you. She knows where the cots are kept and where you're to sleep and I dare say she'll be happy to show you to the kitchen. You'll have to fend for yourself, mind you, our kitchen staff are daily and they left on the last transport back to town. Goodnight, Mr Glossop.'

Knowing himself dismissed, Glossop reluctantly left Matron's office and went out into the darkening night. And it was still too damn hot by half.

CHAPTER THREE

At nine o'clock Red Cross Transport Driver Sarah Warne swung the Mount Seager bus round Gold's Corner into the last stretch of the route, known locally as the Long Leg. From Gold's Corner to the bridge the Long Leg ran straight for fifteen miles across the plains towards the foothills. Before the blackout she used to be able to see the hospital lights for the whole way but since Japan came in the front windows had gone blank. In the aftermath of twilight Sarah could just make out a black mass of buildings against the royal texture of the hills. Behind the hills, the main range, touched on its pinnacles with perpetual snow, awaited the night against a luminous sky. Although the sun was now below the horizon the cusp of Mount Seager was tinctured miraculously with clear rose. The windscreen of the bus framed a vast landscape quite free of human interest, unscarred by human occupation, moving because of its remoteness.

The road was unsealed and from time to time pieces of shingle flew up and banged against the floor of the bus. Sarah knew where the worst pot-holes lay but could not always avoid them. Every time they bumped across a gap or skidded in loose shingle the VADs screamed cheerfully, if a little less loudly than usual because of the young man who sat beside Sarah in the front seat. This was Mr Sydney Brown and they all knew that he was going up to the hospital because his grandfather had been asking for him for weeks and now the old man was nearing the end. Sarah spoke to him once or twice but whatever her observation his replies could be guessed before they were uttered. 'It is, too,' 'I couldn't say,' 'That's right,' he said in offended undertones. Sarah thought that perhaps, unlike her, he had not yet seen death at first hand and was sorry for him.

The mountains assumed an incredible depth of blue and the foothills turned more darkly purple. Their margins, folded together in a pattern of firm curves, were faintly haloed with light. The road ran forward into nothingness. The plains on either side of the road and stretching out behind them had taken on a bleached look, seeming to fade rather than to darken as night fell, turning the whole scene into an other-worldly monochrome. Sarah watched the road and her petrol gauge. With one layer of her mind she attended to her job, with another she saw that the landscape was quite beautiful, and with yet another she hunted for things to say to Mr Sydney Brown, or shout to the VADs. Further back, in a hinterland of half-conscious thoughts she wondered if Dr Luke Hughes would come into the Transport Office for his letters that night when she had sorted the mail she carried in addition to her passengers. This last conjecture gradually took precedence in her mind so that when unexpectedly Mr Sydney Brown spoke of his own accord, it was a second or two before she realized that he was joining in conversation with the VADs.

'Lordly Stride,' said Sydney Brown.

'I beg your pardon?' cried Sarah.

'Lordly Stride came in and paid a record price,' said Sydney. 'I heard it on the air while I was waiting for the bus. Rank outsider.'

An instant babble broke out in the bus.

'She's done it! That's Farquharson's horse. That's right, it's her horse!' And then the attenuated inevitable coda to most of the VADs' dialogues: 'Thass raht.'

'What are you all talking about?' Sarah demanded. She was answered immediately by each of her eight passengers. Miss Rosamund Farquharson, the Records Office clerk who usually worked days, had swapped her duty for the overnight shift, and had gone to the races down-country. She had travelled into town on the morning bus and told everybody she was going to back Lordly Stride in the last race. 'We all said she was mad,' the VADs explained, but the truth was Rosamund Farquharson was in a mess and needed the money, so much so that what might have felt like a steep gamble to her colleagues had seemed a genuine lifeline when she laid the bet, fingers crossed and whistling hope.

'You *are* a lot of gossips,' Sarah said mildly.

'It's not gossip, Transport,' shouted one of the VADs. '*She* tells everybody about it. She's not fussy, she doesn't care who knows. That dress she bought for the races—well, *bought!* She said herself there was only one shop left where they'd give her credit.'

'She's mad,' said a small nurse profoundly.

'I'll say.'

'Did you hear about her and old Comfort?' asked a solo voice.

'Eee—yes!' the chorus chanted.

'No. What?' the nurse demanded.

'She caught Rosie kissing one of the boys when she brought the mail round.'

'She's mad.'

'Comfort or Rosie?'

'Both.'

'I'll say.'

'But Roz is being a fool to herself.'

'No need to ask which of the lads it was.'

Mr Sydney Brown cleared his throat. The voices faltered and were obliterated by the grind of tyres on shingle, body rattles from the bus, and by the not inconsiderable racket of the engine. Sarah began to wonder uneasily on the subject of their discussion. She was surprised to discover in herself a violent distaste for this gossip about Rosamund Farquharson; surprised, because their friendship was a casual affair based on a similarity of experience rather than of taste. They had met properly in the Mount Seager Records Office. Each of them had returned to New Zealand after a long absence in England but while Miss Farquharson perpetually bewailed the lost gaieties of her glorious exist-ence in the London of art school and galleries, Sarah tried very hard to avoid such lamentations. Since the outbreak of war she too had suffered from a painful nostalgia for the old days. Where Rosamund had attended art school, Sarah had three years at Oxford and one at a dramatic school under her belt, in addition to another two years spent struggling to find small pickings in indifferent compa-nies. While Rosamund's memories were constantly invoked in a rose mist of past bliss, Sarah's were solid and genuine. After exhausting months in weekly rep, in the farthest flung corners of what her parents' generation of New Zealanders still referred to as 'Home', Sarah eventually fluked her way into a West End production and the most poignant of all her recollections were of London. She was called back to New Zealand for a family crisis when her younger sister became ill. The sister had been expected to recover, but her shocking and sudden death made it impossible for Sarah to leave their widowed mother alone in New Zealand. With a sensation of panic, she had stayed on, and then she was trapped by the war.

'You're lucky to have got away. England's a good country to be out of now,' the Mount Seager day porter once said, and Sarah had enormously warmed to Rosamund Farquharson when the usually cynical and smart blonde replied fiercely, 'Do you like to keep clear when your best friends are against it? I should think not. And nor do we.'

A little self-righteously, perhaps, they had formed an alliance. They had few tastes in common. Rosamund had been given two years at the London art school by a generous English aunt. She had, it appeared, been hailed back to New Zealand by her parents upon distracted representations made by this same aunt. Her interests were focused so ruthlessly on young men that she had the air of being a sort of specialist. The leap from small town New Zealand and the humble abode of a school teacher's family to Bloomsbury studio parties, had reacted upon her like the emotional equivalent of an overdose of thyroid gland. Rosamund had listened first with bewilderment, then with encouragement and finally with the liveliest enthusiasm to monotonous conversations about eroticism, at that time the fashionable topic among art-students. She quickly collected an amazing jargon and a smattering of semi-technical information which, like some precocious reincarnation of the Ancient Mariner, she was quite unable to keep to herself. Rosamund was given to using tediously blasphemous and indecent language, and her favourite recreation was a process she called 'waking up the old dump'. At first Sarah had a notion that most of Rosamund's dissipations ruled these purple patches to her telling of them; but with the appearance of Private Maurice Sanders among the recovering men of Military 1 she was obliged to change her opinion.

'This time,' Sarah thought with a sigh, 'I'm afraid she is doing an odd spot of the bonnet-and-windmill business. And with Private Sanders! How she can!'

She switched on her headlamps. About two hundred yards ahead the Long Leg ended abruptly. They had reached the edge of the plains. A great river made its exit from the mountains a mile or two to the west, flowing down from the foothills. With the sheer banks of the riverbed the plains ended as sharply as if they had been sliced away by a gargantuan knife, the foothills rising steeply above and the mountains proper beyond. Sarah changed down. The Long Leg dived into a precipitous cutting and finished emphatically at the deep chasm of the river. The wheels of the bus rattled across the wooden planks of the old bridge. The headlamps found white painted rails and uneven planking, loose boards clattering ominously beneath the weight of the bus. Sarah heard one of the VADs say to another, 'I hate this part of the trip, the bridge is far too rickety for my liking.'

'I'll say,' her pal replied, 'and that wooden rail wouldn't stop a dog from falling in, let alone this bus.'

They giggled nervously as Sarah changed down again

and in the split-second while the gears were disengaged the voice of the river could be heard, a vast cold thunder among boulders below the high bridge. As they reached the far side vague shapes of trees and a roof appeared against the steep hill to their left.

'You can hardly see Johnson's pub in the blackout,' said a cheerful VAD.

'Awkward for Private Sanders,' said the small nurse. There followed a subdued tittering.

'I reckon he could find it blindfold.'

'Shut up. You're not supposed to know.'

'Poor old Farquharson.'

With a vicious jab, Sarah sounded the horn. The VADs screamed in unison.

'What's that for, Transport? Have we run over anything?'

'A reputation,' said Sarah.

After a final short, steep climb she pulled the bus carefully into the hospital driveway and parked with a shout to the VADs to remember that Matron expected the patients in bed and sleeping by now, and not to disturb them. She turned her attention to young Sydney Brown. With a sudden wave of sympathy she saw the hospital as he must see it, not the ramshackle collection of well-worn buildings she had come to know and value as a genuine place of sanctuary for damaged civilians and out-of-place servicemen. To Sydney Brown the scent of carbolic, the hush now that they were between the wild river and the immense reach of the mountains up ahead, this must have felt a place of foreboding, a dark and jumbled site where his grandfather lay dying. She smiled kindly at him, hoping he could see her in the reflection from the headlamps, bouncing off the back of the storeroom and the boilerhouse, the peeling paint on the old weatherboards even more obvious in the light from the headlamps than during the blistering heat of the day.

'I'll take you to Matron, shall I, Mr Brown? We can get you a cup of tea and then in to see your grandfather. I know Father O'Sullivan was expected, so—'

Her voice petered out. What more was there to say?

'I don't want tea, I'll just see the old man.'

Sydney Brown was up and out of his seat, down the steps, and waiting.

Sarah took out her torch, turned off the headlights, and nodded, pocketing the keys. 'Yes, of course, come along.'

Mr Glossop's slow, heavy tread had not long retreated back across the asphalt yard when Matron heard the rattle and squeak of the nine o'clock transport rolling up the driveway and into the parking area. The VADs would take a few minutes to sort themselves out from the journey. Sarah Warne was a sensible girl, one of the few she could rely upon, which meant she had a moment to gather her thoughts before she was needed to brief the night staff with Sister Comfort.

Retrieving the paperwork she had hurriedly tidied out of Mr Glossop's reach, she looked through the papers. Surely he wouldn't have pried into her private correspondence? She frowned, because that was exactly the kind of behaviour she'd expect of the infuriating fellow. Even so, he wouldn't have had time to look through them thoroughly. She sat forward in her chair and spread out the papers before her. Almost twenty-five years here at Mount Seager and, while there had been difficult years, in particular

24

during the influenza epidemic after the last war, when she was a newly appointed ward sister and they had been stretched far beyond their capacity, both to care and to cope, things had never before come to this. The bill for roof repairs to the Surgery was two months overdue. After a dreadfully wet winter, they simply hadn't been able to risk the old corrugated iron roof any longer, it was bad enough in any other ward, but a serious health hazard in the Surgery. A third letter from the local bakery, with a curt note attached from Elsie Pocock, a woman she had known her whole life, and now Matron found herself crossing the road in town to avoid speaking to her. Two further angry demands for payment, one from the farmer who supplied sides of beef '*at cost!*' as he reminded her in the letter, '*at cost!*', and another from the milk factory. The extra beds, the military wards commandeered when the men were sent home with scarlet fever and polio, the more serious complications of burns and amputations for the poor lads who would be forever scarred, all of it meant added work for a dwindling staff as ever more of them left to help the war effort themselves. Every day there were extra patients to feed and laundry bills rising through the rusting roof and the men in charge up in Wellington seemed to have no idea at all how their plans affected ordinary people out in the rest of the country. Her creditors had been patient at first, everyone was having to do more on far less in wartime, but time was running out. Matron would have the respite of the Christmas break, with all but the farmers stopping work for a few days, come January however, she would need to pay up, something had to give.

Matron took up her pen and paper and began composing a letter. As she did so she continued her train of thought.

If she had been as flighty as young Rosamund Farquharson, silly girl spoiling herself with Sanders, she'd have put money on one of the sure-fire bets the men in Military 1 were so keen on, but Isabelle Ashdown had never laid a bet in her life, not even as a young nurse when all of her fellow trainees put a penny each into the sweepstake on who would be the first to bag a doctor husband. She thought then that betting on men was foolish and gambling on horses even more so, and nothing in the subsequent years had proved her wrong. She frowned, until a month or so ago, she might have thought Dr Luke Hughes could be persuaded to turn on the requisite charm. She had warmed to the young man as soon as he arrived. They had enjoyed several late night conversations, and Matron found his approach to his work both modern and a welcome tonic for the hospital. A sherry party at Christmas had often resulted in a New Year windfall to the hospital donation fund, especially if a handsome young doctor could be persuaded to work his magic, but Dr Hughes had been distracted lately, even a little brusque once or twice, she didn't trust his ability to elicit generous donations from frosty older ladies. She shuffled the papers back into a neat pile, and wished, not for the first time, that she might fold away her concerns as tightly as the hospital corners she still prided herself on, decades after her initial training, faster and sharper than any of her nurses. Her worries were interrupted by a low rumble of thunder, high up in the mountains and then another soon after, this one much closer.

Matron finished and signed her letter and waited a moment for the ink to dry. She was about to fold it into an envelope when she had another thought and added a post-script, initialling this part of the letter with a flourish, adding it to her pile to be sorted later. Then she stood, the old floorboards creaking in the heavy evening heat, and reached around the safe to pick up a rusted tin bucket. She carefully placed it beneath the worst of the gaps in the old roof that was the only protection afforded her office against the elements, so many years of being over-heated in summer and chilled to the bone in winter, so many years of tidying up others' mess. She would have to tell the night staff to ready their pails and mops, she doubted that even that latest crack of thunder would be warning enough for them, giddy as they were about the coming Christmas festivities. Many, she knew, had been wishing for a good storm to clear the air, but Matron knew a good storm meant only that a fierce light would be shone on the deficiencies of her hospital. She felt inside her pocket, checked that the safe key was there, warm and protected. She turned off the lamp on her desk. She had her torch in her other pocket and there was no sense risking rain getting through and onto a live electrical wire. She walked out into the night, a smattering of stars were just visible through the rapidly gathering clouds. It was still unbearably hot, but finally the cicadas were silent. The storm would be upon them soon.

CHAPTER FOUR

Rosamund Farquharson had been under orders to return to duty before seven o'clock. Already she was two hours late and had not yet reached the bridge. The bus, she reflected, must be nearly in by now. Might as well be hanged for a sheep as a lamb. Soon there wouldn't be any more petrol anyway. The fat bag on her lap gave her a grand feeling of independence. A hundred pounds! She could see the pay-out clerk peering at her from his window behind the totalisator. 'You can collect from the Jockey Club's offices tomorrow, you know.' Not she! She wanted to feel the notes in her bag. She supposed twenty pounds would have to go to the people she'd bought the car from. And twenty-five to the dress shop. And another five to Maurice. It would be something to be able to pay back that five pounds to Maurice. She'd be very formal when she gave it to him. 'It was awfully kind of you. I shouldn't have let you do it. I've been quite worried about it. Thank you so much.' Or would that look as though she'd noticed the change in him? Would it be better to be casually friendly? 'Oh, by the way, Maurice, here's your fiver. I'm rolling in wealth, did you know? Had a marvellous day.'

Let him think she was having fun without him. Hint at an exciting encounter at the races. She'd go to Military 1 as soon as she got in, still wearing the races dress. It made her feel something special and he could see it for himself. Sister Comfort would be on duty but she'd make some excuse. She'd say she'd put a few bob on for him at the races. Or would he think she was—? A feeling of the most bitter desolation came upon her. She experienced, like a physical sickness, a realisation that no matter what she did there could be no return to the old days. As though her pain was a sort of emotional toothache, she began to explore its cavities for the sheer horror of aggravating the screaming nerve. He had lent her the fiver because he was uncomfortable about her. The Johnson woman down at the Bridge pub had cut her out. He was crazy about Sukie Johnson, crazier than he had ever been for Rosamund herself, and that was because she could offer him far more than Rosamund ever could. When Rosamund met up with Maurice now, it was only because he was a patient and she a clerk here at Mount Seager. 'He's moved on from me,' she thought in a crescendo of pain. And having reached a point where she could endure her self-torture no longer she began to hunt for an antidote. She would after all win him back. He'd see her tonight in this lovely frock. He'd be as excited as she was about her winnings. In less than a fortnight he'd be sent back to camp, training and up to the minute tactics and all that. He'd be shipped out again soon enough, but before then she'd see him admit to missing her, she'd borrow a studio and throw a marvellous party for him, a farewell, and a welcome of sorts, welcome back Maurice. Rosamund began to weave plans, muffling her pain with vivid dreams of reconciliation and renewed happiness. By the time she got to the end of Long Leg, the antidote had worked and she felt a kind of gaiety that almost matched the vibrance of her beautiful yellow dress.

It was quite dark when she finally reached the bridge. Her small car bumped over the rattling, uneven planks. At the far end, the road divided. It turned sharply to the left through a patch of dense native bush making a wide angle with a track that ran uphill ending at the Bridge Hotel one way or straight ahead to Mount Seager. As Rosamund drove on to the hospital, her dipped headlamps picked up six white objects that moved alongside the road, stopped, and darted back again. She pulled up short and switched on the beam.

The white objects were resolved into pyjama-clad shins, cut off at the bottom by socks and boots and at the top by army great-coats, the poor fellows must have been sweltering in them. Rosamund leaned out of the driving window.

'And what the hell do you think you're up to?' she asked pleasantly.

'That's all right, Miss,' said a sheepish voice. 'On your way.'

'Turn them lights off for Gawsake,' cried a second voice.

Rosamund switched off the lights and produced a torch which she turned on the owner of the sheepish voice, revealing a long sallow face with a disgruntled expression and a pair of watchful eyes.

'Private Pawcett, I see.'

'How're you doing, Rosie? You haven't seen a thing now, have you?'

'Who knows?' said Rosamund. 'You're taking a chance,

30

aren't you? This is the third time. You'll catch a packet this trip, Bob.'

'Cut it out, Rosie, be a sport.'

'We'll see. Who are your friends?'

The circle of light shifted. A second face, darker than the first, with smart, bright eyes, blinked nervously.

'Hul-lo!' said Rosamund. 'The pride of Military 1 on the razzle. What's come over our Corporal Brayling? You don't usually let yourself get mixed up in your mates' antics, Cuth.'

An unsteady hand moved across his face.

'He's fed up,' Private Pawcett explained. 'Poor old Cuth's fed up. Look, his missus is going to have a kid and they won't let him off to go and see her. He's feeling that crook about it all he had to do something. Hadn't you, Cuth?'

'I wouldn't of gone to the house,' Corporal Brayling protested. 'I told them I wouldn't go near her. I could've just sent a message. I don't want to give her the fever. I'm OK now anyway, none of us are infectious and we'll get discharged soon enough. Ah, it's all no good.'

'Tough luck,' said Rosamund lightly.

'We brought 'im along for a drink,' Private Pawcett said. 'He needed it.'

'"We"?' Rosamund repeated. 'That reminds me. I haven't met the third gentleman.'

The light dodged about a little, momentarily revealing a bank covered in wild thyme and a thicket of dark leafy scrub, before it found the third figure, coming to a stop upon the back of a sleek dark head.

'Turn round,' Rosamund said breathlessly.

He turned slowly.

The silence was broken by Corporal Brayling digging

31

Private Pawcett in the ribs. 'Come on, Bob, reckon we'd better get a move on,' he said.

'You're right there, mate. OK Cheerio, Rosie!'

'Hooray, Rosie!'

They moved away, their heavy boots crunching up the loose shingle.

'Had a good day, Roz?' Maurice Sanders cried.

Private Pawcett and Corporal Brayling picked up their pace a little, the better to be away from whatever their mate was about to say to the Farquharson girl. No doubt about it, she knew she had a face on her and a fair shift of a shape at that, but Sanders couldn't half push his luck at times.

'He needs to go easy on her, can't play around with a girl like that and not come unstuck in the end,' said Corporal Brayling.

'As if you'd know,' sniggered Private Pawcett.

'I wouldn't want to know, would I? Not with my Ngaire *hapū* and the baby coming soon enough. I'm not like you blokes.'

'Nah sport, sure you're not.'

'I'm not,' Brayling insisted, his step slowing, his voice dangerously low.

Pawcett laughed unkindly, the extra pint he'd downed before they left the pub meant he didn't notice the change in Brayling's tone, 'You mean her old man'd drag you off back to the *pā* and go old-style Māori on you if you cheated his girl?'

Brayling stopped in his tracks and Pawcett realized he'd gone too far. In the faint spill of light from the porch of Civilian 1, the solid and strong Māori man looked as fierce as ever he'd seen him. Pawcett kicked himself, his mother had always said his mouth would get him hung one of these days.

'Mate, I'm sorry,' Pawcett said. 'I didn't mean it, not like that, but you've got to admit, your Ngaire's old man is one hell of a—'

'*Rangatira*? Chief? Too right he is,' Cuthbert Brayling answered his own question. 'And his *iwi* and mine go back a long way, all the way "back to the *pā*", if you like. I'd never muck around with these girls like you lot. My Ngaire, she's a queen, she's everything to me.'

'Cuth, mate, play the—,' Pawcett stopped himself just in time, 'Play the game.'

Their voices faded in the darkness. They'd served together now for almost two years, alongside their reckless mate Sanders, trusting each other with their lives, comrades and brothers, and it was only back in New Zealand that the differences between them became bigger than the bonds forged in action. They were both relieved to be alongside the hospital offices now, it meant they had to hush, it meant they had to work together. If there was one thing they'd learned in the army it was how to work together.

Brayling doubled over and started moaning, Pawcett held him up, they stumbled towards the door of Military 1, making as much noise as they could, no sneaking in, no pretending they hadn't been out playing the wag.

Pawcett called out as they crossed the threshold, 'Hey Nurse, Nursey! Cuth's only been and gone sleepwalking again, we told you what a palaver it was with him over in Africa, give us a hand girlie, will you?'

The little nurse started up at his words and hurried to the porch door, shushing him as she went.

33

Pawcett kept up his loud recitation, well aware that none of the men in the ward would be sleeping yet and they'd enjoy the scene he was about to give them.

'Problem is, Nurse, you lot insist we have an afternoon kip every day, but where's the rest when we've to keep an eye out for Cuth? A caution he is for sleepwalking, honest. And Gawd knows where Sanders has got to. He was worried about Cuth heading over to the river, stone me if we're not in for a flood the minute that storm hits, or worse, what if he'd got into one of those tunnels under here? The place is riddled with them. Be a love and help us out, will you?'

Sanders meanwhile, was offering Rosamund his best self-satisfied grin. Faced with his cheery good looks, his twinkling eyes and the dark curl that fell over his left eye, no matter how often he combed it back, not to mention the knowing smile that Rosamund had promised herself she would ignore, she felt her resolve melting away. The tough carapace of a girl who cared nought for his charms, a girl who was as easily distracted by other young men as Sanders was by Sukie Johnson, faded all too swiftly into that old yearning. It was a wanting made still more painful because Rosamund knew Maurice would have spent his stolen hour at the pub carrying on with Sukie over the bar, hoping that her old man was as daft as he looked. Still, she had rehearsed her lines and she knew her new yellow dress looked pretty darn good, so she gave it her best shot.

'Oh, it's you Maurice, I might have known you'd be out carousing with the boys.'

34

Sanders smiled his lop-sided grin, 'You should have come along, Rosie, plenty of honest blokes in the saloon bar, a lovely girl like you'd have no trouble picking up a beau, 'specially not in a frock like that, showing it off for all you're worth.'

His words stung, but Rosamund brazened it out, 'And get into even hotter water than I am already, two hours late for my shift and Sister Comfort on the warpath? No fear. Besides, the Bridge Hotel's lost some of its allure lately.'

'Blimey! "Allure" is it now? There's a phrase if ever I heard one. Picked that one up in London did you? Fair enough. I reckon a backwater boozer like the Bridge isn't for the likes of you. Mind you, the beer's a darn sight cheaper there than it is back in town, and some of us,' he stepped closer, too close, but Rosamund stood her ground, 'some of us aren't quite as fit in the pocket as we ought to be, are we, love?'

Rosamund smiled and slowly lifted her handbag, she reached in, clicked open the clasp on her mother's red leather purse and carefully peeled away a five pound note from the larger bundle. She planted a deep red kiss right on Captain Cook's face on the outer note of the bundle before she put it safely back in her purse. She was glad to see the sight of the money wiped the smile off Maurice's face, if only for a moment.

'Didn't you hear?' she asked lightly.

'Hear what?'

'I'd have thought it'd be all round Mount Seager by now, can't imagine the girls on the late transport would be talking about anything else, you know how they love a gossip.'

'What would? Where's all that money from, Roz? Who've you robbed blind?'

'My horse only went and came in, Maurice. So here's your fiver, and I'll thank you for the loan, and that's you and I quits, don't you think?'

'Ah, Roz love, come on girl, don't give a bloke a hard time. I'll be given my clean bill any day now and once we're off back to camp I reckon they'll ship us out again quick as you like. You can't blame me for taking my chances, can you?'

Rosamund was about to answer him truthfully, to say that of course she didn't blame him, she couldn't imagine how horrid it must be to be lying out here in the hospital, hating being ill and then worrying even more about getting better, knowing that would mean heading back off to war and still no end in sight, things getting worse by the week if the news from England was anything to go by. The lads might bluster to each other, bluster to the nurses as well, but before Maurice had turned his lovely smile to Mrs Johnson across the bar of the Bridge Hotel, he'd confided some of the horrors to her. His worry that it had made him look soft had only made her warm to him more. She was about to give in, about to step forward, ready to turn off the torch, when a far brighter light shone on the two of them and Sister Comfort's furious whisper saved her from herself.

'Miss Farquharson! I shall see you in Matron's office in five minutes. As for you, Private Sanders, you've had your final warning. I'm taking this to Sergeant Bix, I can promise you that.'

Rosamund shook herself and stepped back, almost glad of the trouble, and Maurice Sanders watched her walk away from him, lit by Sister Comfort's torch. Taking in the line of the neatly-fitting yellow dress he pursed his lips to whistle and only just stopped himself.

'Don't be an idiot,' he thought, 'you've given the poor girl enough of a run around as it is. Let her be.'

CHAPTER FIVE

Sarah Warne was at her desk in the Transport Office. She was trying to work out the shift rosters for the next fortnight and two of her fellow drivers had already called in sick over Christmas and Boxing Days. She didn't blame them, she might have pulled the same trick herself if she hadn't been in charge of the rota, or if she wasn't well aware that Dr Luke Hughes was also working the full Christmas shift. She frowned, Luke had been distant lately, unusually so. There was something going on and Sarah was determined to get to the bottom of it.

Sarah and Luke met when she was in the West End and he in his second year of surgical studies across the river at St Thomas's. She knew herself very fortunate to have made it into a West End cast. It wasn't a major role and in truth, Sarah sometimes wondered if she was a major role sort of actress. She wasn't sure she had the temperament to be a leading lady, and even though she was the right age, she certainly wasn't an ingénue either. Hers was a steady, reliable character, useful for steady, reliable parts, those that held the story rather than the audience's attention. She had been cast because she could do the job and do it well, she was calm and capable when others might fly up into the heights of passion or down to despair, depending on the notices on any given night. The reliable actress was not the most glamorous role in a company, but it was vital and Sarah understood theatre well enough to know she would stay in work a lot longer than some of the glossier girls from dramatic school and weekly rep.

She and Luke were introduced at a post-show drinks party that trekked from their rabbit warren of backstage rooms to the closest pub and on to the Café de Paris. Sarah recalled that she and her fellow actors had arrived, flushed with the success of that night's show and the several drinks they'd had to celebrate. Luke was leaving when the dashing young leading man spotted him, clasped him to his breast and introduced him all around the bar as a dear old school chum. At first Sarah thought Luke Hughes was shy, not used to the noise and bustle of a group of actors, the back-slapping and kissing, at least two cocktails required to bring them down to the level of ordinary conversation. Left alone with him for a few minutes she tried to make conversation but his replies were so taciturn that she changed her mind and decided he was positively rude. She forgave him a little when he checked his watch, saw that it was gone two o'clock, announced himself exhausted from a day's surgical assisting and, ignoring the imprecations of the theatricals, said he must leave them to their pleasures. She forgave him a little more when he leaned in to whisper an apology for his behaviour and invited her for supper to make up for his appalling manners that evening—'Just as soon as these blasted final exams are out of the way'. She was grateful that her fellow cast members were too busy to overhear, fully engaged as they were in outdoing each other with tales of the worst digs they'd endured in provincial tours. Had they heard it, such a proposal would have provoked an inordinate amount of whistling and nudging among her peers and the rather good-looking Dr Hughes would have hightailed it out of the building as fast as his two feet could carry him, with no chance of a slipper on the stair to find him again.

A fortnight later Sarah met Luke for supper and, both keeping such odd hours, both understanding the strains of a team depending upon them—although Sarah well knew that she was not the pivot for matters of life and death that Luke was, regardless of how desperately important her fellow actors believed the theatre to be—a sincere friendship developed. The friendship was definitely edging towards romance when Sarah opened the door of her little flat to a telegram notifying her of her sister's sudden illness and that her widowed mother needed her help. The long journey home took Sarah from soft London summer to a bitter New Zealand winter and her sister's death, and all too soon afterwards came that awful, inevitable morning in early spring that brought the declaration of war. Mrs Warne was even happier to have Sarah home then, far from the horrors that London would surely face, even though Sarah herself would have liked nothing better than to do her bit for the city she adored.

Sarah and Luke became proficient correspondents, sending long, honest letters full of friendship and a growing understanding, letters in which Luke proved himself far more open on paper than he had often been in person. Then came a year with just a postcard or two, Luke stationed at a military hospital close to battle lines and Sarah worried for his safety as the months dragged on and

40

the news became darker every week. Finally there was a glimmer of hope and she was understandably delighted when military efficiency determined that a British doctor serving in North Africa was better suited to accompanying a contingent of wounded New Zealand servicemen than returning to England and, while there, he should take a six month stint at a hospital now dealing with military casualties. That hospital turned out to be Mount Seager of all places.

Luke found his first few weeks at Mount Seager extremely difficult. He was not daunted by the workload, the outdated equipment, the broken-down buildings, or the leaking roofs that haunted Matron's nightmares, these were nothing compared to the hospital tents in which he had been working for the past months. His upset was a champing at the bit of duty. So many of his friends from school were out in the field, the majority of his medical colleagues were caring for wounded soldiers in the heat of battle or coping with the atrocious conditions in London, Birmingham, Glasgow, with wave after wave of casualties coming in from the nightly raids. Luke bitterly missed being in the centre of things and being useful. He spent his first month in New Zealand in a severe funk until Rosamund Farquharson took him to task.

'Don't be such a prig, Dr Hughes.'

Luke had been going through his files just before a ward round and hadn't realized he was grumbling aloud about 'this blasted backwater'. He certainly didn't expect a reply from the office staff, no matter how much Miss Farquharson fancied herself quite the catch.

Never one to hold back when she had something to say, Rosamund gave him a piece of her mind, 'We all want to

41

do our bit, but not everyone can be the hero just because we fancy it, not even the likes of you with your clean white coat and London certificates on the Surgery Office wall. Yes, you probably could be getting your hands dirtier somewhere else, but come on, do you really believe your friends out there, giving their all, would begrudge you this? They're no mates if they would. Looking after servicemen who're doing their damnedest here or anywhere else, it's all part of the work. And by the way,' she added, her well-defined eyebrows raised, a smile on her rigorously carmined lips, 'we New Zealanders might gripe about being stuck way over here when it's going to blazes everywhere else, but you'll find we're not so keen on you Pommie chaps doing the same. Some of those lads in the military wards are going stir-crazy, they're spoiling for a scrap. I'd watch it if I were you.'

Rosamund turned on heels that were definitely not regulation, and flounced off across the hospital yard in a way that several of the recovering servicemen at Mount Seager, taking a breather on the porch of Military 1, found enormously reviving. Even Dr Hughes allowed that being told off by Miss Farquharson was amusing, particularly in conjunction with the way the word 'Pommie' sounded in her accent. Rosamund's New Zealand vowels had been determinedly and intentionally rounded by her years in London. Moreover, he had to admit she had a point. He took note, pulled himself together and, aware that he was now the most senior doctor available to Mount Seager, gave himself to the work with an alacrity that pleased Matron enormously and surprised Sister Comfort even more.

Even though she didn't expect their friendship to feel

the same in wartime New Zealand as it had been in London before the war, Sarah had expected that she and Luke might take up where the letters had left off. Looking back she found it hard to imagine how carefree they had been, even with the constant pressure of Luke's studies. Now she sometimes wondered if they had been deliberately blind, willfully ignoring the growing tensions on the Continent. Her sister's death, her mother's gnawing grief, the awful news that came to them daily, the broken soldiers she met in her work, young men who very occasionally let slip the mask of bravado, all of it meant that Sarah was no longer capable of ignoring the obvious—Luke had changed. He was hiding something from her and it was driving a wedge between them.

Along the yard in the anteroom to the Surgery that he had been assigned for the night, Mr Glossop was also preoccupied, shuffling on his cot, too hot and far too irritated to sleep. Yes, he had seen the eminently sensible Matron pocket the key to the safe. He trusted her, she was a fine woman, without a doubt. The hospital safe, however, in a set of buildings as ramshackle as these were proving to be—corrugated iron roofs rattling in the rising wind, the buckets he'd seen strategically placed by nurses in preparation for the brewing storm—well, that was a hell of a lot of cash he'd handed over and he didn't trust the hospital safe, not as far as he could throw it. Not that he'd be throwing anything, come morning, after a sleepless night on this flamin' cot. He knew there were a few private rooms here at Mount Seager, his great aunt had demanded one years back. She'd come in with some women's troubles

43

and had kicked up a hell of a stink about being in a ward with an old Māori lady. Proper tartar his aunt was, giving the nurses what for, and the doctors. Quick as a flash, Matron had come on through, rattled out her orders, and what do you know, but wasn't the *kuia* given the private room and not his aunt. That shut the old bism up good and proper. Still though, you'd think they'd have given him a room of his own for the night. It wasn't as if he was one of the rowdy servicemen, it was a bit of a cow to leave him to a cot in a shoddy anteroom. And by heck, it was sweltering in here. Damn tin roofs, no good to man or beast.

Mr Glossop was quite right. There were private rooms at Mount Seager, one at the front of every ward, just inside the porch. Wishing to give the dying man the privacy he needed Matron had moved old Mr Brown to the private room of Civilian 3 two weeks earlier. Now she stood outside that room, speaking in hushed and urgent tones with Father O'Sullivan. Young Sydney Brown had been closeted inside with his grandfather for the past fifteen minutes. Matron was about to knock on the door when it opened and Sydney, ashen-faced, stepped out.

'Are you all right, son?' asked Father O'Sullivan.

The young man shook his head, fear and confusion in his face, 'I don't know, he's talking daft, I think I need a—'

Matron took over, 'Go on in to Mr Brown, Father O'Sullivan. I'll sort Sydney out with a cup of tea and maybe a splash of whiskey in that tea, eh Sydney? Medicinal purposes. Come on now, I'll take you to the kitchen and find someone to look after you.'

Matron put a firm arm on the young man's shoulder and propelled him away.

At the porch, she turned back to Father O'Sullivan, 'You'll come to find me, Vicar, and let me know how Mr Brown is doing?'

The vicar and the Matron exchanged a look.

'Yes, of course, Matron.'

When Matron returned to her office she found Rosamund Farquharson and Sister Comfort waiting for her, Farquharson barely shame-faced despite being well over two hours late for her shift and Sister Comfort even sharper than usual. Both women spoke at once:

'Matron, I must insist you speak to Miss Farquharson—'

'Play fair, Sister, let me explain. I had a win, Matron, a real honest to goodness win, so it took much longer to get away, what with having to pick up my takings. I thought about going home to drop off the money, a hundred pounds is a hell of a lot to be carrying round all night, but I'd have been even later for my shift, and I didn't want to let you down, so I just—'

'Let us down? *Now* you worry about letting us down!'

'Enough, both of you,' Matron held up her hand. 'Sister Comfort, I'd be grateful if you would go to young Mr Brown, I left him in the kitchen and promised to return to sit with him, he's quite shaken up. Make him a cup of tea, will you? And here,' she reached into the lowest drawer of her desk, 'add a tot of this to it. He's in shock.'

Rosamund's eyes widened at the image of Matron keeping a bottle of whiskey in her desk and it was only Sister Comfort's immediate complaint that she was not one of the kitchen staff to be sent off to make a cup of tea that meant Matron was angrier with the Sister than at Rosamund's barely-suppressed glee.

Sister Comfort held her tongue and stalked off along the yard towards the kitchen block and Matron finally turned to Rosamund.

'How much did you win, Miss Farquharson?'

Surprised by the unexpectedly bald question, Rosamund responded immediately, 'Oh, a hundred, Matron. A whole hundred quid. I have to give some of it over to a few people that I . . . I need to help out, but all the same, it's put me in a grand mood. I am awfully sorry about being so late and getting Comfort's nose out of joint, I don't mean to be such a bother, really I don't. I guess I'm just not used to such, well, boring work.'

Matron sighed, 'Yes, I can imagine for a young woman such as yourself, saving lives and keeping a hospital going in wartime is terribly tedious. I suggest you leave your winnings here. I'll put them in the safe and you can collect the money when your shift finishes. Minus, of course, the hours I'll dock from your pay for your late start tonight and the several days you've been late over the past weeks. Is ten pounds a fair price, do you think, to keep your job?'

Rosamund's large green eyes widened even further, was Matron really threatening to sack her if she didn't hand over a tenner? Matron was waiting, one hand out for the money, the key to the safe in the other.

'I, well, I—' stuttered Rosamund.

'It would be awfully difficult getting a job right now, don't you think, Miss Farquharson? Let alone without a reference. Still, I'm sure there are some factory jobs, some-where about. Or land work, I believe there are quite a few young ladies working with the shearing gangs these days, what with the shortage of manpower.'

'You wouldn't,' Rosamund was flustered, her face as red as her lipstick, 'I thought—'

'That I was a pushover, just because I'm not vinegar-sharp like Sister Comfort? Then you have another think coming, young lady. Let's be quite honest, shall we?' Matron squared her shoulders and turned to face Rosamund, 'Your behaviour has been abysmal, since the day you arrived. You've made a fool of yourself with Private Sanders, and don't make that face, I could hardly have failed to notice, you have the entire team of VADs gossiping about you, and goodness knows what the soldiers in Military 1 say in private, given their words in public are bad enough. There is a man dying here tonight, alone but for a grandson who, I now discover, barely knows him and chose not to visit him until tonight, despite several requests. You have a chance to redeem yourself, take the consequences of your actions and get to work on a new start. It is the one chance I will give you.'

Matron's voice was low and considered, but her words cut far deeper than Sister Comfort's scolding. Rosamund tried to respond but, when she opened her mouth, she found she had no words to express her shock. Matron nodded in satisfaction.

'Leave your winnings with me, I shall lock the money in my safe and, when your shift is finished in the morning, you may collect the balance of ninety pounds.'

Matron finished her words, emphasising the word 'ninety' to assure Rosamund that she meant to follow through with her threat.

Rosamund clicked open her purse, dumped the bundle

of notes on Matron's desk and rushed from the office. Had she been in any state to slam the door behind her, she would have done, instead the warm wind did the job for her, slamming the door and rattling the whole office with its force.

Matron sat down and looked at the notes, at the key in her hand, and the neatly gathered pile of unpaid demands littering her desk. The small office shuddered as another gust of wind battered the thin weatherboard walls, a shock of lightning briefly lit the sky beyond the bare window, a stronger crack of thunder hard on its heels, and finally the downpour began. Matron leaned back in her worn leather chair and nodded. At least the torrent would keep anyone else from her door for the moment.

CHAPTER SIX

The occupant of the private room at the front of Military 1 was also having a difficult evening. He had been trying for some time to write a letter, a letter that was overdue and yet, for the life of him, he couldn't seem to put pen to paper this evening. Nor had he managed to do so on any of the three evenings preceding. The rain now drumming a fierce tattoo on the corrugated iron roof above, syncopated with that which fell on the curved frame of the porch beyond, might have had something to do with it, but he feared his inability to express himself on paper was the symptom of a deeper malaise. It was just possible that he was homesick.

'My dearest Troy', he began again.

He stopped, looked at the page, crossed out the three words and took a clean sheet of paper.

'Darling Troy'.

Shaking his head, he took up a third sheet of paper and tried once more.

'My Troy'.

Again he faltered. 'You utter dolt, Alleyn,' he whispered to himself, conscious of the ward full of men mere feet away beyond the flimsy partition walls that formed the small private room he had been assigned as the base for this operation.

'Troy is far from being a fool,' he went on, 'she knows very well there is a great deal to do with your work that you cannot say to her and even more that you struggle to say in person, let alone on paper. And God knows when this letter will get to her. Just write the words, you blasted idiot.'

He could not. Whether it was the incessant rain drowning all possibility of contemplation, or the sense of several dozen men beyond the thin walls, few of them sleeping, all with their own worries, all missing their own loved ones, Alleyn knew himself defeated.

He stepped away from the small table that served as a desk, stretching as he did so. He reached for his pipe and lit it, holding the match for a moment in his long, thin fingers. By the light of the match, and that thrown from the dimmed desk lamp, he saw himself reflected in the side window. A tall man stared back, a raised eyebrow rapidly followed by a frown. He rubbed his nose and sighed, cracking the window open a little further to shift the reflection and let in the scent of the drenched roses that were all about the hospital. The roses, at least, would be glad of the rain. Alleyn was glad of it himself, he'd been sleeping badly in the fierce heat of the past week, and it hadn't helped that the secrecy of his task here at Mount Seager meant he had been cooped up in this private room almost the whole time since he had arrived under cover of darkness a week earlier, awaiting word from his superiors. The reason for his arrival at Mount Seager was known only to Alleyn himself, the Chair of the Hospital Board, an old and trusted friend of the most senior man in the New Zealand police force, and a single contact at the hospital. Matron appeared to have bought the story that Alleyn was the Chair's English cousin, a writer collecting traditional tales in the Antipodes, cut off from home by the war and struck down by the kind of nervous distress known only to the most modern of artists and then only those with a private income. The tale was given out that he needed rest and quiet, and so rest and quiet—or as much as the men of Military 1 would allow—had been prescribed. He had been in place for the past week, listening through the partition walls, noting movement beyond this side window and the smaller one that opened onto the porch with a good view of the yard beyond, and studying the notes and observations passed on by his contact. As yet, there had been no development worth reporting to his superiors and nothing at all to write to Troy.

Alleyn looked at the travel alarm clock on his table, it was almost a quarter past ten. The grumbling and subdued guffaws of the men next door would abate soon. He sat down at the table, took up a clean sheet of paper and tried again.

My dear Fox,

As will be abundantly clear to you, my perspicacious friend, I am now well and truly arrived in New Zealand. You know I began my work in Auckland, welcomed rather fulsomely by the estimable local police force of that fair city. You will understand when I say I am grateful to have been spared their enthusiasm any longer. I was diverted almost at once from my appointed city and, that matter dealt with—a longer tale, for another time—I have been sent on dispatches to an altogether different part of this astonishing land. Of course I am not able to indicate precisely where, suffice it to say that were I allowed to have a good look around I should come back to you with tales of glorious scenery and majestic landscapes. There is, understandably, a growing unease to do with matters offshore. For those of us at home in London it has, I confess, been a little too easy to assume these lands at the end of the earth are safe from the ravages of war, but while their cities remain unharmed, their people are a different matter. A great many sons have left for King and Country, and too many have not returned. Those who have returned have often done so in very different health from that with which they left. There is a mix of concern for 'Home' as many of them still call it, an understandable concern for their own young men, coupled with a palpable worry that Japan is edging closer by the day. I must say, I fear they are right and it turns out my superiors in this endeavour hold the same view, with good cause. It is to be hoped that Troy is as accommodating as our own dear Scotland Yard. In addition to the personal trials of being so long from home, I admit to finding the idea of yet another summer Christmas quite absurd, however extraordinary the surrounding scenery. I fear I shall never accustom myself to the idea of good old St Nick in cricket whites. The time, Brer Fox, is quite out of joint.

I shan't go into the details of my current abode, other than to say that my legendary skills have detected not one but two affairs of the heart that are, true to form, failing to run smooth. I have also noted an understandable if tiresome degree of complaint from the stout fellows confined to the ward rather than barracks. The Matron here has a very modern approach to their convalescence, giving them ample opportunity, once they are well enough, to roam the grounds, play card and board games, read from well-stocked shelves. She maintains that distracting them from their injuries and illness will afford them far faster recuperation than the more usual enforced rest. She may well be right, they are very young after all, and young heads can be easily swayed when difficulty hits. Many of these chaps are the good sort who signed up right away, gung-ho and ready to take on the worst that Hitler could throw at them, the youngest among them have had to grow up awfully fast. No doubt they've seen sights akin to those that you and I cannot forget. The bonds forged between unlikely mates are as strong as one would expect and yet once back home it seems their fiercest gripe is an over-strict regime, the cost of a pint or a badly-ridden filly. As if all they have been through were but a dream. What a piece of work is man, eh Fox?

So it is that I end this missive where I began, unable to tell you my exact location, nor why I am here, nor to whom I must answer. I trust that by the time you receive this, the winter nights will be shorter, the evenings drawing out. No matter the world we find ourselves in whenever this war is finally over, I have no doubt there will always be need of the long arm of the law, we will be kept in busy employ.

He signed the letter with a careful hand and addressed the envelope with his customary precision. If he could not write the letter he ought to write, he would at least make a damn good fist of the one he found himself able to complete.

Alleyn looked at the clock for the third time that hour, noted that time was passing no faster than it had yesterday evening or the evening before and took a file of notes from a combination-locked briefcase. He found the pages that had given him pause when he'd first received the file and read them through once again.

In early November a garbled message had been picked up by local services monitoring radio frequencies. It didn't appear to be in code at first, merely a message sent out, quite possibly from a youthful radio enthusiast, in the hope that anyone out there might respond. It was only when the message was picked up once more, and then a third time, each time from a different frequency, that the information was passed up the ranks. Once the counterespionage team had the information they quickly linked the timing of the messages to brief sightings of a Japanese submarine off the east coast. The vessel had been sighted twice, once reliably confirmed, the second time less certain, but when it became clear that the sightings coincided with the despatch of the second and third radio messages, even the unconfirmed sighting was taken seriously. From there it took but a short time to break the code. The actual information in the messages was not of any great substance, for they noted the military presence at Mount Seager hospital which was a matter of public knowledge and the submarine had already disappeared from view. However, the combination of radio messages and the two sightings was felt serious enough for the senior statesmen in Wellington to despatch Alleyn to Mount Seager to pick up what information he could from locals and patients alike. Alleyn and his superiors both understood that they might well be on a wild goose chase, the submarine had not been sighted for over five weeks, no further coded messages had been intercepted, and what the Inspector found was a simple country hospital, a set of army offices and, beyond the usual human dramas that any group of people were prone to, nothing to report. Until a day ago, when Alleyn's contact at the hospital had delivered the latest sealed file. A new message had been intercepted, in a different code, not all of which had been deciphered, but it was now believed that a series of coordinates were to be transmitted in the morning after midsummer's night. There was no information as to what the coordinates might reference, and still no clear understanding of the intended recipient of the messages, but the time factor meant that Alleyn had spent all day yesterday and most of last night on alert and, as midsummer's night began, was no closer to knowing who or what he was looking for. It was all exceedingly frustrating.

'There are more things in heaven and earth—' Alleyn muttered under his breath, the end of the line cut off by a tremendous clap of thunder and simultaneous flash of lightning, illuminating the length of the yard beyond the front window and then the rain took on an even more driving tone. By now, the racket of the downpour was almost farcical, Alleyn decided he was incapable of rational thought and took to his bed. If he must play the invalid, he might as well act the part. There would be no sleep with this noise, but at least he might lay down and read.

Twenty minutes later Chief Detective Inspector Roderick Alleyn of Scotland Yard was happily roaming the blasted heath with King Lear, the wind, rain and thunder outside providing admirable support.

CHAPTER SEVEN

In the private room of Civilian 3 another tragedy was finally played out. Young Sydney Brown had pulled himself together enough to return to his grandfather's bedside and the little nurse in the room had sensibly allowed him the privacy that this time required. Forty-five minutes later when Sister Comfort came to check on Sydney she had found him hunched over a pillow, hugging it to his chest as he looked on in horror at the old man, still and already becoming cold in his bed. Now Father O'Sullivan prayed quietly, the nurse awaited Sister Comfort's orders, Sydney tried not to show his revulsion at sitting alongside a dead body for the first time in his life, and failed miserably.

Dr Hughes knew enough about nurses and their understanding of patient protocols to take his cue from Sister Comfort, so he waited in silence for the older woman to speak. After an appropriate time of silence had elapsed, the exact number of minutes being something Sister Comfort had judged to perfection after all these years, she spoke up and, with no effort to lower her voice or soften her usual strident tone, gave her orders.

'Dr Hughes, wait here, I'll fetch the relevant paperwork

and be with you in a moment. I shall pop in to Matron when I go to the Records Office and let her know.'

Dr Hughes offered to fetch the paperwork himself, but he was over-ruled as Father O'Sullivan sprang up from his hard wooden chair at the head of the bed, 'No need for either of you to divert yourselves, I'll alert Matron. You've plenty to do. I'll go to her straight away.'

He was gone from the small room before Sister Comfort could protest that it was more usual for her to pass on this kind of news and for the vicar to stay with the bereaved.

Her next words to Sydney were sharper to match her frown, 'Mr Brown, if you'd like to go along with the nurse, she'll find somewhere for you to rest for the night.'

'What? Rest? Nah, no thanks, Sister, but I can't be—' he shook his head, 'I mean, I've got to go, things to do.'

Sydney Brown sounded as if he might make a run for it at any moment and Sister Comfort immediately squashed him.

'I'm afraid not, Mr Brown. The next transport is not due to leave until six o'clock in the morning and even then it will depend on the state of the roads. Frankly, I'd be very surprised if anyone leaves Mount Seager tomorrow morning. A storm like this has a bad habit of bringing down a flash flood and making the bridge too dangerous to cross. It wouldn't be the first time we've been cut off by the river and I doubt it'll be the last. Nurse, if you will?'

The shocked Sydney Brown stumbled to his feet, fidgeting with his collar and cuffs as if he might square up for an argument and then, seeing the determination in Sister Comfort's eyes, he followed the nurse, his feet scuffing at the polished floor, his arms still wrapped around the pillow he held as a comforter.

Sister Comfort looked after them frowning, 'Foolish lad, doesn't know when he's well off.'

Dr Hughes was no longer surprised by Sister Comfort's brusque manner. Whatever the situation, whether he would have spoken carefully or forcefully himself, Sister Comfort could be relied upon to crash into any scenario with neither care nor finesse. He noticed now, as he had several times before, that her manner was actually remarkably useful. The little nurse, who appeared as inexperienced with death as Sydney Brown, had assumed the mantle of her office and was now the epitome of efficiency, as Sister Comfort had no doubt intended, while Father O'Sullivan had left with his unusually prayerful demeanour quite put away. In fact, he had looked much more like his regular self, a figure Rosamund Farquharson once mischievously but accurately described as looking 'like a bank clerk who somehow found himself in a priest's cassock and forced to deliver a sermon'.

Sister Comfort turned to Dr Hughes when the others were gone, 'I shall send Will Kelly to deal with the body and get it down to the morgue. We'll have to be fast, he'll not keep in this heat.'

She turned on a silent heel and was gone.

Left alone with the corpse, Dr Hughes shuddered and turned his back on the dead man. He had seen far too much of death in the past two years and even an old man dying of natural causes disturbed him. He tried to calm his breathing, clenched his fists to still his shaking hands, but it was no good, the sight of the dead man took him back to the heat of battle, the stench of war, the bloody and broken young men calling for his help. These were the cries that infested his dreams, interspersed with the awful silence of death, the silence that now woke him whenever he tried to sleep. Dr Hughes became almost faint, quite dizzy and turning into the room, he grasped the foot-rails of the bed to steady himself. He forced himself to open his eyes. Here he was, in the old man's room. There was the corpse. Yes, the man was dead, but he was old, nothing dreadful had happened to him, his was not a life cut off in its prime.

Brought back to the room, he looked about himself and took in the peeling paint at the window, a bucket catching heavy drips of rain. He knew the New Zealanders were finding it hard, sending off so many healthy young men to fight had a real effect on the home front. Early in his tenure he'd innocently remarked on the distance from the theatre of war and Matron's response had been swift.

'We've all we need here in New Zealand to look after ourselves and we're grateful for it, but we're feeling the pinch as our lads go off and we send the best of us away. We felt it in the first war too. There's only so long anyone can give and give before they break.'

Dr Hughes understood that an entire generation of men missing after the first war, the loss of strong young men now, had taken its toll on the nation's spirit as well as its economy. He'd had money worries of his own and understood how debilitating it could be to scrimp and save. His family were very ordinary and his whole way through medical school he had been on scholarships and bursaries. Even so, his money worries were as nothing to the nightmares he now dealt with on a regular basis. He'd taken on the night shift in order to try to avoid the dreams, but they felt even more brutal when they arrived in the light of day and the one person he had confided in had been

60

most frightened of his fears. When Luke tried to explain to Sarah why he was afraid to sleep, fearful of what might come, he saw worry and perhaps even shock in her eyes as he talked of the walking wounded in his dreams, mumbled in garbled language about his fear. The words she eventually spoke were intended to be comforting and she had tried to understand, but he was sure he had said too much. He was worried that she now thought him a coward and, in response, he had closed himself off from her. Luke knew she must be confused and upset by the way he had been avoiding her. Sarah was a lovely girl and she deserved someone better than him, he would have to tell her that. He groaned inwardly, he knew only too well that some lives could seem hopeful on the outside and yet inside it was all turmoil and upset. Take young Sydney Brown for example. All of twenty-one, about to inherit his grandfather's farm, lock, stock and barrel, and seemingly no happier about it than had the entire estate gone to a stranger.

'Thing is, I don't flamin' well want to be a farmer, that's the cow of it,' Sydney had said, whispering across the old man when Luke came in to check on Mr Brown, 'I want to be an engineer, I want to make things happen. I never wanted the farm at all. I can't stand being stuck out here in the sticks. I'll sell it quick as I can and be off.'

Luke's reveries on the uncertainties of fate were cut off by the welcome arrival of Will Kelly, the night porter. Kelly was famed at the Bridge Hotel for his ability to drink gallons of lemonade shandy, his drink of choice, with no obvious effect, yet a single tot of whiskey, rum, or brandy— Kelly wasn't a fussy man—would have him drunk as a lord and twice as foolish in no time at all.

'Ah, it's himself, is it? The young doctor, and good evening to you too.'

Kelly clattered into the private room and halted his forward trajectory by the noisy but effective method of clanging his ancient trolley into the hospital bed. He set to work right away, rolling the covers back from old Mr Brown and readying his trolley and body bag to house the deceased.

As he worked he sang quietly, 'Full fathom five thy father lies, of his bones are coral made—'

Kelly broke off to look at Luke's aghast face, 'Don't you worry at all. Not your fault, this old fellow. Time's the culprit here, nothing you could've done to save this one, don't go blaming yourself.'

'I know that, of course I know it was his time. It was his grandson, he wanted to see Sydney,' the doctor protested. 'We all thought he was holding on for the young man.'

'Well, that's the way with the dying, hang on when you expect them to go, pop their clogs when they're meant to hang on. Never can tell. Tricky ones, the dying are. The lad was lucky to be here when he went, more often than not the family hang around for hours or days, waiting for the final words, the last breath, then the minute they nip out for a cup of tea, there you go, he shuffles off his mortal coil. I reckon they prefer to be alone when they go. He was a lucky young fellow all right. Come on then, old boy, let's be having you,' Kelly said as he manhandled the corpse into the body bag.

Luke frowned and took a few steps backwards, eager to get away from the sight of Kelly rolling the corpse into the canvas bag.

'I have to go, there are forms, Matron has the papers ready and I need to sign them.'

'Death and taxes, always the way. You hurry along to the office, they'll have the paperwork ready and want it signing, always want a name to a death, that they do and yours is as good as any other once you've your fancy letters after it.'

With that Will Kelly finally finished struggling with old Mr Brown, fastened the bag, rolled the bagged body onto the trolley and pushed off and out of the room. Luke heard him as he headed along the yard towards the morgue, hidden away at the far end of the row of wards, singing through the rain.

'Those are pearls that were his eyes; Nothing of him that doth fade, But doth suffer a sea change, Into something rich and strange.'

Luke had to admit that Kelly had a fine baritone, and an apposite choice in his Shakespeare. He turned out the overhead light as he left the room, remarking how especially empty it felt with the dead man removed, as if death really did have a presence of its own. The doctor took a deep breath and forced himself to pay attention to where he was. He was no longer in a field hospital, he was no longer surrounded by heat and dirt and flies. He was here, at Mount Seager and as the ghastly images receded from his mind, he looked across to the Transport Office. The dimmed light was on. Very well. He would sign the paperwork for old Mr Brown and then he would go to Sarah and speak to her. He took a deep breath, squared his shoulders and walked across the yard.

CHAPTER EIGHT

Mr Glossop, uncomfortable on his cot in the anteroom, finally decided he'd had enough. He should have been at home by now in his cosy little cottage, drumming rain outside, his apple trees and the big walnut getting a welcome soaking, a fine night's sleep ahead knowing his work was done and done well. Not tonight. There was something not right, he was sure. It wasn't just the rain, nor was it the heat, heavy despite the sheets of water dropping from above. He needed to be sure the money was secure and he'd move this darn cot down to sleep alongside the safe if he had to. No one would say Jonty Glossop was not a conscientious man. He'd just missed the last war, too young by a year, and while he was not officially too old this time round, they'd sent him home when he offered to take up his papers and serve, told him he needed to get into shape, get fit. The nerve of it, in his prime and told he wasn't forces material. It rankled even now, but he wasn't one to bear a grudge, not Jonty. He found a valuable job, stuck with it, and proved he could do it well, even with all the trouble from the van, the fuss every week to get the rounds done on time, always some hold-up at one of the destinations, you'd think they didn't want paying, some of them. Well, he'd make sure they got paid tomorrow and catch his death of cold for his pains no doubt.

Mr Glossop's shirt was badly stained with sweat when he finally managed to get the cumbersome cot down to a manoeuvrable size. He made a half-hearted attempt to at least wipe off his face before he left the anteroom, she might be a stickler for propriety, but Matron was surely a lovely woman. She had a few years on him, but he liked that in a woman, always had, none of these flighty young things had any appeal, too clever by half and all too ready to come the madam. All right, he would arrive at Matron's door bedraggled with rain, but if she happened to be in residence, he'd rather not be dripping sweat as well.

Standing on the steps to the Surgery, he looked along the yard. The rain was tearing down as expected, but other than the high wind driving the torrent down from the mountains, it was quieter outside than inside. Now that he was not directly beneath the corrugated iron roof the drumming rain seemed less insistent and the asphalt it fell upon sent up a damp heat and the cloying smell of warm, wet tar. He was about to step down and out of the shelter of the office door, when he saw a flash of white in the distance, up by Military 2. Glad he had turned out the lamp in the anteroom, he peered ahead. It was hard to judge in the dark and rain, but Glossop thought he could make out the large shape of a starched uniform, white veil blowing in the wind, scurrying up to Matron's office. She stopped at the door, waited a moment and then scurried back out of the rain into Military 1. A lucky escape, he wouldn't mind pleading his case to Matron, but he didn't fancy having to persuade that mis-named harridan Comfort that she wasn't the only one around here who took her work seriously. He had taken just a few steps into the yard when another blasted light shone out, from Civilian 3 this time, and he ducked back into the doorway of the anteroom. Peering out, he saw a figure, the vicar presumably, judging by the dark coat, heading straight for Matron's office. There was a brief burst of light and then he was inside. Well then, Matron was definitely in situ. Perhaps she'd leave with the vicar, Mr Glossop thought, there would be formalities to be done if the old fellow had died. Not long afterwards, he saw another figure heading towards Matron's office, up to the door and then, after a brief pause, away again. It must have been that fool of a porter, Matron was wise not to open the door to him. Glossop frowned, he could either spend the night in the anteroom or wait a little longer on the step and hope the coast cleared. He thought more clearly about the woman in question. Matron was an efficient woman, she wouldn't be closeted in her office with the vicar for long, she had far too much to do. He now saw another figure heading into the yard from the ward, the young doctor no doubt. All this to-ing and fro-ing in the rain must surely point to the old man popping off, Mr Glossop reasoned. Rain dripping from his bulbous nose, Mr Glossop allowed himself a brief smile as the light fell once more from Matron's door and the vicar stepped out, no doubt he and Matron were heading off again to deal with the old man. Just at that point there was a huge roll of thunder, a crack of lightning directly above the hospital, and Jonty Glossop—who would not have admitted this to a living soul, and hadn't even admitted to himself that his fear of thunder and lightning was one of the reasons he was not happy sleeping alone in the anteroom—turned back into the Surgery, put his hands over his ears and screwed up his face with his eyes shut tight. He opened them only after there had been another long rumble of thunder and the lightning had flamed all around, brilliant light shining through his closed eyelids. When he looked along the yard there was no one in sight. The Matron must have made her way back to Civilian 3 with the vicar and presumably the doctor, paperwork for the old bloke, death had its own offices. Good, it would give him time to set himself up in front of the safe, maybe he'd even play possum and pretend he was sleeping when Matron came back in. She could hardly send him back to that awful anteroom, all the way through the rain, once he was soundo, now could she?

Head down, the rain slicking his greasy curls against his deeply lined forehead, Glossop made his way along the darkened yard. Arriving at the door to Matron's office, he knocked politely. It was possible they had tried to step out when his back was turned or when his eyes were closed, and thinking better of it had gone back inside. He wouldn't want Matron to find him lacking in manners. He knocked again and, satisfied there was no one in the office, he tried the handle and was immensely gratified when the unlocked door admitted entrance. Mr Glossop gave a curious shake of his shoulders, with his enormous belly and his wet curls, he looked for all the world like a drenched bulldog who had somehow acquired the coat of a poodle. Then he launched his bulk and the unwieldy cot into the office, closing the door behind him.

He smiled, talking to himself as he often did on the long drives across the plains between his payroll drops, 'Right then, Jonty Glossop, let's get to work. You get this cot up

67

and give her your best Sleeping Beauty impression when she gets back. By the time she's done with the old man and the vicar and that daft-as-a-brush porter, not to mention the drippy Pommie doctor, she might even wake you with a peck on the cheek, glad to see someone with half a grain of sense in her office.'

Glossop was still struggling to put the cot back together when, in a brief lull in the rain, he heard a woman's voice. He stood stock still, terrified it was Matron returning before he had made up his bed. The voice didn't sound like hers though, it was lighter, younger, and definitely more agitated than he would expect from that august lady. Glossop would not have called himself an eavesdropper, but it was an acknowledged fact that he preferred the company of the ladies to that of his fellow men. It was one of the reasons he had been glad to take on the payroll deliveries, volunteering to be drop-off man when the younger, fitter chaps who might have been a more obvious choice went off to do their bit. Apparently the government that considered him not fit for active service didn't mind him taking the risk of actual highway robbery. His colleagues in accounts thought him both brave and a little foolhardy to give up the cushy nine-to-five and a desk of his own, but none of them had worked out that the payroll drop took him to four hospitals, three schools and the two factories on hush-hush war work. At all but one of these establishments there was either a young lady with a good head for figures—as if that was the most interesting thing about her—or an older lady with a willing ear for his traveller's tales. If Glossop could persuade one of them to pour him a cup of tea after a long drive, then he'd not say no to a fresh girdle scone and a chat into the bargain, before he pushed off

68

again on his lonely route. Despite his eagerness to lie down, Glossop couldn't help leaning closer to the thin weatherboard wall to listen to the woman's voice. It was hard to make out exact words, what with the wind and rain, but the young lady was clearly upset, her voice raised. He strained to hear what was said and to whom, but the wind in the middle of the yard whipped up and span around the office, so much that he was unsure if the voices were coming from the Transport Office on the far side of Matron's or the Records Office he'd passed in his run and stumble along the yard. He caught a clipped tone to the ends of her sentences that made her sound as if she were one of those girls who'd been off to London or Paris and come home to New Zealand determined that everyone should know she had travelled, she was not just another country girl looking for a quarter-acre paradise and nothing more. Those girls he could do without. Glossop was attaching the last leg of the cot and he nodded to himself, he might be lonely sometimes, but loneliness had its compensations.

Whether it was contemplating the compensations of his life, or the lateness of the hour, just past eleven o'clock and he was an early to bed, early to rise man, even on summer nights, Glossop's fat fingers took on a sudden dexterity and with a snap, click, clunk, the cot was whole. Finally he lay down along the length of old canvas, the damp would not deter him now. Mr Glossop gave in to gravity and the fabric beneath him strained, shuddered, but held. The arguing voices were stilled, even the rain seemed to be lessening a little, or perhaps he was simply so used to it now that he didn't notice, and he felt himself relax for the first time since that damned flat tyre this afternoon.

He knew he might be in the bad books when Matron returned, but with any luck she and the vicar would be some time yet. He could rest here, perfectly stationed between the door and the safe. All he needed was forty winks and he'd be right as rain. Glossop chuckled to himself at the absurd term given the weather and the fact that Matron's tin bucket was catching fat drips not two feet from his nose. He reached out his hand to the safe, giving it a solid pat to reassure himself that he was the close guard this moment needed. Disconcertingly, the safe rocked a little beneath his hand. He lifted and dropped his hand again, and again the safe rocked. Glossop opened his eyes, the cot groaned as he raised himself up on his elbows, and he stared at the safe. This time he slapped his meaty palm on the side of the heavy iron frame. As if affirming his worst fears, he heard a gentle click and the safe door swung open. It was empty. Horribly, obviously, empty. Glossop was suddenly very hot and at the same time, utterly chilled. He let out a strangled yelp that turned into a full-throated roar, rolling off the cot and up onto his knees he crawled his way to the office door. He wrenched the door back on its hinges, crying out into the rain and the wind in the yard beyond.

'Thief! Robbers! Safe. Thief. Help! Thief. No!'

It was a few moments before the lights in both Military 1 and 2 came on, the civilian wards took a little longer, the door to the Transport Office was flung open and Sarah Warne rushed out, quickly followed by Dr Hughes. On the other side of Matron's office the Records Office door was opened and Rosamund Farquharson stood back, careful not to let the rain ruin her new dress or her beautifully set curls, careful too to ensure that no one noticed Maurice

Sanders slip past her to join his fellows from the ward as they came rushing out to stare in bemused amazement at the round, red-faced man bawling highway robbery into the tempest from his place on his knees in Matron's office doorway.

CHAPTER NINE

'Mr Glossop!' Sister Comfort managed the impressive feat of bringing to just four syllables, uttered barely above a whisper, a tone both chilling and imperious.

Glossop lowered the pitch of his wails of 'theft' and 'robbery' but he did not desist. Sister Comfort shook her head, walked across the yard impervious to the rain and, to the cheers and applause of the combined ranks of patients, by now all crowding to the verandahs, the windows and the porches leading out from each ward, she hauled Glossop up by the shoulders of his shirt.

'Pull yourself together, man,' she hissed, 'Look where you are, look at the spectacle you're making of yourself. There are people here who are terribly ill, a gentleman has just died and you are howling like a banshee in the door to Matron's office. What on earth has happened?'

Glossop, brought up short by Sister Comfort's mention of Matron, seemed to come to his senses, if only a little. He stumbled backwards into the office, pulling Sister Comfort with him, to ensure she could see the gaping maw of the empty safe. Her solid frame hid the view from the staff and patients craning their necks to see what had happened, so that all they could see beyond the Sister were the white gesticulating arms of Glossop's damp shirt.

Rosamund Farquharson meanwhile, was now on the steps trying to see past Sister Comfort and into the office, 'My winnings—Matron had all of my winnings, the whole damn lot!'

Even in her passion, she omitted to mention that Matron had deducted ten pounds from those winnings, nor did she mention the five pounds that had gone to Private Sanders. Rosamund might be upset, but she wasn't foolish. In her anguish over her loss she also appeared to have lost her nicely rounded vowels.

From his spot on the porch to Military 1, Maurice Sanders watched as Rosamund tried to push past Sister Comfort. He still had a soft spot for Rosie, he didn't want to see her making a fool of herself in front of this lot. At the same time he knew he had already contributed more than enough to tarnishing her name among her peers as well as his own, those VADs could be vicious gossips, and it was this awareness that held him back from actually leaping across the yard to her rescue.

'Lucky get-out there, mate,' he whispered to himself a moment later, when Sarah Warne stepped up to Rosamund's side instead, saving Maurice from a chivalrous side to his character that neither he nor his comrades had previously noticed.

Sarah's voice was calm but her eyes were sharp as she put her hand on Rosamund's arm, 'Let's not make too much noise right now.' She edged closer and whispered, 'Can't you see they're all enjoying it far too much? You don't need to give them what they want, Rosie, not always.'

Rosamund turned to look at the assembled crowd of

patients, the VADs and other night staff, everyone keen to see what would happen next, all of them eager for a scene. She spoke out of the side of her mouth to Sarah, 'Fair enough, but oh, wouldn't I like to give them the full-blown damn and blast it scene they want. All right Sarah, I'll be the good girl. Lead on, Lady Macduff.'

She held out her hand to Sarah and allowed herself to be led meekly into Matron's office. They were just inside out of the slowing rain, when a voice called out from the men standing in the porch of Military 1.

'Oi, Sister, shouldn't someone find Matron?'

The call was taken up by the servicemen in their serried ranks, shouting the same until it turned into a song, *'Fetch the Matron, fetch the Matron, fetch the Matron bring her here, bring her 'ere—fetch the Matron and—Bring—'Er— 'Ere!'*

At the sound of the men's jollity, Mr Glossop finally lost his temper completely, he elbowed Sarah and Rosamund aside the better to direct his ire towards the servicemen across the yard, eliciting a 'Boo!' from the men in the porch, an angry 'Hi, there!' from Dr Hughes and the decidedly more threatening, 'Watch it, you great oaf, or I'll bloody well give you something to moan about!' from Maurice Sanders.

Ignoring them, Glossop took the topmost of the two steps to Matron's office as his dais and launched into a diatribe against the hospital, the road to the hospital, the bridge on the road to the hospital, the clapped-out van he had been given to drive on the absurd road and over the absurd bridge to the absurd hospital, gearing himself up with a stream of furious invective peppered throughout with the kind of language that prompted even the usually taciturn Bob Pawcett to turn to Cuthbert Brayling with, 'Got to admit, Cuth, he's got a turn of phrase. Wouldn't be out of place from a navvy, or Sanders here on a bad day.'

Sister Comfort, incensed by the language and much else besides, grabbed Glossop by the ear, pulled him back into the office, sat him down in the old leather chair and demanded he cease immediately. She silenced both Rosamund and Sarah with a single glance, and then she took charge.

'Where is Sergeant Bix? Well?'

The question, in many ways more a command than an enquiry, was answered by the sound of boots clipping to attention on the asphalt. Those gathered outside Matron's office parted and made way for the sergeant. It was all his men along the wards could do not to cheer. They were fond of Bix, a friendly and capable man who had little truck with the sort of hospital rules that appeared to have been invented purely because Sister Comfort preferred it that way.

'Here, Sister.'

'Indeed. And yet we have all been "here" for some time. Why is it, Sergeant Bix, that my hospital staff are continually required to keep your men under control?'

'To be fair, Sister, it's way past lights out and I've a hell of a—loads of, sorry—paperwork to get through in the office, what with so many of this lot heading off back to duty in a few days.'

Bix's case for the stern leadership of his men was not reinforced when several of the soldiers hanging off Military 1's verandah whistled and cheered their approval at the thought of leaving the hospital. The sergeant turned to the servicemen with an air of a man who had had more than enough of brokering peace between servicemen and nurses in the past few months, and the spectators became quiet, almost as if they were settling into their cinema seats, the main feature finally about to begin.

It was all Sister Comfort could do not to rage at Bix the way she wanted to rage at the men, and it was only her faith in the value of hierarchy that held her back. Instead she lowered her voice and spoke quietly to Bix, 'There has been a theft.'

'Righto, Sister, then we'll need to investigate,' said Bix, stating the alarmingly obvious. 'How much has gone?'

'Mr Glossop's van sustained a flat tyre during his rounds, with several hospitals still on his delivery list. Matron secured the contents of his pay-box in her safe and now we find the safe wide open and Mr Glossop's payroll appears to be missing with four establishments still awaiting their money.'

Bix's eyebrows raised to his receding hairline and Sister Comfort took that as a sincere appreciation of the situation.

'Indeed. Young Miss Farquharson also appears to have lost her winnings from a day at the races, Matron was safeguarding that sum for her as well.'

'So we ought to get a search going, right?'

Sister Comfort frowned, 'Given the large sum involved in Mr Glossop's payroll, I really don't want any of the patients to know what has occurred. Gossip is a most dangerous thing in any hospital.' She paused and glared at Rosamund Farquharson who had opened her mouth to point out that theft was possibly a little bit worse, 'There may yet be an explanation, Miss Farquharson. Let us hope that there is. For now, Sergeant Bix, I'd rather we took the line of least said, soonest mended, so I will recommend to Matron that we pass it off as a search for Miss Farquharson's winnings.'

Sister Comfort then turned to Sarah, 'Miss Warne, drive round to the Bridge Hotel and let them know there has been a theft, and they need to be on their guard, for all we know the thief is trying their luck at every establishment in the foothills.'

Sarah nodded and ran nimbly around to the area behind the kitchen where the vehicles were parked.

Sister Comfort turned back to Sergeant Bix, 'Until we can contact the local police force—and I shall get onto that immediately—I suggest the safest course of action is to get these men back to their beds.'

'Fair play,' Bix nodded and turned smartly to the door, 'Right then,' he shouted across to the men as he strode into the yard, 'We all like a lark, but give it a go, lads, back to bed. Come on now, let's be having you, one two, one two, quick march.'

The men fell sharply into line, allowing their training to take precedence over their understandable curiosity and the civilian patients followed suit.

'You there,' Sister Comfort continued in her mission to bring order to chaos, pointing at the VAD whose head was poking out of the Records Office window, 'Get on the telephone to the police station at Gold's Corner and tell them there's been a robbery. Yes, I know there's only one constable and he'll be off-duty by now' she said, pre-empting the answer, 'but I'm sure he has a direct line to his superiors in town and can alert them faster than we can. Then he can join us here and offer some semblance of order while we wait for the police to sort out what on earth has happened.'

The VAD shook her head, shrugged, and answered with a nonchalance that had Sister Comfort wanting to throttle her, 'No can do, Sister, already tried. The line's down, there's no operator on the line, nothing doing.'

She had barely uttered these words when they heard the bus trundling up the driveway far faster than usual. With a squeak of brakes, Sarah Warne ran back, breathless.

Wind and rain had pushed back her short dark hair from her well-defined face and she looked deeply concerned, 'Sister Comfort, I took the bus up as far as the bridge, but I can't get round to the pub, there's been a washout. Right where the road turns up to the pub, it's all covered in rocks and branches. The river's higher than I've ever seen it and it looks to be going awfully fast. I checked the bridge too, some of the loose planks must have been dislodged in the storm, there's at least one of them totally missing and a couple of others sticking up looking like seesaws. Even without the rain, I daren't risk going over it in the bus, I'd get stuck, or worse.'

Sister Comfort took a deep breath and, while her self-control was admirable, even she had to admit defeat at this juncture, 'Oh for goodness' sake, will someone not find Matron?'

CHAPTER TEN

As the servicemen of Military 1 pulled up their sheets, the occupant of the private room emerged and turned towards the doors leading out to the porch.

'You don't want to do that, mate,' said one soldier.

Another added, 'You missed all the fuss already,' and lowered his voice to add to the man in the bed closest, 'typical bloody officer class.'

'Yeah, take it easy cobber, you might get a strain.'

They laughed and turned in.

The officer-class gentleman held up his pipe as if to say he was simply headed outside for a smoke and the foot soldiers of Military 1 gave him up for a classic chap of the upper ranks, no more sense than he was born with. If he wanted to risk Sister Comfort's wrath and Matron's too, for she must surely be on the warpath by now, then it was his look-out. They'd done their bit with the warning, clearly no one was going to tell the likes of them what was going on, they'd get it out of the VADs in the morning, it was time for some shut-eye.

Alleyn stood in the leeward shadow of Military 1's porch from where he had a clear view to Matron's office. He watched Sister Comfort and Mr Glossop for a while. The fat man held his head in his hands, rocking slightly from side to side, while Sister Comfort took a brief second, unaware that she was being observed, to let down her guard and look about her in dismay. He watched too as Glossop looked up and said something in a voice too low to hear across the yard, and immediately her starchy demeanour was back, any hint of vulnerability shut away. He saw Rosamund Farquharson and Sarah Warne exchange a glance, hold hands briefly, and he watched Rosamund take herself off to the Records Office on one side of Matron's office and Sarah to the Transport Office on the other. Dr Hughes followed Sarah and Alleyn had an idea that the young doctor was asking for a private word, but Sarah turned, said a few words, and Dr Hughes trudged back along the yard to the Surgery, surplus to requirements.

For a second everything was still, the noise of the tempest had dropped to a dull drone and now the loudest sound was that of the swollen, racing river just a few hundred feet away. It was coming up to midnight. Alleyn rubbed his nose. He'd heard the interchange about the telephone line and the bridge, something must have happened that necessitated the intervention of the local police. With no one local to take charge, he ought to get into Matron's office and see if he could help, but he had an odd sense that he'd learn more, as well as maintain his cover, if he could only hold off for a moment. He was also very aware that the midsummer night would be short and his real task was to follow up any possible leads or discrepancies throughout the night. Alleyn saw Sister Comfort lean towards Glossop and was sure he was about to witness something useful when the intimate moment was broken

80

by the squeaking of uneven wheels, the rattle of a trolley that had seen far better days, and an out-of-place love song sung softly in a surprisingly mellow brogue.

Will Kelly stumbled into view from beyond the Porter's Lodge, crooning of his love taken in his arms and how he'd given her kisses sweet. He was pushing a trolley upon which lay a closed canvas body bag. Kelly, the bag, and the trolley had all seen better days. At that precise moment, Father O'Sullivan appeared walking swiftly towards the scene of the fuss from the northern end of the yard. Alleyn assumed he was coming from Military 3 where the particularly damaged young men spent very difficult nights, no doubt some of them needed solace through the storm.

Sister Comfort, alerted by the singing and the squeaking, strode out of Matron's office and launched herself across the yard at the porter, 'What on earth is going on, Mr Kelly? And why is this poor gentleman not in the morgue?' she hissed.

Will Kelly's answer was a tipsy jumble of excuses, including the perfectly reasonable response that he had taken poor old Mr Brown down to the morgue but found it locked on his arrival. 'And it's Matron has the key, isn't that so? I turned to make my way back, leaving the trolley tucked into the porch of the morgue, out of the rain. Not that this poor fella will feel the cold or the wet now, will he, but even so, respect for the dead—'

Sister Comfort tried to interject about his appalling breach of rules that had left a dead body unattended for any length of time, no matter the reason, but Kelly was not to be diverted from his tale.

'I knocked and I waited but there was no reply from Matron's office and I knew she wasn't in the Transport

81

Office or the Records Office because there were rows coming from both and it was the lovely accents of those two girls who've been away in England. So I knew, Sister, that neither were Matron. It's a New Zealand accent she has and proud of it, as well she might be. Well, there I am with no key and poor old Mr Brown, may his soul rest in peace with the faithful departed, left down at the morgue, and I just popped into the room where he'd breathed his last you know, in case Matron was there with the young fella. Awful cut up the lad looked when I saw him earlier, and truth be told, she's a soft heart on her for a fierce woman. Like you I've no doubt, Sister Comfort, a soft heart in there, somewhere—' Kelly broke off for a moment as if he'd surprised himself considering Sister Comfort might have a soft heart after all, and then he was away again, 'But no, she was not there neither. All there was, was that poor young lad, fast asleep and curled up on the floor, his face to the wall, his dear grandfather's pillow to his chest. Heartbreaking. I'd half a mind to cover him up with the blanket off the bed and no matter that you'd scold me, Sister, and my hand was reaching out to it, but then I thought, that's a dead man's blanket Will Kelly, you leave it be. Then what happens next but the whole place is all of a racket with your man Glossop here, screaming blue murder and how was I to get the key from Matron with all that fuss going on, I ask you? How indeed. I took myself off round the back of the wards and made my way to the morgue in the rain avoiding all this fuss in the yard. Dark and spooky it was, the back way, I'll tell you that for nothing. I went to the porch of the morgue and Mr Brown still on his trolley. I waited until the very moment you'd chased them all off back to their beds. Once the coast was clear I came back, not keen to leave him out on his own again. So here we are, your man and I, with our hand out for the key for the morgue. Well, my hand's out, his is likely as not setting fast. I oughtn't to have left him the first time and I was feeling bad enough about it, so there's no need to come it with your reproachful looks, Sister. I stand before you, an old man who wants only to put away his charge, for it's thirsty work this carting about of bodies, yes it is. So, find me the Matron and find me the key and I'll be out of your way in two shakes of a lamb's tail.'

At that, Will Kelly thumped the foot of the body bag, proud of himself for getting through the whole speech. He must have hit the bag more forcefully than he intended, for the trolley gave a terrible screech, lurched precariously first to the left and then to the right, and finally the most uncertain of the wheels fell off and rolled across the damp asphalt of the yard and into the empty space under Matron's office steps, lost in the mess of weeds beneath the office. A mess caused, as Matron could attest, by the need to cut back on gardeners' expenses since the war. As the wheel came to a halt, the whole edifice, trolley and bag and body, slowly and decorously collapsed. Will Kelly stumbled, trying to hold up the body, but his age and state of inebriation made him no opponent for an unexpected wrestling match with a bagged corpse, and he ended up flat on his back, the body bag across him, the trolley atop them and the three remaining wheels spinning in the night.

Alleyn, still on the porch, groaned inwardly at the farce and shook his head at the task before him. With all the elements of a theft laid out in the yard he now had no choice but to reveal himself as a policeman and he must do so without explaining the real reason for his presence

83

at Mount Seager. He looked to the body bag and back to Matron's office with the empty safe. Glossop had taken it upon himself to right the trolley, the better to clear the body from Will Kelly who appeared to have passed out with shock or the exertion of telling his tale, or perhaps it was simply that the night's intake of hard spirit had finally caught up with him. Father O'Sullivan, despite, rather than because of Glossop's help, had scrambled beneath the steps for the truant wheel, wedged it under the uncertain leg and managed to hoist the body back onto the now-upright trolley, assuring the trolley's stability by leaning against it with his substantial frame.

Alleyn grimaced in the shadows, it was time to step forward.

Mr Glossop went even redder in the face before blustering, 'Who's this now, spying on us in the dark? What the hell's going on?'

Sister Comfort advanced on Alleyn, 'Mr Glossop, we have an English writer in the private room, this gentleman is he. I am, however, with you in demanding to know what on earth he is doing out of bed. Speak up!'

Alleyn spoke quietly, 'Thank you, Sister, but I'm afraid the story of my being a writer was one concocted in the hope I would be given complete rest. Very few of your soldiers would be interested in passing the time of day with a writer, I'm sure. The truth is,' he said, looking around at the assembled cast, 'I have been in New Zealand on some police business, thankfully concluded now, but unfortunately I managed to pick up a croup in the process. Mount Seager was recommended as a quiet place for my recovery, which I'm pleased to say it has been. Until now,' he added with a wry smile at those now gathered together in the rain. 'Fortunately, not only do I find that you need my services, this evening at least, but I believe I am well enough to offer them. Chief Detective Inspector Alleyn, CID, New Scotland Yard.'

He stepped forward and, despite the combined protests of Dr Hughes and Father O'Sullivan, Alleyn began to untie the top of the body bag, his long fingers struggling a little with the damp ties. As he did so, he made a quiet note of those around him. Glossop was fussing, Sister Comfort noisily disapproving, the two young ladies at the edge of the circle both hovering slightly closer. He intended to pay even closer attention in a moment when he revealed the stolen bundles of notes he was sure were contained in the bag. It was quite obvious to Alleyn that when the porter had slapped his hand on the foot of the bag, bringing down the entire trolley, Kelly's hand should have met the resistance of old Mr Brown's feet, not the air at the empty end of an otherwise well-filled bag.

So it was that Chief Detective Inspector Alleyn was also in something of a state of shock when, on finally loosening the top three ties of the bag he revealed, not Mr Glossop's bundles of payroll due at four locations dotted across the stark and beautiful plains, that magnificent sum topped up with Rosamund Farquharson's race day winnings, but Matron's cold body.

CHAPTER ELEVEN

From his vantage point at the left of the trolley, close to the top of the body bag, Alleyn noted the many and several actions that followed, each one precipitating the next, as if the whole piece was an impeccably choreographed and rehearsed scene, not out of place on the London stage. Revue, he thought, rather than serious drama.

The first bit of business took place on the sidelines between Rosamund Farquharson and Sarah Warne, a counterpoint to emphasize the central motif. At the revelatory moment, when the canvas bag was finally opened, Rosamund screamed rather more theatrically than was necessary and Sarah let out a low moan, which struck Alleyn as far more appropriate to the scene, although he paused to remind himself that it was Sarah who was the trained actress, not Rosamund. The two young women turned to each other, forming an elegant tableau, the tall and shapely blonde with her arm around the shoulder of her dark, petite friend, the pair backlit by the light from the open Records Office door.

Alleyn also noticed that Dr Luke Hughes turned to step across to the small brunette as soon as she let out her soft moan, but apparently he thought better of it, twisted away and turned instead to the inanimate body on the trolley. The detective watched as the doctor appeared to both reach out to and shrink from Matron's inert body on the trolley before them.

'Should I . . .?' he asked Alleyn, uncertainly.

'You could check for a pulse, I think, Doctor,' Alleyn said cautiously, 'I fear this is now a police matter rather than one with a purely medical concern.'

Alleyn watched closely as the younger man seemed to steel himself to touch the Matron and saw that when he did so his hand was trembling, ever such a little. It must have been difficult for the doctor, for all of them, she was their superior after all.

The doctor stepped back with a shake of his head, 'Nothing there.'

Alleyn nodded in response and, indicating the ties, said quietly, 'Please, close up the bag, if you will?'

Father O'Sullivan, who had only recently regained his footing after the absurd interval with Will Kelly and the trolley, was now watching in abject horror as Dr Hughes stepped back. The vicar uttered an unintelligible and extremely guttural mumble of horror, and was again drawn to the earth, his knees giving way beneath him. He staggered backwards, collapsing on the first of the two steps up to Matron's office.

Alleyn noticed that Sister Comfort herself staggered for a moment, seemingly torn between shock and distress at the sight of her adored superior laid out on the trolley and the deeply-ingrained sense of duty that drew her to Father O'Sullivan's aid. It would have been bad enough had it been Mr Brown's body abused in this way, but for it to be her beloved Matron was patently too much. In the split-second that Sister Comfort vacillated, Alleyn allowed himself a grim wager on which way she would leap and was pleased to note that he won his own bet. Sister Comfort took a sharp intake of breath, jolted a little as if an unseen hand had slapped away her incipient hysteria and she stepped quickly to the vicar. She had him back on his feet in a trice and was speaking in a no-nonsense tone that Alleyn admired for its efficacy while admitting that he was no different to the regular soldiers in finding her combination of assertion and aggrieved insistence highly aggravating.

'Right then, Father O'Sullivan, let's get you into Matron's office. I'll have you seated there and we can work out who is responsible for this appalling incident. This is all too much.'

Alleyn held out a hand to stop her, 'If you don't mind, Sister—'

'Mind? There's plenty to mind, don't you think, Inspector? I'm simply trying to do my job.'

'And quite right too.' Alleyn's tone was both charming and very clear. 'However I must also do my job and given the circumstances in which we find ourselves, it seems that mine takes precedence over yours.' She began to bluster and he spoke over her in a cool tone that allowed no argument. 'I'll need to take a close look at that safe before anyone else enters the office I'm afraid, and I'd also like to look at the papers there on Matron's desk.' He indicated beyond Sister Comfort to Matron's desk where a mess of jumbled papers were rudely scattered. 'Given the conjunction of theft and well—' Alleyn shook his head looking down at the trolley, and everyone present was grateful he chose not to be any more specific, 'the *confusion* in which we find ourselves, I think we had best assume that Matron's office is out of bounds for now.'

Sister Comfort was clearly put out, but decades of training had left her not only susceptible but also partial to a well-defined hierarchy and it was obvious that the detective quite outranked her at this juncture. She nodded her head making no effort to disguise her irritation and settled Father O'Sullivan on the top step, not quite inside the office.

No sooner had the vicar taken up a more comfortable position than Mr Glossop demanded the spotlight for his own oratory.

'Now look here,' he said to Alleyn, 'I've no flamin' idea who you think you are, coming over the big I-am, but this is New Zealand, God's own country you know, and we've our own police who're among the best in the world, same as our soldiers and our sailors and our air force come to think of it. It's all very well you playing the great white chief, but there's four payrolls gone missing here tonight, and now God only knows what's happened to Matron, a better woman you wouldn't find if you searched from here to Cape Reinga, right across the Tasman too I don't doubt. So I reckon if anyone is to—I mean, damn it all to hell, but—well—,' he seemed suddenly to run out of steam and took a long slow breath to puff himself up again. 'Well,' he tried once more, and Alleyn noticed Mr Glossop was sweating still more profusely than he had been even moments earlier, there were great beads of perspiration dripping down his face and onto his damp shirt, 'It's all fine and good you taking the reins and, and all that, but— but Matron and the money and dammit, where is the old fellow's body? Eh? Where's the bloke we knew was dead? What the flippin' blazes is going on round here?'

With that the fat man's too solid flesh seemed to melt, indeed so gradually did his legs give way beneath him, his lungs run out of breath, his words lose their splutter, that he was still speaking as he collapsed slowly to the ground, for all the world like a deflated hot air balloon, elegantly coming to land.

As Sister Comfort left the bewildered Father O'Sullivan, stepping over Will Kelly to tend to the gibbering Glossop, Alleyn looked at the scene before him and, thinking that the New Zealand women were proving themselves far stronger than their menfolk, he checked his watch and gave his orders, turning to Sarah Warne and Rosamund Farquharson.

'The storm appears to have very nearly blown itself out, but I take it that even a reduction in howling torrents and formidable wind is unlikely to make a difference to the possibility of a working telephone line or a passable road into town?'

Sarah Warne disengaged herself from Rosamund's protective arm and stepped forward, 'That's right, I'm afraid. Olive who runs the exchange in town is bound to have worked out that the lines are down by now, she'll have let the engineers know, but they start at that end and then work their way out with repairs.'

'All the way out here in the middle of nowhere? It'll take all night, if then,' Rosamund interjected.

Sarah Warne spoke over her friend, 'That's not fair, Rosie, it's not as if there are dozens of men available to do the work.'

'You're telling me,' Rosamund answered, with a wholly inappropriate wink in light of the circumstances.

Exasperated, Sarah turned back to Alleyn, 'We're not quite the backwater you might think.'

'I don't think that at all, far from it. I very much appreciate the necessity of checking lines of communication thoroughly and in such a manner that no vital points are missed.'

'And to be fair,' Rosamund Farquharson added, taking a small step forward herself, 'there's nothing anyone could do about the bridge losing its planks, not even the Met's finest.'

There was something in the young woman's tone and demeanour that set Alleyn's teeth on edge. He looked sharply at her, and was astonished to see a sly smile play about her lips, her green eyes sparkling.

'I don't imagine I'm the Met's finest, merely the only representative of any police force at hand,' he replied shortly, hoping to dampen her spirits before her colleagues were drawn far enough from their morbid reveries to notice her inappropriate impertinence.

'That's not what the papers have been saying about you,' she grinned again. 'You're not going to go all false modesty on us now are you, Inspector? Not in our hour of need?'

'If I can be of assistance then I shall certainly do so. Given the situation in which we find ourselves, it behoves each of us to do our best to sort this matter as quickly as possible. Don't you agree, Miss—?'

'Farquharson, Rosamund. Rosie if you like.' She said, holding out her hand to Alleyn who took it in a state of bemused interest. 'And there's no need to come over the stuffed shirt with us,' she went on, giving him back his hand after a warm shake, 'We're not in Belgravia now, Inspector.'

'Quite, Miss Farquharson. We're at the Mount Seager Hospital, standing in the dregs of a tempest, contemplating a major robbery, the missing corpse of an elderly man, the found body of the most senior and longest-serving staff member in the hospital, along with an impassable river and a useless telephone line, both of which preclude any endeavours by the local constabulary to deal with the incidents of the past hour. I frankly doubt that even the most traditional of the supercilious detectives found in a certain type of crime fiction would maintain a stiff upper lip in the face of such a bizarre contrivance of events. Time then, to take control over circumstance.'

All of which would have made a perfectly elegant curtain to Act One, had not Will Kelly awoken, taken in the scene around him, let out a long and loud belch, and demanded of the gathered players, 'What's for tea? I do believe it's time for me tea.'

CHAPTER TWELVE

Alleyn lost no time in giving his commands.

'Sergeant Bix, is it? I'd like you to instigate a thorough search of the hospital premises, take only the most trusted of your administrative staff with you.'

'Righto, Sir. There's a couple of lads, real good men but neither passed for field duty, very unhappy about this office work, damn hungry for action.'

The detective supressed his impatience and nodded his approval, 'Tell them, and anyone you may meet in the course of your search, that you are looking only for Miss Farquharson's winnings. The men in the military wards obviously know that a theft has occurred, Mr Glossop has made sure of that and their wards are directly opposite Matron's office so they have already seen a great deal more than I'd have liked. I'd rather we didn't alert the entire hospital to the full extent of our concerns. Meanwhile, letting those who are aware see that a search is in progress might, with a good wind, keep their natural curiosity at bay and allow us to sort the rest of this chaos as quickly as possible.'

Alleyn was all too aware that the real reason for his

presence at Mount Seager still took precedence, no matter that the situation before him demanded his attention. He briskly gave the rest of his orders. Matron's office was to be out of bounds until he had taken a good look around. The door was closed, locked, and Sister Comfort reluctantly handed over her own full set of keys to the hospital buildings. Until Matron's keys were found, Alleyn was determined he would at least have one full set about his own person. He acknowledged to himself that it was quite possible that her own keys were on Matron's body, somewhere in that blasted body bag, but now was not the time to once again reveal the cold body of their beloved superior to the contingent of horrified onlookers. Will Kelly was ordered to sleep off the effects of the spirits he vehemently denied drinking, his brogue becoming stronger with each denial, 'Lemonade only, I tell you, I'm a shandy man,' and Sergeant Bix frog-marched him down to the Surgery anteroom to overcome his vapours.

In the few moments they were gone Alleyn made a hasty calculation as to possible culpability and decided Bix was also the safest bet to remove Matron's body to the morgue. Until he was able to interrogate those standing in the yard, he knew that anyone present might be hiding something about the theft or Mr Brown's missing body or even what had happened to Matron. Bix had been at the furthest distance in the army offices and he seemed a very regular sort of sergeant. Alleyn heartily approved of a regular sort of sergeant and felt he had no choice but to trust him.

On Bix's return Alleyn took him to one side, lowering his voice, 'How secure is the morgue?'

'One way in and one way out, Sir,' he replied.

Alleyn considered the friendly, open-faced man before

him for a moment and then he decided, 'It's highly irregular and I'd very much like to look over the morgue first myself, but nothing about this evening is proving regular, so let us take the line of least resistance in this case.'

'Sir?' Bix asked, genuinely perplexed and not a little awe-struck at Alleyn's presence and easy assumption of status.

'Forgive me,' Allen replied, 'I've been too long from straightforward detecting and tonight's events have caused me to slip back into the easy manner I have with my own sergeant, a shorthand in which we often seem to understand what the other is thinking.'

'Right you are, Sir. So you'd like me to—?'

'Take Matron's body to the morgue. Leave it there, on the trolley, just as it is now. Until we can establish exactly what has taken place, I don't want her disturbed any more than absolutely necessary. Lock the morgue door and return the key to me. You and I will go down together as soon as possible, to ensure the morgue is as secure as you attest, and once I've had a chat with Dr Hughes about his where-abouts this evening, we can let him attempt to ascertain the cause of death.'

'And then I'll get on with the search, but only say it's for the young lady's missing winnings, not the payroll?'

'Exactly that.'

'Very good, Sir,' Bix replied, and taking the key from Alleyn he marched himself along the yard between the offices and the wards. Alleyn watched him go and wished for some of the excitement Bix clearly felt at being involved in a criminal case. His own over-riding sense was one of frustration that this incident had interrupted an already disturbed night, coupled with distaste for the upset he would undoubtedly bring to those still awaiting their own orders, at least some of whom must be entirely innocent of any wrong-doing and yet question them he must, prying into their lives regardless of innocence or otherwise.

He turned and surveyed the group before him, 'Miss Warne, the offices look to be almost identical in size, am I right?'

Sarah quickly divined the reason behind Alleyn's question and gave him the kind of fully-informed answer that eased his frustration a great deal.

'The staff offices are, but they don't all have the same amount of space inside, it depends on how many desks and chairs and whatnot they've got in them. The Surgery is smaller, to make space for the anteroom where they keep the anæsthetic preparations, iodine and all the other necessities for surgical procedures, medicines and such. They're all locked away, of course,' she added hastily.

He warmed to her immediately, 'Thank you. In that case, between the Transport Office and the Records Office, which will afford us a modicum of comfort in the task that lies ahead?'

Sarah allowed that her own Transport Office was likely to be both tidier and slightly more comfortable due to the absence of the extra desk in the Records Office and the presence of an ancient divan, set aside for ambulance drivers who needed a rest after a night on the road.

'The Transport Office it is,' Alleyn cried and herded his suspects up the two wooden steps and into the squat weatherboard building. Sarah led the way while Rosamund Farquharson, Dr Hughes, Mr Glossop, Father O'Sullivan and Sister Comfort complied with varying degrees of willing. Once they were all crammed into the office, Alleyn took the floor, standing by the open door.

'Thank you all for coming along with me. I'm sure this does feel heavy-handed, for which I apologize. I had no intention of coming over all Scotland Yard on you, but with the payroll theft and a certain concern over what has happened to Matron—'

'Certain concern?' interrupted Glossop from the leather chair at the desk where he had taken the most comfortable seat, 'Matron was a picture of healthy womanhood and now we find her laid out cold on a trolley commandeered by that drunken idiot. There's a thousand pounds missing from the safe, not to mention the body of the old bloke gone astray. I'd say that's murder and theft, not a "concern" for Gawd's sake.'

Rosamund spoke up, her vowels now as rounded as Sarah Warne's had necessarily been when on the London stage, albeit with an additional touch of breathlessness which Sarah would never have essayed, even for the most laboured of ingénue roles, 'There's my extra one hundred pounds actually, Inspector, Matron was looking after my winnings. She was most insistent about it.'

'Well there you are,' Glossop added, 'no place for your ever-so-English understatement, no place for it at all.'

Alleyn held up his hand to stop any further interruptions and tried again, 'Thank you both.' He turned to the furious fat man, who was mopping his brow with a handkerchief that must surely have been too damp to do any good, 'I agree, it certainly seems as if we are looking at two crimes here, crimes which may or may not be linked. Yes, thank you, Miss Farquharson,' he added, eager to avoid Rosamund interrupting again, 'Three, if we consider the theft of Miss Farquharson's own sum in addition to that of the payroll. I am very sorry to say I have to agree with Mr Glossop at this point, that it is also possible Matron has met with foul play. We need to know, at the very least, how Matron's body came to be on the trolley and where Mr Brown's body might be found, ideally before his grieving grandson discovers him missing.'

There was a brief pause when even Mr Glossop appeared to recall the death of the elderly gentleman and the need for some courtesy to his next of kin.

Alleyn went on, 'For the moment, and until Dr Hughes can give me a clearer indication of what may have happened to Matron, I'd like to begin by interviewing each of you one by one.'

'Oh, please, Inspector, I'm no pathologist,' Dr Hughes said, holding his hands up in dismay.

Alleyn frowned, looking at the earnest young man in front of him. Hughes's high forehead was furrowed in serious worry, his eyes were a deep grey framed with long dark lashes that would not have looked out of place on a fashion plate like Miss Farquharson, and even so did not diminish the obvious sincerity with which he spoke. Alleyn wondered for a moment if perhaps Hughes was more upset about the events of the evening than was warranted and then dismissed his thought as unfair, for all he knew Mr Brown's death was the straw that had broken an unknown camel's back. No doubt that camel would reveal itself as the night progressed.

'That is unfortunate, Dr Hughes,' he said at last, suddenly aware they were all waiting on him and wishing, not for the first time that evening, that he had his trusted Sergeant Fox on hand. 'But in lieu of a full post-mortem, indeed without your own local police force until either the telephone line or the bridge can be repaired, we shall all have to muddle through as best we can. Until we know what has happened to Matron and to Mr Brown's body, I am forced to treat this as a murder case, in addition to one of theft. At the very least there is something extremely unusual in substituting one body for another, unusual enough to suggest the certain possibility of criminal activity.'

Alleyn paused, the office was silent and, finally, so was the world outside, the howling winds that had so recently abated to a soft lull were now entirely absent. He wished himself anywhere but here, doing anything but what he was about to do. Beyond the thin wooden walls and the corrugated iron roof of this cramped office were the wide plains, encompassing the small, sleepy towns and stretching towards the ocean in the east, while in the opposite direction, mere miles from where they now stood in the foothills, there were range after range of mountains, their jagged peaks still glistening with a dusting of snow even now, on midsummer's night. If he had to be awake he would wish to be outside, gazing up at the misplaced Southern Hemisphere stars. Alleyn had taken to studying the unfamiliar constellations since his arrival and those that were new to him had become even more alluring as he grew to recognize their hidden forms, while those he had known since childhood seemed still more brilliant in this darkened and distant primordial land. The group stared at Alleyn, waiting for him to speak. There would be no star-gazing tonight.

'As each of you admits to having spent time with Matron this evening, and indeed several of you were with her privately in her office, I shall need to speak with you all individually. Until then, and with my sincere apologies, I must ask you to remain here in the Transport Office. I intend to trust you to keep an eye on each other, but should anyone choose to leave the office without my permission, I may be obliged to lock you in. If necessary I shall ask Sergeant Bix to post one of his men on the door. Is that clear?'

It was clear, but not at all uniformly approved.

Glossop muttered under his breath and finally blustered forth, 'It's a flamin' cheek's what it is. My bosses trust me to drive that pay-box week in, week out, across the plains, by myself mind you, I don't need no bloody—excuse me ladies,' he nodded to Sarah and Rosamund, both of whom were biting their cheeks in an attempt not to smile, 'I need neither a chaperone nor a guard to make sure I keep the money safe and I have to say I'm browned off that you, Inspector or Detective or whatever it is, don't have the same trust in me that my bosses do. The actual Government of New Zealand, I'll have you know. Not to mention that you've already made up your mind that one of us is a thief or, God forbid, a murderer, and yet you want to lock us all up together.'

Alleyn waited until Glossop had finished and responded quietly and patiently, 'The title is Chief Detective Inspector. It's a cumbersome mouthful, I agree, Mr Glossop, however I willingly answer to Inspector, Detective, Mr Alleyn, Alleyn, or even "hey you", if necessary.'

Alleyn caught Rosamund's eye and her twinkling nod of approval as he turned to Sister Comfort, who was already gearing up to give him a piece of her mind, no doubt prompted by Glossop's failure to include her when he apologized to the 'ladies'.

'What you don't seem to understand, Inspector,' she said, 'is that you are asking me to leave the supervision of my nurses to a subordinate. With Matron, I mean with Matron—' for a moment Alleyn thought that the steely woman before him might lose her composure and he noted that everyone else in the office seemed as horrified by the prospect as he himself felt and hoped he did not show. Fortunately her years of diligent training took over once more and after a moment in which Sister Comfort seemed to steady herself, the way a dinghy might right itself in the hands of a skilful sailor, she went on, 'I am now in charge of the hospital. I must be allowed to discharge my duties.'

'I appreciate that, Sister Comfort,' he said, not unkindly. 'Regardless, the duties I must discharge insist that you cannot. On his return I shall send Sergeant Bix to fetch your next in command and you shall have a word with her, deputising where necessary.'

The others were easier to deal with, while Father O'Sullivan fretted that someone ought to be with young Sydney Brown in case he awoke, he was content to wait in the office for now. Alleyn privately made a note to fetch Sydney Brown to the office as soon as possible, he too had spent some time with Matron this evening, albeit with the vicar in attendance. Young Mr Brown must be added to an already alarmingly long list of interviewees. Dr Hughes reluctantly agreed to offer his best guess as to what might have happened to Matron, although he protested once more that he was no pathologist. Sarah Warne declared herself willing to use the time to get on with the rotas for the week, if Glossop could be persuaded to allow her to sit in her own chair at her own desk.

Only Rosamund Farquharson seemed positively pleased with the situation, 'I very much want my money back and I'll do whatever needs doing to make sure I get it. You can count on me, Inspector,' she added brightly, with what Alleyn thought was a wholly unnecessary and quite charming smile.

There followed a little business as Bix returned, was sent to find Sister Comfort's subordinate, came back with the stoic nurse and orders were given, though not quite as quickly as Alleyn might have liked.

'Very good,' Alleyn said, once matters were finally accomplished to Sister Comfort's satisfaction. 'Now, Miss Warne, I have a task for you while Sergeant Bix escorts me down to the morgue, your bus had how many passengers this evening?'

'There were ten of us in total, Inspector, myself and nine passengers. Eight VADs and Sydney Brown.'

'Very well, I'd like a list of your passengers and a further list noting the patients and staff in each ward. I gather, Sister Comfort, that even the patients who are about to be discharged are confined to wards from seven in the evening?'

'That's correct, Inspector. Matron and I pride ourselves on running a tight ship, we like to know where everyone is at all times. We have a nurses' station at the entrance to each ward, and a night nurse on duty from 7 p.m. sharp, so we can give you full lists of all those servicemen and civilians who were safely in bed and certainly unable to commit the theft or anything else—'

Sister Comfort's composure left her for a moment and Alleyn stepped in quickly.

'It would be an unconfined joy to eliminate such a large number of people from my list of potential suspects.'

'Leaving just us I suppose?' Glossop asked, still red-faced with anger at the suggestion of his culpability.

'Not just us, Mr Glossop,' Sister Comfort interrupted. 'Three convalescent servicemen were given leave to walk to the front gate this evening, they're due for release any day now and we encourage active exercise before they return to service. The three in question are particularly incorrigible.'

'That's one word for them,' Rosamund couldn't help herself and Sarah Warne dug her friend in the ribs.

Sister Comfort went on, 'I know they were not in the ward at seven o'clock which is when they were due, in fact I'd not be surprised if they weren't back a good deal later.'

'Which ward?' Alleyn asked.

'Military 1.'

Alleyn nodded, 'Of course, right in the middle of all this evening's alarums. In that case, I think we might ask Sister Comfort's newly-appointed aide-de-camp to bring those three men along to join you here. And ask her to rouse young Mr Brown and bring him too, I might as well have all my chickens in one coop.'

Glossop started to bluster further about contagion from the convalescent soldiers, but Sister Comfort cut him off with a sharp reproof, had he not heard her say that the men were due for discharge and perfectly well?

'Then we're all set,' Alleyn said brightly, clapping his long hands together to hold their attention. 'Sergeant Bix, if you'll accompany me back to the morgue we can ensure that the place is free from any concern before Dr Hughes begins his analysis and then we can at least leave Matron in peace for what remains of this brief night. We'll then send you off on your search of the premises. We may even find that our friend Will Kelly put a girdle round the hospital in forty minutes and the missing Mr Brown awaits us in the morgue. I admit that I'm sorely missing my fingerprints man Bailey right now, we can, however, at last set this investigation in motion. As soon as the telephone lines are reconnected and the bridge once again passable, I hope to have something of use to hand over to your fine New Zealand constabulary,' he directed the latter remark at Glossop. He looked around at those gathered in the office, 'This may be the shortest night, but I fear it may well seem the longest. I suggest you make yourselves busy, and those with no business will just have to make your-selves as comfortable as possible. After you, Sergeant.'

CHAPTER THIRTEEN

Alleyn allowed Bix to lead the way into the yard. He closed the door behind them, sorely tempted to lock it but stopped himself.

Bix spoke up, 'Trusting of you, Sir.'

Alleyn smiled, looked down at the short, stocky man, his receding sandy curls slicked back neatly, his boots as brightly polished as if he were headed for the parade ground, 'If I were to take a guess, I'd say you were a student of human nature, am I right, Sergeant?'

'I try, Sir. Always useful to understand what makes your men tick.'

'I completely agree.'

In the dim light from the office windows Alleyn watched Bix first frown and then nod, smiling, 'So what you're trying here is something of a ruse then?'

'Is it?' Alleyn asked amiably.

'Well, you said you trusted them, but you can't really, not every man Jack of them.'

'Or Jill. Indeed. But I didn't say I trusted them all, Bix, I said I trusted them to keep an eye on one another.'

'Too right you did, Inspector. Might it be more likely

you're trusting them to notice if one of them is a bit off?'

'It might indeed.'

'And holing them up in there, on what's turned out a lovely night after all—' Bix added, peering at the diamond-sharp stars above.

'Lovely,' Alleyn repeated, looking up. He was enjoying himself enormously, he'd missed this kind of back and forth with Fox.

'Someone's bound to have a pop, aren't they? Sooner or later. Likely sooner, I reckon, what with you closing the door and that window in Transport having been stuck for most of the past year.'

'Is it stuck?' Alleyn asked lightly, 'I'm sure I didn't notice.'

'Of course not, Sir.'

'However, I rather expect someone will "have a pop" as you say, Bix. Human nature being what it is, sometimes the company of other people is all the irritant required to form a pearl of revelation. We can but hope.'

They were walking along the yard at a good pace, the scent of roses even stronger after the drenching the land had taken earlier. The wards were fully silent now, the covered lamps at each nurses' station offering just enough light to delineate the windows, the half-glass porch doors, and the broader shape of the buildings. Beyond the wards, Alleyn felt the solid presence of the foothills and then the immense strength of the mountains, stretching back and westward, forming the spine of this long island. Whatever the night held, the midsummer sun would rise on those peaks soon enough.

Bix stopped after they had passed the Surgery on their left, 'Here we are, Sir.'

'Here?' Alleyn questioned, peering ahead into the darkness, 'I thought your new army buildings were ahead of us at this point? I must be more disoriented than I thought.'

'They are, Sir, a wee way on, but the morgue's to your right. Sorry, I'm so used to getting about the place in the dark most nights, always some emergency or other, I'd say I can see my way with my eyes closed.'

'How useful,' Alleyn spoke quietly into the night.

Bix flicked on his torch and shone it to their right. Alleyn saw that they were twenty feet or so from the morgue, which was set back and away from the wards. It was a squat building with a shallow roof, hidden by the porter's hut and yet another impressive row of roses.

'The roses work well to hide this statement of mortality from the patients,' Alleyn said.

'They do, Sir, too many flamin' roses if you ask me. It's like a *pot-pourri* of death, draws even more attention to it and I know that's not the plan.'

Alleyn smiled to himself. Bix's French accent was only slightly more alarming than that of his own dear Sergeant Fox. If he had to be abroad tonight, he was glad to have Bix at his side.

Bix shone the torchlight on the morgue door, allowing Alleyn to step forward and unlock the building, and then he gestured to the detective, 'After you, Sir.'

The door opened into a small entrance area, beyond which was a steeply sloping passage, perhaps three times the width of the old trolley that had caused so much distress and no more than ten paces of Alleyn's own long legs. The passage opened out into the morgue itself.

'I took the liberty of leaving the trolley in here, Sir,' Bix said, indicating the ancient trolley, hard against the wall immediately to their left. Alleyn asked him to shine his torch on the body bag for a moment and he had a sense that they were both holding their breath as he opened the ties on the bag and confirmed that Matron was indeed still lying there. Alleyn stared at her face for a moment and then carefully closed the bag. He waited as Bix lit each of the gas lanterns attached to the walls, the room becoming both starker and smaller as its limits were defined.

Between the descending gradient of the passage and ascent of the ground immediately behind the building, Alleyn estimated that the space in which they now stood was more than half built into the earth. It was clearly a worthy achievement to create a morgue this cool in the long hot summers of the plains. Alleyn thought that he would have enjoyed a chat with the architect over a pipe, assuming there had been an architect, this far from the big towns. Perhaps the place had been crafted by a canny builder, someone who understood the shape of the land. He stood in the centre of the morgue and took in the room around them. Directly before him were eight cavities for the dead, each with a short, plain linen curtain in front hanging on brass rings from an identical length of dowling. The curtains were no doubt for the proprieties of the living rather than those already returning to the earth. He looked from the holes carved into the rock to the trolley.

'These appear to be trolley height, is that right, Bix?' Alleyn asked, advancing towards the dark recesses that seemed to open into the land itself.

'They are Sir, Will Kelly brings in a body and he—I'll admit I'm guessing, I've not seen it myself. My guess is he just slides it in.'

'Hopefully managing to avoid tipping himself in at the

same time,' Alleyn responded. 'Hand me your torch, will you?'

Alleyn shone the torch into the first three cavities. They appeared to reach a good seven feet back, and were as wide and long as the largest of men. He thought again of Fox for a moment and felt a primal shiver reach across his shoulders. He brushed it away with an impatient sniff.

'Looks like it ends in rock back there, Bix?'

'That's right, Sir. The old boys who built the hospital knew what they were up to.'

'Old boys?'

'Farmers mostly, settlers. Those blokes could do anything you like with a yard and a half of Number 8 wire, but they took it seriously, all right, and there was one old boy—' Bix paused and scratched his head, waiting to see if a little more scratching would help. When it didn't he went on, 'Sorry, Sir, his name's gone in all the excitement, anyway, he got himself halfway through an engineering degree, proper examinations and all that malarkey, up in Wellington, and then the Boer War came and he was off with our lads over there. Well, they wanted engineers, obviously. They said there was nothing he didn't know about building a bridge across a raging river or digging deep into the earth to find water, no matter how dry it looked. The story goes he never finished his degree, the war took it out of him, as it does some men. He didn't become an engineer as such, but he was the one who told them they ought to build the morgue right here, and they all knew, because it was him who'd said it, they'd better listen. Told them it might look like a wooded slope up the back, but beneath the bush was the foothills, solid and proper. Too right. 'Course there was no electricity out here back then, that came long after, so this was the spot they chose. They dug down and let the rock do the insulating for them. Dry in winter, cool in summer.'

Alleyn took in the information from Bix's soliloquy, then indicated the lanterns, 'And is there no electricity in the morgue still?'

'I reckon Matron never saw the point, that and the bills were piling up. You can't rob Peter to pay Paul in a hospital, Sir.'

'No?' Alleyn said, almost wearily, and checked himself. If Bix had a great deal to say, at least he was offering it willingly. Eliciting information about the scene of a crime was a basic technique taught to every constable, he must be losing his touch if he'd almost silenced a witness. 'Do explain.'

'A hospital is a world unto itself, not unlike the army. Or the police force, I don't doubt. My mother was a nurse, before she married my father, so I knew it for a fact before I came here. The hospital is ruled by the Matron. She says what's what and even the fanciest of surgeons works that out for himself after a while. Everyone knows it's right that she's in charge, 'cause they live and breathe the hospital, it's all they do. They weren't meant to get married you see, back in the old days, and if they did they had to leave the job, so those that stayed, they'd pretty much given their lives to it. This Matron does, or she did, anyway, I mean—'

Bix stopped, looking to the body bag on the trolley.

'Go on,' Alleyn asked.

'I reckon she figured, Gawd bless her, there's no point spending money putting electricity in the morgue when the roofs are leaking and bills want paying. She's the one who'll get it in the neck from the patients in the end. My point being, she can't—I mean she couldn't—rob herself, could she?'

'And it's not as if those resting in the morgue will complain of the lack of electric light?'

'Exactly, Sir,' Bix smiled, delighted to be in the company of someone who cared for his musing.

Closer inspection revealed exactly what Alleyn had expected from the start, the morgue was disappointingly ordinary. It was small, as befitted a rural hospital that had, at least until wartime, dealt with little more than farming accidents and the routine life events of welcome births and the expected deaths of those whose lives had run their course on this fertile land.

He turned to a sturdy table set against the wall opposite the cavities. The stainless steel cladding that covered the wooden surface reflected and added to the light from the lanterns. No doubt it was upon this table that post-mortems were carried out. To the right of the table was a small desk with a heavy ledger on top. Using his handkerchief as a glove, and careful only to touch the cover and pages by the top corner, Alleyn lifted the cover and flicked through several pages, revealing dates, names and causes of death in a clear, rounded hand. The last date was in October this year.

'Private Patrick Fisher?' he asked Bix.

'Paddy Fisher. Big West Coast family. Great kid, Blue they called him, on account of his red hair, you know?'

The Inspector allowed that he didn't and Bix went on.

'They brought him back covered in burns. We thought he'd make it, you know? Thought he'd get through, but burns like that, compromises the whole system, doesn't it? Smallest thing and you're gone. The kid was beginning to turn the corner, picked up a cough one week, it was pneumonia the next. Poor bugger.'

Alleyn nodded, turned away to leave Bix to his thoughts. Alongside the ledger were several large hide-bound books of anatomy, a shelf above held the usual quantity of surgical spirit, embalming fluid and the like, including half a dozen glass vials of various liquids alongside a set of different sized syringes, each of the vials individually labelled both 'Poison' and 'Do Not Ingest'. Alleyn found himself gruesomely thinking that those for whom the liquids were destined probably did not need the warnings. The glass door to an adjacent corner cupboard showed a set of weights and enamel dishes that had no doubt held organs and guts in their time. The whole place appeared to have been polished to within an inch of its life, gleaming with a dull sheen in the lamplight and the detective had to concede that even Bailey would have had trouble getting fingerprints from a room as thoroughly cleaned as this.

'How well do you know the morgue, Bix?' Alleyn said.

'Not well, Sir, but I've been in here on occasion, supervising one of the lads come to fetch a fellow soldier.' He paused, 'I know it might feel that we're out of it over here, to those of you who've been in London, but as well as the lads we've lost in action, there's been blokes sent home in the hope of getting better after losing a leg, or a chunk of their guts blown out, maybe they've had some time on one of the hospital ships, Sir, but even so, they've been no-go in the end. So I don't know it well, but I've been in here more often than I'd like.'

'There's nothing out of the ordinary?'

Bix looked around.

'Sorry to let you down, but nothing seems off that I can see.'

'Not at all, Bix. And is it always this spotlessly clean?'

'The whole hospital is, Sir, if Matron has—sorry—if she had her way. All that cleanliness next to godliness palaver, a tartar for it she is. Was.'

Alleyn took Bix's torch and shone it again into the empty cavities one after the other, noting the absence of dust, the smooth shine on the chiselled-out spaces, each one finished on the base with a dull steel which shone in the torch beam.

He stepped back, 'I can think of worse places to be laid out than nestled at the foot of your astonishing mountains.'

'You sound like one of our Māori lads, Inspector, always on about the land and how it's a living thing, they are.'

'A healthy respect for natural forces does none of us harm, Bix.'

'Fair enough, Sir.'

Alleyn returned the torch to its owner and rubbed his long hands together, it was definitely cooler in here than the rest of the hospital, the settlers had done a good job.

'Right Bix, we'll get Dr Hughes to come down and see if he can't establish a cause of death. I'll set you to keep an eye on him, if you will.'

Bix looked horrified, 'Ah, come off it, Sir, you don't suspect young Hughes, do you? Surely not.'

Alleyn shook his head, 'Whether I suspect him or not is irrelevant. One of the worst aspects of this blasted job is that one is obliged to treat absolutely everyone with suspicion. A certain style of modern detective fiction might show our hero rushing to a terribly clever supposition by page sixteen and spending the rest of the novel proving himself

113

right, but for your long-suffering actual policeman there is merely painstaking elimination and solid detective work, which means questioning every possible suspect. That will be my next task. Let's just look over Matron's office first, shall we?'

CHAPTER FOURTEEN

It was testament to the resourceful settlers in whom Bix had such pride that the noise of the fracas from the Transport Office struck them forcefully the moment the sergeant opened the heavy morgue door into the asphalt yard. Alleyn grimaced and declared that Matron's office could wait, while Bix broke into a run, throwing the torch back to the Inspector in an underarm pass that Alleyn deemed worthy of New Zealand's famed rugby players. As Bix hared off to deal with matters in the office, Alleyn took his time locking up the morgue. He had no doubt who was causing a fuss back at the Transport Office, nor did he have any concern about Bix's ability to handle the matter. He studied the key in his hand, felt the smooth turn of the lock as he tried it, and the deft, certain click of the dead-bolt sliding into place in the dark. Safe as the grave. He winced at his appropriate turn of phrase and turned back into the yard, past the porter's lodge. Several of the night staff had left their lonely posts to come to the porches of their wards, while a number of newly-awakened patients were peering into the dark from verandahs and windows.

Alleyn whispered to the nurse in the first porch he came

to, the sparsely populated Civilian 1, 'I'd get your charges back to bed, if I were you, Nurse. I'm sure you don't want to hear from Sister Comfort about the proper care of night wards?'

He had almost invoked Matron in his warning and thought better of it as the words were forming in his mouth, not only was Sister Comfort on the premises and at least available to be presented to the staff, she was plainly a more daunting prospect than Matron.

'Oh no, I wouldn't want to worry Sister Comfort, not at all,' squeaked the nurse and Alleyn could almost hear her blanching at the thought.

'Sergeant Bix has it all in hand,' he added.

'It did sound like an awful row,' she answered, backing away slowly.

Alleyn smiled in the dark, his voice light and soothing, 'The sergeant seemed to think a possum might have found its way into the Transport Office, feral creatures, I gather?'

'Crikey yes,' she answered, satisfied with this answer and called to her fellow nurse, one ward up, 'Possum they reckon, Sandra, no cause for alarm.'

'No cause for alarm?' Sandra answered with a hearty laugh, 'You've obviously never had a possum eat right through your telephone wire!'

The message was passed along the porches and verandahs, the night nurses resumed their posts, the patients their beds, and Alleyn smiled with pride at a lie that came so easily and was so apt for the location.

By the time he was at the other end of the long yard, the wards were again hushed but for the grunts of their inhabitants and the Transport Office itself was as silent as one of the many dormant volcanoes Alleyn had observed in his travels throughout New Zealand. As silent and as potentially lethal.

'Thank you, Sergeant,' he said to Bix as he stepped into the tight confines of the office, tighter still since Bix's man had brought over the three hastily-dressed soldiers from Military 1.

Bix nodded and stepped aside, allowing Alleyn to take up his position beside the door.

The Inspector looked around him at the small company crowded into the office, the faces that stared back were a mixed bag. There were masks of fury, resentment, guilt, dismay and, he was intrigued to note, amused boredom playing on Rosamund Farquharson's freshly lipsticked mouth.

'I'm most awfully sorry to have kept you waiting all this time,' Alleyn began, playing up the reticent Englishman, he had an idea that a mask of his own might come in useful as the night progressed. 'I'm sure you're all feeling a little concerned by the events of the evening so far.'

'Concerned?' expostulated one of the soldiers, a tall, sallow chap with a surly expression, 'I'll say we're flamin' well concerned.'

Bix raised a hand in caution but he was ignored and Private Bob Pawcett went on, 'We've been dragged from our kip in the middle of the night with no reason and no call for all this high-handedness either, I might add. We get here and Rosie fills us in on the god-awful scene with the Matron. No one's telling us anything other than it's not even our own police who are playing the Almighty giving out orders like nobody's business. Glossop lets on it's some Pommie bloke and then you turn up, the fellow that's been skulking about Military 1 for the past week and never even made any damned effort to introduce yourself to us, thinks he's above the likes of an ordinary soldier, you've made that quite clear.'

'I do apologize,' Alleyn spoke coolly, 'I was not at liberty to reveal my identity, and as a military man yourself, you'll understand the need to obey rules.'

There was a pointed tone to Alleyn's voice when he mentioned rules, prompting a hurried, 'He does that, we all do,' from the good-looking Private Sanders who also took the opportunity to kick his mate in the shins.

Pawcett was not to be silenced, 'You pull rank all you like, Sarge,' he nodded to Bix, 'I'll take it from you, you're my boss after all, at least you are here at the hospital, but I'm damned if I'm going to be kept in here all night with no bloody reason given and no idea when we're allowed back to our beds either. *And* all three of us still recuperating.'

'That's a very good point, Private,' Alleyn agreed. 'And of course, I'm sure that you and your fellows here have fastidiously stuck to the regulations regarding recuperation, have you not? No late nights, no card games when you could sneak past the night nurse, no going out beyond the hospital boundaries? That *is* right, isn't it?'

Pawcett had the sense to shut up then, there was something in Alleyn's tone that suggested a military past and a soldier who did not suffer fools gladly, whether they were seniors or subordinates.

Alleyn was about to continue when Rosamund spoke up, a twinkle in her pretty eyes, 'Don't you even want to know what the row was about, Inspector?'

'Not especially, Miss Farquharson. You see, I doubt very much that your account would accord with Mr Glossop's, or his with that of the Private here, so I'd prefer to leave that for the moment and concentrate on the less salacious but rather more pressing duties ahead of me.'

Alleyn turned to Bix and they quietly exchanged a few words, the sergeant nodding his head from time to time and taking notes in his military notebook. Finally, Bix nodded assent one last time, left the office, and Alleyn turned back to the chorus of expectant faces.

'Now begins the most irritating of police tasks. I shall have to interview each of you, one by one, to better understand what has happened here tonight.'

Alleyn saw that Glossop, even redder in the face than before, was about to protest, and he held up his hand, 'I am sorry, Mr Glossop, I fully appreciate that as you personally have the trust of no less than the Government of New Zealand, you find the suggestion you might be guilty of anything at all both preposterous and insulting. I expect all of you feel this way to some extent.' He smiled ruefully, 'Almost all of you. Police procedure is a dreary thing and yet it must be followed. Dr Hughes, if you'll follow me, we can get started and then Sergeant Bix will take you down to the morgue to see if you can't find any answers regarding Matron. I'm hoping that while I conduct these interviews Bix will complete an investigation of his own and find either the missing money or the missing Mr Brown Senior, preferably both, and we shall all be safe in our beds before long.'

Dr Hughes raised an eyebrow, 'How likely do you think that is, Inspector?'

Alleyn shrugged lightly, 'No less likely than a theft, a missing body and a spare turning up out of the blue. Shall we?'

Dr Hughes stood and Alleyn noticed his quick glance to Sarah Warne who was avidly studying the transport rota at her desk. He noticed too that Hughes darted an even quicker glance to Rosamund Farquharson and the surprisingly half-hearted smile she gave back. Despite his brief acquaintance with Miss Farquharson, it did not seem in keeping with her character for her to smile quite so wanly in response.

Alleyn made a mental calculation and followed it with a brief announcement, 'I'll speak to Father O'Sullivan after Dr Hughes, and then you three soldiers,' he said to the men of Military 1, 'You might as well all come along together as you seem to be so happily in each other's pockets. Bix will fetch you when I'm ready.'

'We can find our way to the Records Office,' Pawcett mumbled.

'I'm sure you can, but the earlier disturbance has underlined a necessity for security, so I shall lock this door after Dr Hughes and myself.'

'But, but—' Glossop spluttered, 'what if that means you're locking us in here with a murderer?'

Alleyn smiled as he held open the door for Dr Hughes, 'It could be, Mr Glossop, that I am locking him—or her—out. You might feel more comfortable if you look at it that way. Now please, do behave yourselves, we've a great deal to get through yet.'

CHAPTER FIFTEEN

Dr Hughes followed Alleyn back into the yard and he made for the Records Office, but Alleyn held out a hand to stop him, 'I'd like to take a quick look at Matron's office, if you don't mind accompanying me?'

Hughes nodded his assent and they stopped at the steps to Matron's office. Alleyn crouched down and peered at the boarding on either side of the steps.

'All of these buildings are raised off the ground, are they? Offices, wards and army buildings?' he asked.

'Yes,' Hughes said, 'I noticed it too when I first arrived. It seems to be very common out here, many of the buildings are raised a foot or two off the ground rather than dug into foundations. They add this skirting effect with boarding to cover the emptiness beneath the building. All of it made of wood, of course.'

'Less likely to come down in an earthquake, I suppose?'

'Exactly.'

Alleyn shone Bix's torch on either side of the steps and along the shallow fence of skirting described by Hughes. 'I see what you mean. It's almost as if the offices were just dropped into place by a child playing at building a hospital.

They've blocks to hold them off the ground. That keeps out the damp as well as potential flooding, I imagine, then this odd little bit of fencing around the bottom to cover the gap and give the illusion that the outer walls go right to the ground. Ingenious.'

Hughes smiled wearily in the dark and Alleyn could hear the resignation in his tone, 'As I've found in my time here, Inspector, there is a great deal in New Zealand that is built on illusion and much of it ingenious indeed.'

'You shall have to tell me more later, Hughes. For now, would you mind terribly cooling your heels out here while I have a quick look inside Matron's office? Bix and I meant to give it a once-over on our way back from the morgue but we were dragged away by that damn fool fuss playing out with Glossop at the centre. I shan't be long.'

Pulling the keys from his pocket, Alleyn let himself into the office. He crossed deliberately to the desk and, after covering his hand with his handkerchief, he reached carefully for the desk lamp. He smiled to himself at the extent of the care he was taking and he thought, 'There's likely any number of jumbled prints on the lamp, and no certainty the thief needed the light, but I don't want to put the noses of the local police out of joint before we've even met.' He found and turned on the lamp. Returning to the door he said to Hughes, 'An awful bother, I know, but you wouldn't mind standing in the light here, would you? It won't do for me to lose my first suspect before interrogation.'

'When you put it so nicely,' Hughes responded drily, shifting a step to his left and placing himself in the faint line of warm lamplight.

'Good man,' Alleyn nodded pleasantly, turning to continue his study of the office.

It was exactly as they'd left it just over an hour earlier, the safe door wide open, Matron's leather chair upturned where Glossop had sent it flying, the pile of papers fanned out on Matron's desk. Alleyn knelt before the safe and shone Bix's torch into the empty space, confirming what they all knew, the safe was indeed quite empty.

He stared at the open safe for a minute longer, wishing Fox was alongside him and then looked down to Dr Hughes in the yard, 'Odd, don't you think, Hughes?'

'Which part, Inspector?' Hughes replied with a look around him and an incredulous shrug, 'I have to say, it all feels very odd to me.'

'Yes, of course,' Alleyn answered distractedly, a deep furrow dividing his high brow, 'I meant that the safe was left open, unlocked. The lock was not forced, which means the thief had a key and yet they did not lock the safe after them, which would at least have ensured the theft remained undiscovered until Matron came to return the payroll to Mr Glossop in the morning. Odd.'

'Perhaps someone disturbed them? Or they lost it in the act of transferring the payroll?'

'Perhaps,' Alleyn acceded and then turned his attention to the mess of papers on the desk.

He leafed through the scattered pages using his pen to separate them. There were a few letters to do with medical matters and specific patients, but the bulk of the papers were bills and quite overdue ones at that. The sums in themselves were not enormous, but the accumulated total was such that any establishment would find it difficult to repay without a serious windfall or a generous benefactor, ideally both. He sifted through the letters again, carefully checking the dates at the top of each one. While they were

123

not in the tidy order he might have expected given Matron's attention to duty, they were, more or less, dated consecutively, as if someone had been through them hurriedly, pushing the papers apart to find one they sought above all others. Eventually he found one letter that was neither a medical letter nor a bill. He carefully inched it out from the pile and frowned as he read it. When he turned to the post-script he whistled softly to himself. 'Oh gods. That poor woman.' Alleyn checked himself. He'd instructed his men often enough that it did no good to feel pity for anyone at this stage of the game, not when there was much still to discover about the players.

Alleyn carefully folded the letter, the handkerchief covering his long fingers, and slid it into another envelope from the stack on the shelf beside Matron's desk. Once it was safely stowed, he folded the envelope and put it in his pocket. Touching his pipe, a thought occurred to him.

'I wonder, Hughes,' he said, crossing to the door where the doctor waited, 'if you might accommodate me? I've been cooped up all evening in that private room in Military 1—'

'On your mysterious "other business", Inspector?'

'Quite so,' Alleyn replied briskly. 'And I'd very much like a tour of the grounds. If you don't mind we could walk and talk, and I'll take the opportunity to smoke a pipe.'

'Do you always offer your potential suspects the choice of location for their interrogation?' Hughes asked, finding himself a little relaxed for the first time that evening and thinking that perhaps, under other circumstances, he might rather enjoy the company of his fellow Englishman.

'Only those I feel have something they'd like to say.'

'Oh,' Hughes said with a frown, his shoulders and

stomach instantly tense once more. 'I had no idea I was so very obvious.'

'Now then, young cub, don't go all petulant on me,' Alleyn rejoined. 'I'm just rather well practised at this bit of detecting, and I far prefer to speak with one who wants to talk than with those from whom I am forced to poke and pry their secrets. What do you say?'

'Do I—do I have a secret to tell you?' Dr Hughes stuttered, sounding shaken.

'Would you like a walk, Hughes?'

'Ah. Yes. I would. Yes, thank you, Sir.'

'Good-oh.'

Now that the wind had swept away the clouds of the evening, the combination of a newly-risen half-moon and the vast sweep of the Milky Way led Alleyn to decide there was enough light for them to walk without the torch. He had an idea that Hughes might be more willing to talk in less light.

'Are you all right without the torch, Hughes?'

'I prefer it, Sir. Especially if you're to interrogate me.'

'I imagine a villain might feel the same,' Alleyn said lightly.

There was a wry smile in Hughes's voice as he replied, 'But would a villain have the sense to point it out?'

'A canny one might, hoping to take the old man for a fool.'

'But you are neither old nor a fool, Inspector.'

'You flatter me. Let's begin.'

At first Dr Hughes responded monosyllabically to Alleyn's questions about his training, his work in the field and his initial reluctance to stay in New Zealand. He opened up when he admitted that, adept as he had become at patching up young men to send them back to war, he did so with a terrible ambivalence.

'I want to heal them, that's my job, my calling you might say. I've wanted to be a doctor for as long as I can remember and a surgeon ever since I started my training. But at the same time I feel very strongly that I want to keep them safe, and I know they're safer here, in hospital. Not that they'd thank me for doing so.'

Alleyn asked, 'Do you also wish to keep yourself safe?'

'I'm not a coward, Inspector,' Hughes bridled at the suggestion.

'I know that,' Alleyn said simply, 'but you have seen action. It wouldn't be wicked to wish to preserve your own life, just as you wish to preserve the lives of others.'

Alleyn knew it would be useful in the coming hours to use the payroll theft and the revelation of Matron's body to ask questions that might also shine a light on his espionage inquiry, and Hughes seemed to be labouring under a painful self-imposed silence. Just as Alleyn was gearing himself up to play the hard man, Hughes stopped in his tracks.

'I need to tell you something, Sir.'

'And must we stand still while you do?'

'Oh no, I'm sorry. Of course not.'

They walked on along the yard and around to the main entrance where Alleyn had previously noted a well-placed bench. The sound of the swollen river ever closer, Alleyn felt rather than saw Hughes's fear, heard it in his careful step, his fretful sigh. He'd hoped the young man would simply blurt it out, whatever it was, but it was not to be.

'Honestly, Hughes, do you really want me to probe? I will if I must, but I find that part of the business awfully distasteful and I'd far rather not.'

'I'll say it. I've been a damned fool, Inspector.'

'A fool but not a thief?'

'You shall judge.'

Ahead in the darkness the river sung out its swollen speed. Alleyn imagined it must be very high now and wondered how much of the storm had taken place up in the mountains themselves, if there was still a great deal of water to flow downhill towards the hospital, crashing over the brutal boulders and biting at the riverbank. They took their seats on the bench thoughtfully provided for hospital visitors who might need a break from the bustle and worry inside the complex of buildings. The two men sat companionably as Alleyn carefully filled and lit his pipe, took a long draw, waited for Hughes to light his cigarette, and finally the detective spoke into the night air, 'I've been as patient as I can, Dr Hughes, but there are several others awaiting their turn in the confessional. Come on now, spit it out.'

'Very well. I love Sarah, Inspector. Deeply. But I know I am not good enough for her.'

'Indeed?'

'I had a terrible time of it on my last trip out. Dreadful. And now I fear I am broken. I wake in the night, crying and sweating, I see visions of the men I tried, and failed, to save. You know, Inspector, Matron is, oh damn it all, she *was* a great boon to me. She's been a nurse for many years, she listened to me. Sometimes people don't want to know how it is, but she let me speak. I told her some—' he hesitated, 'some tales. I told her some of the things we were forced to do out there, by circumstance, you understand.

127

There were methods we employed, unorthodox methods. I became skilled at putting men out of their suffering, often for all too brief a moment. On many occasions my surgical skills were useless. Very often the best I could offer was relief from pain and perhaps, sometimes . . .'

His voice broke off and Alleyn spoke into the night, careful not to look at the young man on his right, 'Do try to remember, I am a policeman, Hughes.'

'I do, but you have seen battle, I think?'

'Yes. And I have known many men use their professional skills to do what they could for the injured, the broken, and those beyond salvation.'

'So you know what I—'

Dr Hughes heard the warning in Alleyn's voice when the detective interrupted brusquely, 'I know only what you tell me.' Alleyn waited a moment and then prompted, 'Men have suffered terrible things in war and come home broken, and women have still loved them, stood by them. Are you sure that's all there is to say?'

'All?' asked Hughes in despair, 'I'm a wreck. At first I hated being here in New Zealand, hated feeling as if I'd escaped while my fellows were still in the thick of it. But then I hoped that the quiet out here might help, the nightmares might stop if I concentrated on doing my best for the men in these wards.'

'Did it work?'

'For a while, yes, all was calm, but for the past month or so, in fact since I began to settle here ever such a little, the nightmares have come back with a vengeance. I cannot stand to look at a corpse, I start shaking if I'm alone with a body. I could barely cope with the old man's death earlier tonight and you saw me funk your order to examine

Matron's body. I can't . . .' He stopped and his voice was very quiet when he said, 'Sarah deserves better than me. She deserves a man who is not a coward.'

'Have you said any of this to her?'

Hughes shook his head, 'I can't. I've mentioned concerns about money, let her believe I'm in debt. I thought perhaps if she thought I was less of a—'

'A catch?'

'Oh no, she's not like that, not at all.'

'But even so, you're willing to treat her as if she is "like that", rather than explain what is truly troubling you?' Alleyn waited a moment before he went on, and when Dr Hughes did not respond his tone was very stern, 'I don't know Miss Warne, but she doesn't strike me as the charmed life sort of girl. I imagine she might be very understanding if you could bring yourself to tell her the truth—the whole truth, mind,' he added quietly.

Hughes turned to Alleyn in horror, 'Is that what you'd do?'

Alleyn groaned, 'Dear God, you don't want to know what I'd do, it's what I'd advise. My own record of speaking my heart to young women is neither here nor there. You're being a fool, Hughes, to yourself and to Miss Warne, and you know damned well what I'm talking about.'

'I don't—I'm not—'

Alleyn listened as Hughes attempted to claim otherwise and then gave up in the throes of the attempt. He spoke firmly, 'You are and you do. There's something else you're not telling me and it's as plain as day. As plain as Orion up there,' he said, pointing to the vivid constellation above. 'You really ought to say it yourself, it will be much nastier if I have to dig.'

'Damn you, Alleyn, I can't,' Hughes muttered, bent forward, his head in his hands covering his face, 'Even if it means you suspect me all the more, I cannot say it.'

Alleyn sighed, 'Then we'd best get back and I'll take on the next initiate. I'm sorry you're suffering, Hughes, you're not the first man to do so and you won't be the last. There will no doubt be many more like you before this blasted war is out. I truly do not think a case of shell-shock or whatever they're calling it these days is any reason to disqualify yourself from happiness with a young lady you say you love. I'm going to stick my neck out here and say that your bad case of guilty conscience may have less to do with the heat of battle or the events afterwards than you imagine. I'd hazard a guess that you've been the kind of idiot that gives young men a bad name. I'll also state that you're continuing to behave like an idiot by not telling me the whole truth.' Alleyn stood up swiftly, stretching his long legs, and spoke over his shoulder to Hughes as he sped up, leading them back towards the hospital buildings, 'I shall take my next victim to the Records Office, and while I'm hard at it, you and Bix must go down to the morgue, he can keep an eye on you and you can take a quick look at Matron.' He spoke over Hughes's demurral, 'I'm sorry to ask, but you need do nothing more than assure me that she did not get knocked over the head or have her throat cut, anything else we shall leave to the local officers. Do you think you can manage that if Bix is with you?'

Hughes muttered an unhappy assent and Alleyn asked, 'Now, who do you think I ought to question next? Our good vicar, the three boisterous soldiers, or perhaps one of Helena or Hermia?'

'I'm sorry?'

'It's midsummer night, although I fear there will be no dreaming for any of us. Which young lady shall I interview next, the tall and fair Miss Farquharson or the small and dark Miss Warne?'

Not sure whether or not to consider himself in disgrace, the young doctor spoke into the dark, 'Oh, well, I really couldn't say, Sir.'

'No, I rather thought you might come over all coy at that question. Look here, Hughes,' Alleyn stopped himself, he was already overstepping his boundaries in taking this case on in the middle of the night, with Bix as his only support, then he shrugged and said it anyway, 'In for a penny—look Hughes, I simply think, and I'm no expert on the ways of love or of women, but I do believe in making a clean breast of things if at all possible. Be honest with the girl, tell her what you feel, your situation, your fears if you can. What have you got to lose by coming clean?'

'Everything, Sir, that's the problem.'

Alleyn shook his head at the young man's words, 'In which case I imagine you're not keen to be locked up in the Transport Office with everyone else?'

'Not especially. There is another pressing issue though.'

'More pressing than a visit to the morgue?'

'I really ought to check on the wards, I have a few patients I like to see at this time of night, they're in a great deal of pain and don't sleep at all well. Sometimes it helps to have a friendly ear.'

'Ah, so you're medical doctor turned father confessor?'

'If it's useful. I want to be useful.'

'I'm sure you do.'

'We usually check on the night nurses around this time

too, make sure everything is in order. It wouldn't do for them to suspect something's going on, would it?'

Alleyn rubbed his nose, 'No it wouldn't, well thought. Although I rather fear the cat may be out of the bag before dawn. Very well, take Sergeant Bix on your rounds with you, and as soon as you're done, the pair of you can head down to the morgue. I know,' he said, as Hughes started to protest, 'I'm asking you to take on what I know must be an extremely distasteful task, one any friend of Matron's might blanch at, let alone a young man ostensibly in her employ, because I need your help. Given what you've told me, or rather what you've not told me, I should think you'd be more than willing to find a way to get on my good side. Am I right?'

Alleyn was glad to hear him muster a solid enough, 'Of course, Sir.'

'Good. Then find me when you have something to report, I shall make the Records Office my interrogation room. I may be there for some time to come.'

CHAPTER SIXTEEN

In their absence Bix had roused the sleepy young Mr Brown and sent one of his trusted men with him to the Records Office. When Alleyn found them the youthful soldier was waiting patiently, Sydney Brown sitting alongside, hunched over the pillow he still held, his head sagging almost onto his folded arms, which were resting heavily on his thin legs, a perfectly posed picture of exhaustion and dejection. Alleyn had a quiet word with the soldier, thanked him for his duty and elicited a smile both shy and proud for his thanks. The soldier tripped away, his lop-sided gait giving the reason for his serving at home rather than abroad. Alleyn stood quietly for a moment at the door and stared after the young man, a peculiar expression on his face. Then he shook his head, squared his shoulders and advanced into the small office.

Sydney Brown proved as monosyllabic with Alleyn as he had been with Sarah Warne on the journey out to the hospital. Alleyn expressed his condolences, Sydney Brown mumbled, 'Yip.' Alleyn asked had he travelled far, Sydney muttered 'Nah'. Alleyn sighed, frowning. There was something strange in the young man's demeanour, something that didn't quite fit. Even with Sydney's clear espousal of the New Zealand working man's taciturn delivery, with his grandfather so recently deceased, Alleyn had expected some show of sadness or upset.

'Look here, Sydney, I don't mean this to sound quite as brutal as it no doubt will, but were you and your grandfather close?'

Sydney's dry lips levered almost into a sneer, his dark eyes clouded even more and he muttered, 'Nah, we, you know, nah. Not us.'

After a frustrating interview, Alleyn had ascertained the barest of details about the young man. His father and grandfather had fallen out many years ago which was why Sydney barely knew old Mr Brown, Sydney in turn had fallen out with his own father, 'old bugger's a brute, haven't seen him since I left school at fourteen'. Although he had joined up as soon as he was able, he had been invalided out of service after just nine months, shot by one of his own troop in a training exercise. He lost more than half a lung and, with no love lost between Sydney and his father and nowhere else to go, he was sent home to his grandfather's farm to recuperate.

'Not that I was welcome there, the old man didn't give me the time of day, just wanted me fit and working the farm.'

'That must have been hard.'

'Hard? It was bloody awful. The lot of it. I should never have been shot in the first place. We had a Sergeant Major dim as they come, handing out guns left right and centre to a bunch of flippin' townies, most of them'd never seen one end of a rifle from the other. Some of us, lads like me, we knew what we were about, but oh no, the brass think they know it all. Cockies like us are neither here nor there, no one listens to a word we say. So they sent us out on this stupid flamin' exercise and the next thing I know I'm flat on my back and can't even breathe to call for help. Three months in hospital being poked and prodded like a prize heifer and then it's the long way home for me when the last damn thing I want to do is be a cow cocky like my dad or a flamin' sheep farmer like the old man. Farming's no bloody life unless you're one of that lot who had it handed down to them generation after generation and you've got the likes of me doing all the flamin' work for you. It's hard yakka day in day out and no flamin' thanks for it either, backbone of this country they used to call us, but now—' he stopped to draw breath and his last words came out as a sigh, 'Ah, what's the use. I'd just hoped the war might be my way out, a way into something better.'

'I am sorry,' Alleyn spoke quietly, interested in what else the young man had to say.

'I don't want your pity,' Sydney growled back, his hand punched into a fist in the kapok of the pillow. 'And I don't want theirs either.'

'Theirs?' Alleyn asked.

'The blokes in charge, the bosses, the brass. That lot up in parliament for instance, sucking up to good old England and getting us into the war like we didn't give enough in the last one. None of them have a blind bit of sense about what they're doing, carting our boys off and sending telegrams home in their place. Windy bunch the lot of them, not as if they're taking up a post on the front line, is it? No worries about sending us off to do it for them though. They've never had a care for the working men of this

135

country, we're just cannon fodder to them, always have been, always will be.'

Sydney Brown had run out of words. The rest of his answers in response to Alleyn's questions about the fuss that had taken place in and around Matron's office, were met with a shake of the head, a shrug and Sydney's repeated insistence that he had been 'having a kip', that he was 'wiped out'.

Alleyn thanked the young man and stood to escort him to join the others in the Transport Office. As he did so he asked, 'The Bridge pub, do you know it well?'

'It'll do for drink if you're thirsty enough, I reckon. At least they're not worried about kicking you out at the six o'clock swill.'

'So I've heard. Is there anyone there who is a friend? Someone you join for a drink?'

Sydney's eyes darkened again, 'Nah, I keep myself to myself.'

'Not even a chat with the barmaid to pass the time?'

Sydney shrugged, 'Sukie Johnson's all right, but her old man and her brother are another thing altogether. They reckon they're the big men round here.'

'And they're not?'

'They've got the money all right, but that doesn't make you the be all and end all, not that they'd know it. Bastards the pair of them.' He spat on the ground as he said it.

They reached the door to the Transport Office and, having unlocked it, Alleyn held out his hand, 'Once again, I offer my condolences.'

'Yeah. Right. Thanks.'

Alleyn was interested in the force of Sydney's handshake, for someone who looked as weak as he was thin, the young man had a surprisingly firm grip. He may have despised working on the farm, but it hadn't done his strength any harm. Alleyn had met several farmers in his time in New Zealand and found them to be generous men with a deep understanding of the land they worked. It was on the tip of his tongue to say that he hoped that Sydney would one day understand the value of a life of good, hard work, but the young man had rushed on ahead into the office before he had the chance. Ignoring the others, he slammed himself on the floor, bunching up the pillow behind his head, his eyes tight shut. Alleyn thought it was no doubt better that he said nothing, no young man angry at the world ever found solace in the advice of his elders.

As Sydney Brown was swallowed into the warm fug of the crowded Transport Office, Alleyn extricated the over-heated Mr Glossop from the group. Much as he found himself tempted to leave Glossop until last, rather in the manner that a picky child might leave an unpleasant morsel on the plate in the hope he won't be forced to eat it after all, the man's ruddy complexion and mounting fury meant that he simply couldn't risk it. Alleyn didn't need another medical emergency on his hands, not even one as well-placed as this. As Bix was now back in attendance, Alleyn generously allowed that the office door might be left unlocked, letting in a little of the cooler night air, even as he led out a grumbling Mr Glossop.

In his interview Glossop quickly confirmed the exact sum that was missing and, at Alleyn's request, he wrote up a list of the specific locations that awaited their pay in the morning, having missed out on the delivery this evening.

'You don't think they'll be surprised you didn't turn up? Worried for you?' Alleyn asked.

'I'd already rung up Central Office to let them know about the blasted flat tyre, damn the roads out here, and it's not as if I haven't told them about the bridge a dozen or more times. Once the storm broke I'm sure they'll have let the other payroll drops know I wasn't going to get anywhere tonight,' Glossop paused, sighing and mopping his brow, 'Or at least, I darn well hope they did. They're the idiots who sent me out in that rackety old van, even though I'd told them time and again that the tyres needed seeing to, the bridge was in a terrible state and the roads, well, I know I've already said it, but you'd better believe me, it's even worse once you get on past the next—'

Alleyn cut him off before he had to listen to another long list of Mr Glossop's tribulations, 'Which means no one is expecting you until tomorrow morning?'

'Not now, no. Ever so lucky you turned up, aren't we, Inspector? Charging in like the cavalry and then making sure to lock us up with God knows who might want to murder us all in our beds.'

'No beds for any of us for now, Glossop,' Alleyn demurred and probed a little more, but there was not much to be had from Mr Glossop that hadn't already been ranted in public at some point over the past few hours. He was angry, he was tired, his bosses were fools, the soldiers were rogues, neither of those girls in the office were any better than they ought to be—no, not even the quiet little dark one, demure as she might paint herself—and only Jonty Glossop himself had the true measure of what was going on. A good woman, a fine woman was dead, a vast sum of money stolen, and the Inspector himself was right now

138

wasting his time interrogating the only innocent man present.

'You don't think Father O'Sullivan is an innocent man, Mr Glossop?' Alleyn asked lightly.

Glossop snorted his derision, 'I no more trust a vicar because of his dog collar than I do a policeman because of his badge, Inspector. It's the measure of a man that proves him, not his job title.'

'Clothes do not make your man?'

'They do not.'

'Very wise.'

'Nor a starched veil, if you get my drift,' Glossop added pointedly.

Alleyn demurred with a slight nod, 'It is true that Sister Comfort does not live up to her name as fully as one might wish.'

'I'll say she doesn't. Goes out of her way not to, if you ask me.'

It was on the tip of his tongue to say he hadn't asked, but Alleyn bit it back. If his long years of uncomfortable interviews had taught him anything, it was that in offering least, he gained most. He waited a moment, and another, and finally Glossop could contain himself no longer.

'I've a good head for faces, Inspector, always have. Not so bright with names, which can be a rotten trick, but I'm smart with faces. Now, I've seen Sister Comfort many a time and I've tried to get out of her way many a time, I'll admit, but there was something odd earlier on this evening. I saw her in a certain light, can't even tell you what it was, but I had a feeling something wasn't right, felt like she was spying on me. Caught a glimpse of her skulking in the shadows and damn odd it was too.'

'Odd?'

'Off, something was off with her. Out of sorts.'

'Or out of joint, as so much at Mount Seager appears to be. Do you think I ought to ask if she was quite well, Mr Glossop? Or if there was a problem, perhaps?'

'You must do as you like,' Glossop was back to his blustering self, 'you're the one's put yourself in charge and keeping us from our beds, even if that blasted cot is nothing like a bed. All I'm saying is that Sister Comfort was snooping around this evening and I saw it. No idea what she was after, but I tell you, I saw it.'

'I'll bear that in mind. Is there anything else I ought to know before I return you to the dubious comforts of the Transport Office?'

'Well yes, you haven't asked what I heard when I was in Matron's office, have you?'

Alleyn's voice was dangerously cold, 'Go on.'

'I'm not as green as I'm cabbage looking, Inspector, though no doubt your Pommie education and fancy elocution would think otherwise, and I pay attention to what's what. I was looking out from the Surgery anteroom and I saw Sister Comfort head for Matron's office, get up to the door, and turn away again. I saw the vicar head across and into Matron's office. I saw the Irish rogue hanging about the door too, though no one let him in, and then, after he'd gone I saw the door open and Matron and the vicar came out.'

'You saw them leave Matron's office together?'

Glossop blanched at the thought of explaining his fear of thunder and lightning to Alleyn, 'Ah well, not as such,' he stuttered, 'but they were definitely on the step and the next time I looked the yard was clear. When I got up to

Matron's office it was empty, so they must have headed off together. But my point is Matron and the vicar were in the office after all. So why do you think Sister Comfort thought better about knocking or even opening that office door?'

'I have no idea, but I'm sure you do.'

'I do now you come to mention it, I reckon Sister Comfort was wanting to get a look at all that money and once she heard voices inside realized she'd better scarper and quick.'

'What about Will Kelly?'

'Him? For all I know he was already tipsy and couldn't remember what he was doing at the door. You can't take his word on anything, that much is clear.'

'You appear to have very strong opinions of all of your fellows here tonight, Mr Glossop.'

'*And no wonder!*' he shrieked. 'My money's gone! Just like that! And it could have been any one of them. Matron is—was—a good woman through and through, the rest of them, I wouldn't trust them as far as I could spit.'

'You have made that quite plain.'

'With good reason. Once the coast was clear and I did get up to the office with the damned cot under my arm, I heard one hell of a row.'

'Really?' Alleyn asked.

'Ah, now you're interested, aren't you?' Glossop grinned in delight. 'Oh yes, it was a proper barney all right. One of those two girls it must have been, all "how now brown cow" with the A-E-I-O-U fancy like that, going at it hammer and tongs with some chap, not that he could get a word in edgeways, so I'd no chance of making out which of the men it was, or where it was coming from, Records or Transport. I couldn't make out a word either of them was

141

saying with the noise of the storm and the wind, so no point you asking me, but I'd lay odds that one of those young ladies isn't quite what she seems.'

'Goodness, Mr Glossop, Matron's office appears to have been a veritable Piccadilly Circus. Unfortunately with no Criterion Bar where Dr Watson might meet a chum,' Alleyn added with an almost wistful sigh.

Glossop frowned up at the tall detective and mopped his brow, 'I've no idea what you're on about, but there was a load of coming and going, a row as loud as you like, and as far as I can see, any one of that lot might be your thief and your murderer.'

'Matron too?' Alleyn asked lightly, wishing the moment he'd spoken that he'd held back.

Glossop swore heartily, declaring himself done and dusted with this farce. He stood up and after grumbling about his back and the indignity of being locked in that office with Gawd knows who, he stated that he damn well hoped Alleyn was as good at his job as that Farquharson girl had been telling them.

'She has?'

'You didn't ask us to wait in silence until you were ready for us, Inspector, and we are adults, the usual way to pass time is to talk. Natter. Bang on and on in the case of that flighty tart.'

'Tart, Mr Glossop?' Alleyn asked sharply.

'The blonde. You don't need to be a detective to work her out, but I gather you're more than any old detective, turns out you're quite the renowned sleuth back in London?'

'I don't know—'

Glossop interrupted him, holding up a pudgy hand to

stop Alleyn in the middle of his usual self-deprecating flow. Alleyn found it so disarming he almost gave a small smile.

'Now look, you need to hear this. Of course the money matters, it's—'

'Government money, yes.'

'But Matron, well—' Glossop paused, went even redder than Alleyn would have thought possible and finally he stammered out, 'She's, is—was—a fine woman. Damn fine. One of the best. I can't, can't bear, I can't bloody bear to think—'

'Quite,' Alleyn nodded, clapping Glossop on the back and sincerely regretting his earlier moment of facetiousness, 'I'll get on with the job, then, shall I?'

Glossop gulped, nodded and, head down, the rolls of his chins pushed into his chest, followed Alleyn into the yard. By the time they had taken the twenty paces from one office to the other, Glossop was back to his blustering, arrogant self, but Alleyn found he felt a little odd about the angry, fat man. He felt almost sorry for him.

After he returned Glossop to the Transport Office, the detective popped in to the Surgery anteroom, hoping to have a quick word with Will Kelly. He leaned over the prone figure, caught a strong whiff of what smelled like pure alcohol on the man's breath and, disturbing him in the climax of an almighty snore, he shook him awake. The interview was short and sweet. Kelly was deeply befuddled, insisted he had taken no drink all night but lemonade, appearances and fumes to the contrary, and confirmed Glossop's statement that he had tried to find Matron but that there had been no response to his knock on her door.

He muttered a few more sentences, each more incoherent that the last and then collapsed back down on the scrubbed linoleum floor. Alleyn gave it up as a bad job and went to fetch Father O'Sullivan.

This interview too was brief and to the point. No, the vicar had not seen anything untoward during the evening, he had been far too preoccupied ensuring that old Mr Brown's last hours were as peaceful as possible.

'And after that? Once the gentleman had passed?'

'I went to fetch Matron so she could begin the requisite paperwork.'

'Did it take you long to find her?'

'Not at all, I went to her office and gave her the news.'

'And then?'

'Oh, well then we returned to the private room.'

'How much time passed, do you think, between your arrival at her office and the two of you leaving together?'

'Five minutes at most. Matron had, of course, had the paperwork prepared for some time. Old Mr Brown had surprised us all by declining rather more slowly than expected, we had imagined him ready for death several weeks ago.'

His answers to the rest of Alleyn's questions were equally crisp. No, there was nothing of concern in Matron's office when he went to fetch her, nor anything unusual in her demeanour, and yes he would have noticed if there were anything to report, a vicar for several decades, he was likely as well-trained in understanding human frailty as the detective himself.

'And in spotting matters awry?'

'What do you mean?'

'I understand there are financial problems here, at the hospital.'

The vicar bristled, 'I wouldn't know anything about that, Matron always ran a very tight ship as far as I could see. It is wartime, Inspector. As a nation we have given up a great deal, despite our distance from the war in Europe. And Japan has now brought a terrible worry to our own shores. It hardly seems surprising that there are financial concerns everywhere you look.'

Alleyn's response was dangerously smooth, 'Indeed, but there seem to have been a number of your congregation gathered here who would have been very happy with an unexpected windfall, from young Miss Farquharson to several of the young soldiers to the hospital itself.'

'I must say, I really don't like your tone. I know these people, they are good, hard-working souls.'

'Every one of them, Father? A theft, Matron's demise, and a missing body would seem to indicate otherwise.'

Alleyn found Father O'Sullivan's response irritatingly pompous when he declared, 'Perhaps so, Inspector, but I choose to believe the best in people. It may be that our respective paths in life indicate that particular choice rather more clearly than any words. Now, if you'll excuse me, I should like to return to those members of the congregation you have confined to a small and uncomfortable office.'

Alleyn smiled, hoping that his voice did not betray his irritation, 'Of course, and I'm sure they will be grateful to have you back among them.'

They walked together to the Transport Office, and Alleyn excused himself for a moment to cool his heels outside. It wouldn't do to let the rest of them see how much the vicar had riled him. Something was not right with the man, but he was damned if he knew what it was.

'Oh, for a muse of fire, or good old Brer Fox.'

CHAPTER SEVENTEEN

Alleyn returned once more to the Transport Office and asked Sister Comfort to accompany him back to the Records Office for her interview. They had just taken their seats when there was a knock at the door. With an apologetic glance to Sister Comfort, Alleyn answered it and to his consternation he saw the earnest face of Sergeant Bix looking up at him.

'Any luck?'

'None at all, Sir, and we looked everywhere we could think. I mean, they might have got further away than the wards and the offices, whoever it was took the money, but I can't see how, what with the storm and the bridge being out.'

Alleyn agreed, frowning, 'Not to mention how little time elapsed between Matron locking away the money and Glossop finding it gone.'

'Exactly, Sir.'

'Very well, we have another conundrum to add to our puzzle. Thank you, Bix, I'll leave you to get back to your duties, but stay close by, will you? I may need you again.'

Sergeant Bix nodded, hesitated, seemed about to say

something and then shook his head, stepping back into the yard.

'What is it? Is something wrong?'

'No, it's just, I thought, if I might, I'd quite like to—'

Alleyn was perplexed as the forthright Bix stammered to a halt and looked sheepishly up at him. 'You'd like to what, Bix?' he asked.

His question was answered by a sigh from Sister Comfort who suggested, in a withering tone, that perhaps Sergeant Bix was hoping to pick up interrogation techniques from the great detective himself.

'The Sister's got it in one,' Bix answered with a disarmingly eager grin.

Despite the fact that Alleyn very much did not want a witness to his interview with Sister Comfort, he nonetheless felt obliged to invite the sergeant to join them in the office, he hadn't the heart to send him away once Sister Comfort had unmasked his shy enthusiasm.

Their audience settled and with his notebook in his hand, Alleyn began his questioning and observed with some amusement that Sister Comfort appeared to be playing up to Bix for all she was worth. Her peroration so completely mirrored Mr Glossop's pattern, that Alleyn felt they might have been the patter act at the start of an old Vaudeville show. Where Glossop had blustered about being cooped up with a potential killer, she blustered about being cooped up with Glossop. Where the pay-box man had cast aspersions on the good nurse, she pointed out that Glossop could not possibly be as wholly blameless as he insisted, he had long known how difficult the roads were out here, he complained about them enough, and as Sarah Warne and her Transport team managed

147

perfectly well, she wouldn't have been at all surprised if he hadn't engineered the flat tyre himself.

Bix jumped in at this point, 'As a way to steal the money, Sister? But he'd need an accomplice in that case, surely? He must have known Matron would insist on locking away the payrolls, so why do you reckon Mr Glossop engineered the flat tyre, so close to Christmas Day, at such a— what'd'you call it? Inopportune moment?'

Sister Comfort again looked at Bix as if he were the most dense of fools, 'Inopportune? The man is infatuated with Matron. He could think of nothing more delightful that having to spend a full day and night, or more, in her company. We all knew a storm was brewing, didn't we?'

'True enough,' Bix agreed.

Alleyn looked from one to the other, 'Someone might have told me. If I'd have known I'd be hiding from a hurricane coupled with a monsoon this evening, when I have become accustomed to taking a walk, I'd have taken out my pipe this afternoon instead of spending my time writing letters. Or failing to do so,' he added under his breath, 'But how did you know the weather would be bad?'

Sister Comfort glanced pityingly at Alleyn, 'We live in the shadow of the mountains. Anyone who understands the country would have known a storm was on the way, it was quite clear from the close calm of the late afternoon.'

'I see,' he said, not seeing at all. The afternoon had simply felt as stiflingly hot as had every afternoon of the past week, no different at all and yet, like every night before, it had yielded a clear sky and the merest hint of a breeze from the snow-capped peaks far above. 'You'll accept that local weather is not my forte.'

'Hang on a minute, Sister,' Bix interrupted again, 'I don't

quite see what you mean about Mr Glossop and Matron, are you suggesting they were having an affair?'

'I certainly am not. Matron would never—how could you, Sergeant? Matron is far removed from any of the nasty, sordid behaviour that this hospital, that our Mount Seager, has been witness to recently. When I think of our plans, our hopes for this—'

Sister Comfort stopped, pulled herself up short. Alleyn had to admire her self-control, it was quite astonishing. She smiled, as best she could, a crooked tooth protruding from her upper lip, her shoulders, neck and jaw tight with the effort of holding back, holding in. She smiled again, her snaggle-tooth almost endearing in her effort to seem light and charming, 'Honestly, Inspector, what is the problem with men that they cannot see the method in other men's behaviour?'

'The method in their madness? I expect we're blinded by fellow feeling. I have long believed women to be far more sensible than men, certainly more thorough in their thinking.'

'Exactly,' she responded. 'Now, have you finished your questions for me? I'm worried about the night staff, no one has checked on them and I'm sure you don't want them coming over to Matron's office to ask where we've all got to. They're used to a midnight round.'

'Well noted, but there's much to do before we sleep.'

'We're all busy, Inspector,' she said with a gloriously arched brow, 'I have a list of patients I particularly want to look in on.'

She reached into her pocket and pulled out a folded piece of paper which Alleyn politely and promptly took from her, 'Thank you, Sister.'

Sister Comfort pursed her lips as if he were an exceptionally trying serviceman she was about to admonish for cheek, and then seeing a particular glint in his eye she thought better of it, adding simply, 'If you don't trust me to go alone to the wards, I will allow you to accompany me, as long as you are quite silent and don't disturb either my staff or my patients.'

'Ah, but there's no need for your rounds, Sister,' Bix piped up, 'I took Dr Hughes over to check on everyone and we're just done. He was worried about the midnight round too. All sweet and soundly sleeping over there.'

Alleyn nodded his thanks to Bix and smiled at Sister Comfort, 'That being the case, I think we must trust the good sergeant that all is well for now. If you're still worried later, you and I might take a walk over to the wards together. As you rightly said, we don't want to alarm anyone else just yet. Shall we?'

He nodded to Bix who stood up smartly, giving Sister Comfort no option but to allow him to escort her back to the Transport Office. Alleyn waited until Bix had closed the door behind them and then opened the sheet of paper he had taken from Sister Comfort. He stared at the words as if he couldn't quite make out her writing and then he nodded, folding away the paper and tucking it safely into his pocket along with his pipe and the letter from Matron's desk he had stowed earlier. He opened the door and took a deep breath of the sweet night air. A morepork hooted from the patch of thick bush away to the north of Military 3, where the hospital grounds stopped and the rich land reclaimed its rightful place. In the silence he could hear the rush of the swollen river, he imagined the wild water, swirling beneath the old bridge, wind pulling hard at the uneven planks until one was wrenched loose and the bridge became impassable. Sometimes all it took was one element for the rest to begin to make sense. Alleyn stepped smartly down the thin wooden steps to the yard, a smile on his face. Suddenly he felt more awake than he had all evening.

CHAPTER EIGHTEEN

Rosamund Farquharson studied Chief Detective Inspector Alleyn from her usual chair at the Records Office desk. She had followed him into the office determined not to let him put her at a disadvantage, staking out her place at the desk, arranging her pose just so. Even though it was hours since she had set her hair, Rosamund knew exactly how best to set off her determinedly pretty face and with a practised toss of the head she ensured her curls sat charmingly on her shoulders. Then she leaned back in the chair and gave the detective the benefit of her full attention. It was her experience that men found a frank look either disarming or utterly charming. As he was about to interrogate her, she preferred to begin the exchange with as much information about the detective as possible. Inspector Alleyn was a good-looking man, there was no doubt about it, even if his austere air was a little too monkish for her tastes. He was well-spoken and plainly quite smart, that much was clear from the way he had spoken to the soldiers, warm enough to include them, his tone commanding enough to gain respect, but with just a touch of self-deprecation which meant even the perennially frowning

Bob Pawcett hadn't flown off too angrily when Alleyn took control. She had also detected a hint of humour and would love to know in which direction it lay. Even so, and despite considering herself an acute judge of men, Rosamund couldn't quite make him out. The detective had all of the finesse of certain fellows she'd known, just down from Cambridge and living the life before the war, but he seemed to have none of the stuffiness those chaps usually revealed, Englishmen in particular, the moment a girl spoke up for herself. The way he'd come into the Transport Office just now, he'd had every reason to pull rank, especially once Glossop started on again about how tired everyone was and couldn't they at least have a cup of tea, and Sister Comfort moaning about how her nurses needed proper supervision and the hospital would go to rack and ruin overnight, yet it seemed water off a duck's back to him. He simply smiled politely, ignored their complaints and elegantly asked Rosamund if she might accompany him to the Records Office. He might have been asking her what she liked on the midnight menu at the Café de Paris.

'You're scrutinizing me, Miss Farquharson?'

'Rosamund, please, "Miss" sounds rather too much like a frowsty old maid and I pride myself on getting on with all sorts.'

'Rosamund, then.'

'Thank you. And yes, Inspector, I am rather scrutinizing you.'

Alleyn made a quick judgement, Rosamund Farquharson was sharp. If he asked her about anything other than the theft, he was sure she would notice. However, it was clear that she knew the soldiers, the hospital staff and the surrounding area very well, if he let her take the lead, she might have something to say that could shed some light on the matter he was actually supposed to be investigating right now.

'Go on,' he said.

'You don't quite fit the mould.'

'So I've been told.'

She went on, 'For one thing, you're clearly what they'd call a "gentleman" back Home, a fully-fledged blue-blood aristocrat, I'll bet.'

'I'm surprised to hear you call England "Home"?' he spoke lightly, ignoring her offer to discuss his ancestry.

She grinned at the deflection, with a slight incline of her prettily shaped head, 'Only when I want to irritate other New Zealanders, I've been doing it all night to dig at old Glossop. My mother's generation called it Home, they honestly felt it was. Those who'd come from there I mean, especially those who had the money to get back and visit every now and then.'

'But not your generation?'

'My generation are all honest-to-goodness New Zealanders, salt of the earth, hard-working, proud to be from God's own country, dinkum jokers the lot of us. You only need to spend half an hour in the saloon bar of the Bridge pub to know the ones I mean.'

'I'm not sure I do.'

'Here's an example. I upset Snow Johnson no end a week or two ago. It's his pub you know, and we're right out here, only locals ever go in, even so it's the closest there is to an actual bar. All I did was ask for a "port and lemon with ice, just as they serve it in London", you should have heard the mouthful I got in return.'

Alleyn extended a hand to suggest she should continue.

'Oh yes, a long lecture about how we'd given so much to England and England should be giving back, not the other way around. That I was lucky to be here, lucky to be a New Zealander, should never have left in the first place. And on, and on, and on.' She shrugged, 'I'm proud of my country, of course I am—'

'And yet you left?'

'You can't even imagine the frustrations of small town life, can you, Inspector? How it feels to stand out, always.'

'You did just infer that I am not a typical copper.'

'Fair enough, I did. I just knew I had to get away, right from when I was a little girl in primary school.' She leaned forward now, warming to her story, 'New Zealanders are not very kind to those of us who leave, you know. It's all fine and good to travel, see a bit of the world, but we're meant to come back chastened, vowing we'll never leave again. We're only meant to go away so that we can come home and attest to the certain belief, firm in this nation's soul, that New Zealand is the only place on earth anyone could wish to be.'

'But not you, Miss Farquharson?'

She frowned, 'I've always wanted more, bigger, louder, faster. Perhaps it's a flaw in me that I could never be content with a small town life.'

'There are small towns in England.'

'Yes, but they're only a train ride from London, from the lights and noise. A day's journey at most from bars that stay open until dawn, from dances and galleries and theatres and—' She stopped, shook her head, 'What's the good? I'm back, and nothing to be done.'

'You will content yourself?'

'I will accommodate, as Matron likes—sorry, liked, to

155

say. I will accommodate myself to my circumstances. There is a war on after all, as if we could ever forget.'

'Do you miss London?'

'Fearfully.'

The passion she brought to the single word was enormous and Alleyn had the odd sensation of finally seeing the young woman behind the striking dress and the deep red lipstick, behind the carefully arranged curls and the insistent mask of indifferent pride. For a brief moment she almost looked her age and then suddenly the shutters were down and she was the brittle, manufactured Rosamund again, back into her stride.

'Admittedly there were a few—I'll call them "scrapes"— in my time away, but all the same, I miss London like the blazes. I can't bear to think what's happening to that lovely city while we're stuck here, moaning about our rationing, when it's nothing compared to what's going on back there, getting our news days or weeks later, fearful of an invasion that's never going to come.'

Alleyn wanted to assure her that fear of invasion was far more valid than she might suspect, but he very much wanted to speak with that girl again, the open and trusting one, so he prompted another recollection.

'I imagine you and Sarah Warne were friends in London?'

'We knew each other a little. We weren't really in the same set. I guess to people like you, someone with a usual job, the arts and theatre all seem the same, but they're not really. Theatre people like to work in groups, packs almost, they hang around together, eat together, play together. They're all about the company, a spirit of many as one. Artists are quite different, solitary creatures.'

Alleyn nodded, thinking of Troy, 'I recognize the people

156

you describe, and yet, if you don't mind me saying, you don't seem the solitary type.'

Rosamund opened her mouth to reply and stopped herself. Her hands were still in her lap, but they were also rigid, as held as a cat about to pounce. He could tell she wanted desperately to talk to him, to unburden herself. Despite, or perhaps because of the carefully contrived carapace, Rosamund seemed the kind of girl who would always want to talk to men, forever hoping that one of them might finally take her to task, make her drop the mask and welcome the woman he found revealed.

Alleyn reminded himself that there was no time for pity, 'Or have I got you all wrong, Miss Farquharson?'

Rosamund looked directly at Alleyn, her guard fully up and yet almost transparent at the same time. He felt ashamed of the way he was playing her and yet there was more to uncover, so play her he would. He stared directly at her, knowing she would say more if he waited, reveal more if he gave her the time to do so.

'No Inspector, you haven't got me wrong at all. I'm no artist. I was at art school neither to find my talent—I have my blind spots, but I'm not foolish enough to think I have talent—nor, as so many of the mindless girls were, was I there to bag myself a husband. I was at art school to have a damn good time. After all, I'm just a silly tart, shallow, flighty, no better than she ought to be.'

'I don't believe that for a moment. We've all made our mistakes—'

'Have you?' she asked.

Her genuine interest was disarming and Alleyn was surprised to find himself wanting to tell her the truth, 'Of course I have, but we're talking about you, Rosamund.'

She smiled at the use of her name, softened, and gave in, 'So we are. Unfortunately my mistakes have been all too obvious. I've no doubt someone has told you about Maurice?'

'Private Sanders?'

'I made a right fool of myself there, throwing myself at him because he seemed—'

She stopped, unsure. Alleyn couldn't tell if her uncertainty was because she didn't know how much to reveal about her dalliance with Sanders, or if she was worried it would reveal a side to her she didn't want to admit, not even in the relative privacy of the interrogation confessional.

Feeling wretched at having to probe and probing none-theless, Alleyn gently pushed, 'Was it perhaps that Private Sanders seemed fun and back here in New Zealand, missing London, missing your friends, you were looking for fun?'

Rosamund shrugged, grateful for his intervention, 'All right, that'll do. He seemed fun. And it was great fun, honest, until Maurice decided that Sukie Johnson was a better bet. Certainly she's better connected.'

'Mrs Johnson at the Bridge Hotel?' he asked lightly.

'Oh yes, *Mrs* Johnson. I know she has her attractions, but I can't help thinking Maurice and his mates found her a great way to get to her husband and her brother. Maurice is a good-looking fellow, Inspector, and he's fun to be with, but business is his real love. He's getting his fingers in as many pies as he possibly can, lining himself up for after the war. He's dead certain that radio is going to take off when we get back to fun and frivolity.'

'Radio?' Alleyn kept his tone light and conversational and Rosamund chattered on.

'Duncan Blaikie, Sukie's big brother, owns a part-share

in the radio company in town and Snow Johnson's got a great tract of land, runs right up from the back of the hotel to the edge of Blaikie's big old farm at the top of Mount Seager. Most people would think the land was only good for sheep anyway, but Maurice is sure there's a deal to be struck, radio masts put up after the war. He reckons it's the future. Sukie's brother and her old man are both useful for Maurice, whereas I'm just a girl from a hick town who's travelled a bit and likes a bit of a bet herself. I've none of the connections he's after.'

'Do you think I should look more closely at Sanders?'

'What, for the theft of Glossop's payroll and my winnings?' She shook her head, 'Goodness, no. Maurice likes a lark, a dabble, but he's no thief.'

Rosamund's fingers were agitated now, her hands twisting convulsively. He knew there was something more she wanted to say, someone else she wanted to speak about and he was confident he knew what it was.

'You're very certain. Is there someone else perhaps, someone who has been acting out of character, someone with something to hide?'

She looked up at him sharply and then looked back down at her hands, 'No.'

'I don't believe you.'

Alleyn's tone was brusque and Rosamund started, shocked.

'You're very good at this, aren't you, Inspector?'

Alleyn didn't respond and finally she spoke up, 'Luke— Dr Hughes— he's in love with Sarah. I know it, he knows it, she knows it, but he's been ever so odd with her recently. He's put it down to wanting to ask her to marry him, wanting to buy her the ring, set them up with a fine future, all those things young women are supposed to want, the future every girl dreams of.'

'Do they really?'

She frowned, 'Some girls do, I suppose. They must do or they wouldn't all say yes, would they? But the money story is just an excuse, so even though it's what he's been giving out, I cannot possibly believe he'd stoop to stealing the payroll.'

'Do you know what is troubling him?' Alleyn asked, well aware of the truth.

'Fear, Inspector. It's always fear, isn't it? Fear of being a coward, fear of being thought a coward, fear of pain, fear of causing pain. He's had an awful war and it won't let him be.'

'How do you know all this?'

She looked down at her hands in her lap and stilled them with great effort. When she looked up at Alleyn she was, finally, quite revealed. He thought she looked very young and very hurt, 'The good doctor cries out in his sleep, Inspector, and when he wakes he is shaking in terror.'

Alleyn tidied up the interview after that, there was no need to embarrass the young woman any more than necessary and while Rosamund was capable of brazening out any amount of sly nudges from the young VADs or even some of the soldiers, it was clear somehow that revealing herself to him had been exquisitely painful.

He rather admired her courage and told her so, 'You know, Rosamund, I do wish that your generation of young people were more willing to embrace openness and simplicity, you're quite marvellous when you do. I'm sure it would be all the better for you.'

Rosamund laughed a genuine, open laugh, 'Did your

generation do that? Isn't it more likely that every litter of young people tries to appear older, wiser, more cynical, than the one before?'

'You know, I think you're right, even when the world is in such a parlous state.'

'Perhaps especially then?'

'Perhaps. You're a smart girl.'

'Clearly not smart enough, Inspector, or I wouldn't be one hundred pounds and one broken heart the worse off, more fool me.' She grinned ruefully, shook out her fair curls and checked to see that they fell across her shoulders with a satisfying bounce, 'Are we finished?'

'We are. I shall lead you back.'

'Just in case I run off to fetch the hidden cash?'

'Quite so.'

CHAPTER NINETEEN

With Sanders, Brayling and Pawcett following, Alleyn walked ahead thinking about the nervous tension in the Transport Office, the manner in which each of the possible suspects had assumed a guilty aspect when he pushed open the door, and how much he disliked locking the door on them again.

Sanders muttered to his mates as they fell into line, 'Here he comes, the Pommie prince, playing the big I-am.'

'Shut up, Maurice,' Pawcett whispered. 'We've got to play this right or we'll all be in the doghouse.'

'Too right we do,' agreed Brayling, 'I want to get off this weekend, take my Ngaire over to stay with her people. I'm going to tell the truth and be done with it. We didn't do nothing wrong.'

'*You* didn't, Cuth,' Sanders said.

'And neither did you or I,' Pawcett whispered, his voice sharp, 'All right?'

'All right, calm down,' Sanders agreed, 'but let's go easy on the truth, the whole truth and nothing but the truth, eh, Cuth? You tell your bit if you reckon you need to, but keep me and Bob out of it.'

162

Alleyn turned to watch as the men reached the steps and slowly walked into the Records Office. He took in the Māori man's sharp glance to Sanders, Pawcett's dark look as he nervously chewed on his lower lip, Sanders's own deep frown. Alleyn took a moment to wonder whose story was going to collapse first.

He was surprised that it was Private Pawcett who gave them up, after a gentle nudge when Alleyn wondered aloud whether he ought to invite Sergeant Bix into the interrogation.

'Ah, it's no good, Maurice,' Pawcett said to Sanders, 'we're going to have to tell him, I can't chance Bix running to the brass with this, I'm in enough bother as it is. Nothing serious,' he added, assuring Alleyn, 'It's just that I've never been too good with the old "Yes, Sir, no, Sir" if you know what I mean.'

'I've come across that in my time.'

'I bet you have. Right, Inspector, well, the thing is—'

Pawcett looked at his comrades once more, Sanders shot him a filthy look but said nothing and Brayling nodded his go-ahead.

'We've been running a racket, Sir,' Pawcett said.

'A racket?'

'On the races, you know, running a book,' Sanders added.

Alleyn bit back a smile and managed to nod seriously at the confession, 'I see.'

'None of the lads could get out to put on a bet, could they?' Pawcett went on, 'And we had a friend—I mean, Maurice here had a friend—at the pub,' he faltered, wondering if mentioning Sukie Johnson's name would get him even deeper in his pal's bad books.

Alleyn saved him from worse, 'You needn't kick your

mate, Private Sanders, I'm not investigating a nefarious gambling den. Not tonight at least. I don't need to know the name of your contact at the pub, whoever he,' he paused, clasping his long hands together, 'or she, may be. What I do need to know is where all three of you were this afternoon and into the evening. Let's proceed, shall we, soldiers? A quick, precise report and I can get on with my job.'

Standing to attention, each man gave an account of himself and Alleyn found he almost felt sorry for them. Pawcett was clearly headed for trouble before long and admitted both setting up the book and running the bets.

'I had in mind to make a little on the side from a gambling racket right from the start, you see. I mean, not when they first brought me back, I was awful crook at first, but after I started to perk up a bit I ran a sideline on the nurses.'

'On the nurses?' asked Alleyn.

'Yeah, you know, how often we could get Sister Comfort to storm off to Matron, how many times we could get one of those little VADs to run squealing at the suggestion of a mouse. Harmless stuff.'

'Unless you're Sister Comfort or the VAD in question,' Alleyn said lightly.

'Come off it, it was just something to pass the time.'

'I've no doubt, but it's not quite the behaviour one might expect from a man proud of his countrywomen.'

'Hold on a minute, boss,' Pawcett bridled. 'I'm flamin' well just as proud of the New Zealand lasses as you are of your English girls back home, I'll tell you that for nothing. They've done a damn good job of keeping things running here while we've been sent off Gawd knows where, and some of our mothers doing it for the second time in their lives, I'll have you know.'

'Quite,' Alleyn agreed, the mildness of his tone at odds with the cold steel in his eyes, and Pawcett remembered where he was and to whom he was speaking. He also took Alleyn's point.

'Ah, yeah, I see. Well, when you put it like that, I reckon it's not—only we—' he stuttered to a halt.

'Let's move on, shall we?' Alleyn said briskly, 'Private Sanders, tell me your reasons for being involved in this racket, as your friend calls it.'

Maurice Sanders told his own tale of needing a few bob for 'this and that', Alleyn chose not to enquire. He also noticed that Sanders steered clear of mentioning any of the nurses, the VADs, or Sukie Johnson from the Bridge Hotel. He was simply helping his mate Bob run a book, that was all.

'No harm meant, no harm done.'

'So you all keep saying, and yet you're very keen that Sergeant Bix doesn't know any of this? Despite your assurance of "no harm done"?' Alleyn asked.

Sanders snapped out his answer, making no attempt to soften his tone, 'What we're keen on is getting out of this blasted hospital and finally taking the spot of R and R we were long promised and we've all been denied by damn well getting sick—in the course of duty, mind—in the first place. What's more, we'd quite like that flamin' R and R before the educated idiots in charge pack us off again to their blasted war. Sir.'

It was on the tip of Alleyn's tongue to snap back, everything in his bearing urged him to pull rank, Sanders's tone and attitude were both quite out of order, but all of a sudden he felt for the man, he felt for all three of them. Young men, their lives ahead of them and already tainted with what they had seen and done in war. There was a brief moment when the three soldiers awaited the icy blast of a superior's ire, until Alleyn, aware that a compliant informant was far more useful than an irate one, answered simply, 'I'm sure you would, Private. And no doubt it would do you all the world of good, nothing like a holiday to set the world to rights. And you, Corporal Brayling, what's your story?'

Brayling's tale was unexpected. The Māori man told of his love for his Ngaire, the importance of being on hand to welcome his child, to safeguard that the correct proto-cols were carried out for the woman and child, ensuring the baby knew its place in the family and on the land. Brayling had simply gone along with his mates' gambling racket as something that kept the other men happy to turn a blind eye to his visits with his wife.

'Not close enough to get her sick, Inspector. I'd never do that, 'specially not with her *hapū*, baby on the way. She kept to her side of the river and me to mine. That old river, it runs way down to her people's *marae*, Sir, their land. It knows her *iwi*, her people, knows mine too, I reckon. It wouldn't have let me get across to her, even if I wanted. The river's smart, knows just where to twist and fling you back up on the old rocks. I wasn't going to get close, on my oath I wasn't, I just needed Ngaire to know I was all right and I'd be there when it was time for the baby to come. You know?'

Alleyn noticed that the two *Pākehā* men listened politely to their friend speaking of the river as if it were a living thing. He might have expected a raised eyebrow or even

166

a laugh, but neither man behaved as he'd seen other white men do, dismissing their Māori compatriots' beliefs as flights of fancy. Perhaps they were better soldiers, more of a team, than their antics had led him to believe. He told them to wait outside where he could see them from the doorway while he took a few notes in his small notebook, then he would escort them back to the Transport Office.

The comrades went out into the welcoming night air, their relief palpable, and Alleyn heard two matches strike as they lit up their cigarettes, deep breaths in and then long exhaled sighs, the sweet smell of tobacco marking their stay of execution. He scribbled down a few lines, stared at what he had written, paused, and looked up. He caught sight of himself in the blank window opposite, saw the deep frown cutting across his forehead and sighed, it was no good minding, there was a good deal of poking and prying to do yet. Alleyn felt certain that the two cases were connected somehow, at the very least there was the matter of the intercepted radio signals and Private Sanders's interest in Duncan Blaikie's radio company, the possibility of high land from which to send a signal. He rubbed his nose, looked down at the page, crossed out all three of the lines he had just written and wrote two short questions to himself. He closed the notebook, put it and his pen back in his breast pocket, and waited a moment while Sanders, his whisper a little louder than intended no doubt due to the shock of their reprieve, gave his opinion of the detective.

'What did I tell you? 'Course we thought he was coming over the big chief when he started this malarkey, ordering everyone about like he owned the place and talking with

167

more plums in his mouth than Aunt Daisy puts in the Christmas pudding, but stone me, it's another thing entirely when he's got a bit of history of his own. He's been a soldier, I reckon. Hark at how he talked to us. What's the betting he was in the first war? He'll do.'

'For a Pom,' Pawcett added, grudgingly.

'For a *Pākehā*,' Brayling added.

They chuckled and fell easily into line behind Alleyn as he walked down the steps and, paying no attention to the men or their whispers about him, turned towards the Transport Office.

They had not taken more than half a dozen paces when a white-faced Dr Hughes attended by an equally horrified Sergeant Bix overtook them.

In a move worthy of a prize sheepdog, Bix rounded on the night walkers and came to a halt directly in front of Alleyn.

Pawcett grunted an angry sigh, would have spat on the ground in front of him if he had dared, 'Right. And after all that he's called the sergeant out, all guns blazing. Thanks very much for nothing, Inspector.'

'Hellfire, what now?' Alleyn whispered to himself and, ignoring Pawcett and his chums, took a quick look at the faces of the two men before them, lifted an eyebrow to Hughes, and in a delicate sleight of hand simultaneously raised a thumb backwards, in the direction of the morgue. Hughes had the presence of mind to hold his tongue and simply nod. Alleyn didn't yet know what the nod meant, but he knew enough to take charge of the situation and fast, before Sergeant Bix blurted out whatever disaster in the morgue had brought them to this pass.

Alleyn addressed the sergeant in a light and measured

tone, 'Bix, I was about to lead these gentlemen back to the Transport Office so that I might begin my next interview, however I think it's best if you and I head on down to the morgue. Miss Warne will have to wait a little longer.'

Hughes was plainly preparing to interrupt, whether it was at the mention of Sarah Warne's name or in a fluster about whatever had sent them running, Alleyn wasn't sure, but either way, he chose to stop the young doctor before any damage could be done, 'And Dr Hughes, I expect you know the ins and outs of the hospital rather better than many of your patients, I wonder if you might take the men here to the kitchen?'

'The kitchen?' Pawcett spluttered, incredulous.

'I was thinking it's time we woke up the night porter, Mr Kelly. A good strong dose of coffee ought to do the trick, if such a thing is available.'

'There's Camp Coffee and Chicory, it'll have to do,' Sanders muttered.

'Delightful,' Alleyn proclaimed, 'Dr Hughes, I trust you'll be so kind as to administer the medicine?'

Hughes started to protest and then he nodded uncertainly, aware that the detective was handling the situation and, Alleyn noted with relief, sensibly chose silence as his best course of action.

Alleyn went on, 'And perhaps a pot of tea and whatever they have in the way of biscuits for those back in the Transport Office? I'm sure Mr Glossop, in particular, has had enough of being cooped up with no sustenance. I believe they drill young constables these days with the maxim that a man will give up any number of secrets if he's hungry. However, I rather fear that keeping a New Zealander from his cup of tea is a step too far.'

'We're not a bunch of short order cooks, you know,' Pawcett blurted out.

'Indeed, but you have also assured me that you are not at all unwell. I suggest, therefore, that making yourselves useful is the most valuable thing you can do this evening. I've been led to believe that the New Zealand digger is the most resourceful soldier of them all—'

'Too damn right,' Sanders nodded vigorously.

'Marvellous. Tea and biscuits all round. A veritable midnight feast.'

Alleyn cheerily trotted the few dozen paces to the Transport Office, popped his head into the office to tell those assembled that sustenance was on its way and his faith in their New Zealand love of a good cup of tea meant he trusted them to remain in the office. Leaving the door ajar and a row of astonished faces looking after him, he walked briskly towards the morgue with Bix.

The three servicemen looked after them, even more surprised to hear the Inspector whistling as he went.

'What the flippin' heck was all that about?' asked Corporal Brayling.

'Dunno mate,' answered Private Pawcett, shaking his head, 'The bloke's daft as a brush if you ask me.'

'No one's asking you, Pawcett,' Dr Hughes said sharply as he rounded up the soldiers and led the way to the kitchen.

CHAPTER TWENTY

'She just wasn't there, Sir. Here. She wasn't here.'

Bix gestured expansively in his shock and his several shadows danced against the walls, arms conducting an unseen orchestra of amazement.

'Matron wasn't here?' Alleyn repeated, his own voice betraying shock and something closer to anger.

The evidence before them was all too clear; the old trolley once again overturned, the morgue resolutely empty and, despite the evidence before them, Alleyn's incredulity rose as Bix repeated his story.

'We came in, me and Dr Hughes. I lit the lamps just like before. We turned to have a look at the trolley—well, I did, the doctor was staring at it in shock. Or horror, yeah, I'd say it was more bloody horror, 'scuse my French.'

'Excused,' Alleyn said, automatically, staring at the trolley himself.

'And, as you can see, no Matron.'

'No Matron,' Alleyn parroted, inwardly kicking himself for his dense responses, 'You're quite sure we locked the door behind us when we left?'

'Quite sure, Sir. And I've had Sister Comfort's keys on me all this time.'

'Who else has a key?'

'The only keys out here at the hospital are Matron's, they're the ones we haven't yet found, and Sister Comfort's keys that you gave me to lock up with here.'

'No spares?'

'There is a spare set, but it's in town, with the Chair of the Hospital Board, just in case. Matron always had the keys about her. She isn't—wasn't—the losing things type.'

'Indeed, to lose one body might be considered carelessness.'

'Sorry, Sir?' Bix asked.

'Nothing at all.' Alleyn frowned, 'And so a midsummer night's dream becomes a winter's tale.'

'I really don't follow.'

'Don't mind me, Bix, I become facetious when perplexed. Right now I am perplex'd in the extreme. I fear there are only two possible reasons for this preposterous situation.'

'Go on then,' Bix looked at Alleyn with all the enthusiasm of a smart Labrador offered the chance of a long walk and a good many rabbits, and Alleyn was sorry to have to disappoint him.

'I assure you Bix, it is not that I don't trust you. Given that I have chosen to work with you this far, it would be quite foolish of me not to continue to do so now, but I find myself hard up against my training. I've been taught, and largely obeyed the teaching, to speak my mind only once I am in possession of at least a modicum of facts. Facts are decidedly thin on the ground just now.'

Alleyn stopped, abruptly crouched to the floor and scanned anew for footprints. Nothing seemed changed from when they were in the morgue not an hour ago and yet he had the clear sense of something having moved. It was neither the trolley nor Matron's missing body, but something about him was ever so slightly out of kilter. 'But I'm damned if I can say what it is,' he thought, tapping the cold rock floor with his fingertips. He stood again, more slowly this time, looking about them as he did.

'That being the case, Bix, at this juncture it is wise to move on.'

Alleyn clapped his long hands together as if to provoke himself to action and looked up surprised at the dull suggestion of an echo. 'Hullo!' He clapped again as Bix looked on. 'Sergeant,' he said to the perplexed soldier, 'I shall enlist you. Run back to the Transport Office and make sure that Hughes breathes not a word of this to anyone else, not one word. Once you're sure they're all contained, fetch me a length of good rope.' Alleyn paused, moved closer to the cavities in the rock, clapped his hands once more and, screwing up his face as he made a quick calculation, he said, 'Forty foot, or perhaps fifty. Yes, that ought to do it.'

'Forty or fifty foot of rope, Sir. Very good.' Bix nodded, for all the world like a secretary checking dictation and Alleyn congratulated himself on his choice to trust the sergeant.

'Exactly the thing. We'll also need a pair of new torches if at all possible, the best you can lay your hands on. Good man, step to it.'

Alleyn waited a few moments just to be sure the sergeant was well and truly gone, and then he bent down to remove his shoes. While close to the ground he looked around again, the floor was not quite as smooth and clean as it had been a little earlier, but without a proper forensics man there was no saying if the scuff marks and dusty prints were anything more than those created by Bix and Hughes's size nines leaping about in shock at discovering Matron's body was missing and their subsequent scurry to reveal the next element of this increasingly fantastical night. Alleyn was about to stand and continue readying himself for Bix's return, when he noticed something in the far corner that appeared to have slipped into the hair-thin gap between the sloping natural floor and the dug-out wall that held the cool cavities for dead bodies. He leaned down as far as his long legs would allow and, with his handkerchief covering his fingers he carefully tugged at what he now saw was the edge of a piece of paper. It held tight for a tantalizing moment and then came free. As it did so it also fluttered very lightly in a breeze that could not have come from the closed door to the morgue itself. Alleyn smiled and held the paper up to the light. It was, as he had suspected, a pound note. He turned it over and saw James Cook, all serious thought and good sense.

'Captain,' he nodded.

He had carefully folded the note into the handkerchief when Bix returned to the morgue, a hefty length of rope over his right shoulder, 'Fifty foot, Sir. As ordered.'

'Very good,' Alleyn nodded and, walking to the left-hand side of the row of vaults, he adroitly dived headfirst into the gap and began to shuffle his frame into the coffin-sized hole in the rock.

Bix looked on in shock as Alleyn's muffled voice came back to him, 'If you'll be so kind as to tie the rope around my ankles, good and tight, Bix, that will do nicely. Do make sure you're holding on. If I come to rock in a few inches you can help pull me back out again, if not, I'd rather not go shooting off head first into the underworld without some sort of counterweight.'

Unable to trust himself to utter any suitable response, Bix simply did as he was told, securing the rope firmly around his own waist so it had plenty of give, but he could also stop it short at the slightest word.

Alleyn continued to shuffle slowly towards the end of the cavity, doing so with a mounting sense of unease, he had never been particularly comfortable in enclosed spaces and this was, perforce, more enclosed than most. With just a few inches to go before he reached the end of the dug-out space, he carefully manoeuvred his hand up, past his head, and pushed his palm against cold rock. He explored it with his fingers, searching for a draught, for cooler air, anything that might suggest there was more beyond his hand than the heavy bedrock of the foothills. Eventually he gave up.

'We'll need to be quicker than this, even three cack-handed diggers can rustle up a pot of tea in this time,' he thought, then raised his voice and shouted back, 'Pull gently on the rope now, Bix, make it a spot easier for me to get out than to get in.'

Bix did as he was told and Alleyn repeated the procedure once again. By the time he'd reached the end of the fourth cavity with no change, Bix was rather enjoying himself and Alleyn realized that his new companion had been craving some of the excitement he'd been denied by working on the home front, the same excitement Bix's younger charges yearned for and now, as their recuperation was almost over, were no doubt remembering to fear, if only a little.

'If you don't mind, I'd be happy to give it a go myself?'

The solid, stocky man looked up at Alleyn all keen and eager, and the detective was sorry to turn him down, 'It can't be, Bix, we may be here in Ninny's tomb, but I fear you make a better Wall than a Thisbe to clamber through and speed is of the essence.'

Bix shook his head, 'Sir, I think you just said no, and fair enough, I'm no beanpole like you, but that means you're in again for number five out of eight and I reckon you'd better rattle those dags if you're going to get a shoofti at it before that lot back there finish their brew and come knocking for us here.'

'And I think you just told me to get a bloody move on.'

Alleyn laughed and went again head-first into the cavity. He had not quite entered up to his knees when he realized it felt different, cooler.

He shouted to Bix, 'Hang on tight, my friend, this might be the one.'

'Yes, Sir!' Bix called back and the rope took on a re-assuring pressure.

Not for the first time in his life Alleyn thanked his lucky stars for a good adjutant and headed forwards into the pitch dark. His stockinged feet were scraping the edge of the hole when he heard a commotion in the morgue chamber, he rapidly pulled his legs into the cavity as fast as he could and waited, his breath held, while he heard Bix speaking in the entrance area. The voices were too muffled to make out what exactly was said, but Alleyn was convinced by the barked tone and ready measure of the sergeant's voice that he must have been talking to one or more of the soldiers.

A moment later Bix was back and he whispered to Alleyn in the vault, 'Daft buggers the lot of them, thought we'd fancy a brew ourselves, so they brought it on down, all done up on a tray and fancy with a doily cover, like they think you're Jean flippin' Batten. Mind you, with it being no go, you might fancy a cuppa about now, boss?'

There was no answer and Bix watched the rope move inch by inch into the cavity, he quickly snatched it up again and held on until he heard the sepulchral voice of Inspector Alleyn, seemingly coming from all three of the last holes in the wall, 'I rather expect I will have a cup of tea, Bix. Just as soon as I get back from investigating this chamber. Roll that torch through to me, will you?'

CHAPTER TWENTY-ONE

Once the dumbfounded Bix had rolled the torch into his waiting hands, Alleyn shone the light about him. In his briefing before he arrived at Mount Seager, he had been told about an old tunnel leading from the Bridge Hotel, beneath the hospital, and emerging somewhere in a set of caves to the north of the hospital, long overgrown with native bush. His contact on the Hospital Board assured him that the tunnel showed no sign of being used in any possible espionage. Apparently it was firmly locked where it joined the Bridge Hotel cellar and had been impassable for many decades at the cave end, as the morgue was always kept locked it was simply a closed space. He was further assured that the search had been conducted in such secrecy, that no one in the hospital or at the Bridge knew that there was any interest in matters below the ground. This information was repeated on the page that had given Alleyn pause when he was first handed the file and he had been itching to get into the tunnel since his arrival, but had been unable to do so without alerting the hospital staff to his quest. The theft and Matron's body missing from the morgue provided him with the perfect opportunity to snoop about the grounds without anyone thinking his actions unusual, and the moment he heard the echo of his clapping hands, he guessed the morgue might be another entrance to the tunnel.

He was able to stand, so whoever had chosen to dig out this area behind the wall of tombs had done so with grown men in mind, no Nordic troglodytes here, nor whatever was their Māori equivalent. He made a mental note to ask his old friend Dr Te Pokiha about his people's folklore, and then brought himself back to his surroundings. With the rock of the morgue wall behind him, standing at his full height, and relieved there was a good hand's width between his pate and the rock above, Alleyn looked about him. The torchlight shone bright, but even so, the dense rock seemed to soak up all illumination, allowing a clear picture for no more than a four-foot radius before the light was swallowed into the earth. Slowly and carefully Alleyn took a few steps to either side, making sure not to travel too fast and tug the rope from Bix's hands. The good sergeant was no Ariadne and Alleyn had no interest in confronting a primordial minotaur in the dark.

The tunnel itself was fairly narrow, he knew his own limbs to be long, but even so, he could put his shoulder to one wall and touch the opposite with his palm. The width then, of Will Kelly's ill-fated trolley, with just a little room to spare. He allowed himself a brief smile as he realized he was standing, literally, within the foothills of the mountains he had so admired in the past week. The smile rapidly left his face as he recalled his reasons for being here, one of which was ticking relentlessly closer. It seemed to Alleyn that far too much of the theft and missing bodies conundrum seemed to loop back to his espionage investigation. It was vital that he either keep the two apart until the latter was neatly folded away or find the links, and quickly. As soon as the telegraph wires were mended and the bridge passable, the local police would be alerted, and while he would be glad to hand over the matter of the theft, Matron and old Mr Brown's body, he was loath to risk revealing the real reason he was at Mount Seager. Secrecy had been the watchword of this game from the start and Alleyn wasn't about to allow a single night of mischief to ruin the hours of painstaking work that had led to this moment.

He rubbed his nose and wondered again about taking Bix more fully into his confidence and then shook his head violently, 'Get on with it, man, make haste!'

Facing the waist-high cavity that led from the morgue on one side and with his back against the rock on the other, Alleyn shone the torch in both directions, north towards the hospital buildings and south towards the Bridge Hotel.

'Hi there, Bix?' he called to his man in the morgue, 'I appear to be in the tunnel that leads to the Bridge. What's beyond the army offices? Are there any other buildings, or does the road simply go on to the Bridge Hotel? I'm wondering if this heads there directly.'

'Might do, Sir. The pub isn't far, half a mile on from our offices, if that,' Bix replied, his voice oddly altered in its passage through the tomb, muffled yet strangely echoing through the rock.

'With nothing in between?'

'There used to be a few sheds for the hospital groundsman, a garage that was the stables when they kept horses, but they were knocked down when the war came and the bosses decided to station us out here along with the wounded servicemen. Caused a flamin' fuss it did.'

'I can imagine some of the patients found the building noise difficult?'

'Perhaps they did, I was thinking more of the gardener and Will Kelly, boy oh boy did they kick up a fuss. They looked like a bunch of shacks but you'd have thought we were demolishing their old homesteads the way they went on. Some men can be pretty damn odd about their sheds, Sir. Mind you, Matron wasn't happy either.'

'No?'

'Up in arms about it, not like her, usually she's the unflappable type. Sorry, she was. That one's going to take some getting used to.'

Bix's voice faded and Alleyn prompted him, 'Go on, Bix.'

'Yes, Sir. See, I reckon Matron's problem was she thought the hospital would have to fork out for the new shed, paths, asphalt and all that. The big bosses said they'd foot the cost, military taking it on the chin again if you ask me, but even so, she was still put out. In the end they left a lean-to for the gardener, she was adamant about that.'

'I see,' Alleyn replied, his mind made up, 'Now listen Bix, I know the tunnel heads towards the Bridge, under or skirting your offices. I'm going to have a look in the other direction.'

'I heard it's blocked that way, Sir.'

'Yes, I've heard the same. Regardless, I'm going to try. I'll count aloud at a steady pace, one step for each count and I'd like you to do the same. Keep counting even if you can't hear my voice, will you? When I get to whatever is at the end, I'll turn and come back, still counting.'

181

'Count out loud, Sir, I can do that. Any chance of telling me why?'

'I could, Bix, and I promise I will, but right now I'd rather like to get on with working out what's down here before those three soldiers come back knocking on the morgue door with a Victoria sandwich to provide ballast for our cups of tea. Ready? One . . . two . . . three . . .'

'One . . . two . . . three . . . four . . .' Bix started as an echo and quickly matched Alleyn's pace, even as the detective's voice became faint, fainter, and then silent.

It took just over two hundred paces, always marching forward, always looking ahead, before Alleyn noticed any change in his surroundings, the gradient beneath his feet felt as if it tipped upwards a little and he raised his hand above his head just in time to stop his forehead cracking into a small jut of outlying rock.

'I take that back about the troglodytes,' he thought to himself, continuing to count aloud but lowering his voice, aware that he must be beneath either the wards or the offices by now. For the next sixty steps the gradient continued to rise, until Alleyn found he had to bend his head, always holding his free hand above his forehead to take care he didn't knock himself out. The length of rope had long come to an end and he was debating whether to keep on towards the caves in this uncomfortable manner when the hand he held above his head registered an end to the stone and then the sure sign of rough wooden boards as a wicked splinter pierced his knuckle and announced a change in roofing material rather more brutally than necessary.

'Damn and blast it.' Alleyn was reaching for his handkerchief to stem the flow of blood when he remembered what else was in his breast pocket and how often he had already used the handkerchief as a careful glove. 'Nothing for it, I shall have to be a mewling boy and suck at the thing to get it out.'

As he carefully removed the splinter Alleyn looked about him in the torchlight. He couldn't be sure, but he had a sense that the tunnel hadn't run quite true, he fancied he'd felt a subtle shift to the east. If that was the case, and judging by the number of steps he'd taken so far, he might be nearing the staff offices, perhaps even directly beneath them. The low wooden ceiling above and the possibility that he might be nearing the Transport Office where he had temporarily incarcerated his cast of suspects was hugely enticing, perhaps this was his chance to unpick some of the tangled threads. Taking care to move even more quietly, with the torch low to the ground in case the boards above were not entirely covered by the rich earth of the plains, he moved slowly forward, still counting as he went.

One hundred and thirty-nine steps later his care was rewarded when he heard a low rumble that gradually morphed into several different murmurs of various pitch, and was finally discernible as half a dozen voices, more than one of them passionately raised. He made his way still more diffidently, edging silently towards the sound, his neck and shoulders stooped to the point of discomfort. Eventually he was close enough to determine one voice from another. When looking at the fencing around the bottom of the offices, enclosing the space where they were raised off ground, he'd noticed weed-covered earth beneath, but it must have been a finer layer of soil than he had assumed. It took a few moments for his hearing to adjust to the distortions of distance and density, but eventually he was able to make out a number of different voices, filling in the gaps with guesses of his own where he couldn't quite make out their words.

'Unbearable,' the voice said, followed by a few more words in the same tone, further adverbial furies Alleyn guessed, 'That we should be . . . well, you know what I mean, that we . . . it's unbearable, when my bosses hear about this . . . been treated, there'll be hell to pay. Starting with that . . . Pommie . . .'

Alleyn nodded grimly. Glossop was still on his high horse and Alleyn himself the object of his ire. Several other voices responded. One of them, a man's voice, was in assent, Father O'Sullivan perhaps. Two others, both lighter in tone, the young women's voices, were demurring.

'What else could he do? Matron dead . . . that money missing . . . someone out here . . . culprit.'

'And . . . forget, there's . . . winnings . . . too.'

So the first must have been Sarah Warne, the second Rosamund Farquharson.

Then another voice took her up on the matter of her winnings, '. . . always about you, Miss Far . . .' clearly Sister Comfort was still in a state of high dudgeon, '. . . patients and staff alike . . . our duty to the hospital . . . beloved Matron.'

He waited a little longer, hoping to eavesdrop something that might be more useful than the usual gripes, but it seemed the only discussion going on above his head was to do with Maurice Sanders's opinion about the folly of allowing a Pommie Inspector to take the helm. Rosamund Farquharson opined on the foolishness of thinking they could afford to wait until the local constabulary were able to join them and Glossop grudgingly agreed that the matter was far too important to wait until the lines and the bridge were mended. Alleyn raised an eyebrow, relieved to hear he wasn't considered entirely surplus to requirements.

He turned back to retrace his steps and started counting under his breath to make sure he and Bix had the correct numbers for comparison. Then he caught a brief exchange that gave him pause.

Rosamund Farquharson must have asked something of Father O'Sullivan, perhaps to do with old Mr Brown's death, for the vicar responded brusquely and in such a sharp tone that Alleyn had a sudden image of the previously gently-spoken man as a very different kind of vicar when lecturing from the pulpit, 'Matron and I have . . . working relationship for a dozen years or . . . nothing but . . . welfare of . . . entrusted to us . . . forefront in our . . . You, young . . . judge everyone by your own lights.'

Something in the vicar's affronted tone and Rosamund's sharp retort made Alleyn frown, and then nod, and finally smile as he made his way back along the tunnel retrieving the rope and counting his steps as he went. In another hundred paces the boards above his head once more became the rock of the foothills, and he straightened his neck and shoulders with a sigh of relief. By the time he pulled himself through the cavity in the morgue wall, his face lit by the torch he rolled beneath his chest, he was feeling positively jaunty.

'Eight hundred and fifty-nine,' Bix heaved a sigh as he spoke, the effort it had cost him to keep his count on time and in rhythm showed on his face. 'I never was any good at square-bashing, Sir, they weren't going to make me Sergeant Major, that's for sure.'

'Seven hundred and twenty-four,' Alleyn countered, 'I'm

a little taller than you, so perhaps our pacing was slightly off, but better than that, I stopped for a few moments while you were no doubt counting merrily away.'

Bix peered at his superior, 'You look like the cat that got the cream, Sir.'

'Not quite, but I may have caught a glimpse of a ghost, and that's cheered me enormously. Your turn, Sergeant, take the rope, hold on tight and pop back into the tunnel, will you?'

'To check out a ghost, Sir?' the sensible Bix asked, perplexed.

'I think not, I'd like you to head south this time and ensure that the tunnel does indeed lead in the direction of the Bridge and that there isn't a wide open door welcoming anyone to help themselves to the wine cellar.'

'You'd be hard pushed to find any wine out here, drop of cream sherry maybe.'

Alleyn smiled his thanks and added, 'Try to be a little faster than I was, will you? I fear our worrisome crew in the Transport Office will turn to mutiny if I leave them locked up for an awful lot longer.'

'I'm very happy to head off alone, Sir, if you want to get back to your interviews.'

'I do rather, Bix. Are you certain you're up to it? In the tunnel with no one on the other end of the rope?'

Bix grinned, his cheery face quite animated, 'Sir, we were both in the first war, and glad it was over, damned unhappy when this other fuss started up, but I'd be lying if I said I didn't sometimes envy the younger men their adventures. I'm not scared of ghosts and I'm as sure as you are about where that end of the tunnel leads to. You head off to our merry band of rioters, I'll take the route south and come on back to join you with proof of the pudding if there's any to be had.'

'You're a good man, Bix, thank you.'

Alleyn clapped him on the back and let himself out of the morgue as Bix struggled through the wall cavity and into the tunnel. The detective emerged into the warm night, whistling ever so softly.

CHAPTER TWENTY-TWO

Alleyn took a deep breath as he approached the Transport Office. If anything, now that there was just a thin wooden wall between him and the occupants, the argument within sounded more bad-tempered, simmering tensions closer to the point of boiling over. He stopped, frowning, which way to play it? A show of temper might flush out a few more clues, on the other hand he was tired and frustrated at the vital matter in hand being so effectively derailed by the incidents of the evening. It wouldn't do to let his temper get the better of him at this point, not when so many others were out of control. He quickly made up his mind and just as the noise inside seemed to reach a peak, he unlocked and slowly opened the office door. A witness to the melee within, Alleyn was treated to the choicest snippets of the assembled cast's fight scene.

'You've no flippin' right to talk to me like that, none at all,' Glossop glared at Rosamund Farquharson, his face a vivid puce, a heavy vein throbbing alarmingly in his temple, 'Your loss is pathetic compared to mine, I'm by far the most aggrieved party here—'

'Aggrieving you mean,' interrupted Maurice Sanders,

smirking, with a wink around the room and a flick of his rogue curl.

'You say that Mr Glossop, but mine's a personal loss,' Rosamund said, 'yours is a company loss and the government will take care of that. Who's going to make up my own loss, eh? Tell me that.'

'*Loss*? I didn't flamin' well *lose* all that cash, missy, it was nicked and now I reckon we all know who did it.'

Glossop paused for breath and grunted in Alleyn's direction to let him know his presence was noted.

In response, the detective murmured a cool, 'Pray do tell, Mr Glossop, it will make my night so much simpler.'

His calm tone earned him a mimed round of applause from Rosamund Farquharson which Alleyn acknowledged with a slight nod, his impeccable manners quite lost on Mr Glossop.

'Welcome back, Inspector, a bit damn late, but welcome back. That Māori's run off and you can bet he's taken the whole bloody lot of my payroll back to the *pā* and squirreled it away.'

'Shut it, Glossop,' Maurice Sanders said, with a great deal less charm than he'd exhibited a moment earlier, 'Cuth's our mate and our comrade, and if you accuse him of being a thief one more time I'll shut your mouth for you.'

'We'll have less of the language too, thank you, Mr Glossop,' added Father O'Sullivan. 'There are ladies present.'

'Ah yeah, make a fuss about my language would you? What's it you mind, Vicar? Bloody or damn?'

'Both,' Rosamund and Sarah spoke together.

'Fine coming from the pair of you,' Glossop rounded on the younger women, 'this hospital is going to rack and ruin, Sister Comfort here's got no more control over these soldiers than she has over you girls, the pair of you no better than you should be, and yes, I do mean you too, Miss Warne, all butter wouldn't melt while you cosy up to the young doctor here, and him lapping it up. Don't think I can't see what's going on, you're plain as day, the lot of you. This place is a farce and I can't wait to wake up out of it all, it's a rotten stinking nightmare is what it is.'

'That's enough, Mr Glossop,' Alleyn said, his voice threateningly low. 'Whatever nightmare you believe yourself to be in, I don't think any of us need your inchoate ranting to wake the entire hospital.'

'Maybe it'd be a good thing if I did, about time the patients here knew what a shambles of an outfit it all is,' Glossop grumbled, determined to have the last word.

'If you're quite finished?' Alleyn's fixed smile, contrasting sharply with his cool demeanour finally squashed the fat man, who pulled out his damp handkerchief to wipe his sweaty brow, earning him a disgusted wince from Rosamund and Alleyn asked, 'Now, would anyone like to tell me where Corporal Brayling might be?'

After a moment of blessed silence, Private Pawcett raised wary eyes and mumbled, 'We don't flamin' well know, is the truth of it. He took off about ten minutes ago. Came over all moody and silent and then just said he'd had enough, he had to get out.'

'But you don't suspect him of the theft?'

'Too right we don't,' replied Sanders. 'He's a good mate is Cuth, and we were with him the whole night anyway.'

'Other than the half hour or so you say he went off to speak to his wife, at the bend in the river, where the distance

190

is most narrow, so they could speak across the rushing water?'

'Yeah, sure, but—'

'Unfortunately not, Private Sanders. No matter how well you personally trust your comrade, and well you might, you do not know what Corporal Brayling was doing in that half hour and neither do I—nor do you, Mr Glossop,' he said, pre-empting the fat man's interjection. 'Now, you will listen to me and listen well.'

Alleyn proceeded to tell them calmly and categorically what he thought of their behaviour. It was a lecture he'd been longing to give for the past few hours and he handled it masterfully, reminding those before him of their stations in life and the confusions and upsets they had witnessed in the past hours. His oration was just finished when there came a perfectly-timed knock on the office door. Alleyn opened it to see Bix standing to the side in the dark.

'A word, Sir, if I may?'

Alleyn silently thanked Bix for drawing his speech to a close, he had been on the verge of enjoying himself too much, which would have risked inviting scorn rather than the chastened good behaviour he hoped to invoke in his audience.

He turned back to the room, 'Do try to get along, won't you? *All* of you?'

Directing the last to Glossop, he went out to join Bix in the yard.

CHAPTER TWENTY-THREE

'The tunnel goes to the bridge, Sir, as we figured, but it turns a few times on its way, not as direct as I'd have thought. Mind you, digging around rock, you'd just go the path of least resistance, I reckon.'

'What did you find?'

'No ghosts, not even any spirits,' Bix shone the torch on a dusty bottle in his hand, enjoying his own joke. 'It leads to the Bridge Hotel's cellar, all right, or maybe part of it. I came up to a wide part of the tunnel they look to have commandeered for storage, with a locked door beyond it that I reckon leads to the cellar itself. Take a look at this bottle, Sir.'

He handed it over, shining the torch on the bottle in Alleyn's hand.

'There were dozens of crates of them, all with no label.'

Alleyn shook his head, frowning. He was trying to rein in the irritation he felt with Bix for spinning out this story when there was so much else to get on with and then, looking at the wide grin on Bix's face, he suddenly realized, 'Oh I see, do you think the Bridge Hotel is brewing its own beer and passing it off as stock?'

'Not quite, Sir, I don't think you'd get many of the blokes round this way caught out in a trick like that. We New Zealanders are pretty particular about our beer, but you've heard of the six o'clock swill?'

'Yes Bix, I have indeed been introduced to your country's alarming custom of closing your public houses at six in the evening.'

'And you'll understand that the Bridge sometimes stays open a little later than six o'clock?'

'A policeman's lot would be an even unhappier one were he committed to enforcing the closing times of every public house in either your nation or in mine.'

'You'll get no disagreement from me on that, but Will Kelly said he was drinking lemonade tonight, you remember?'

'I do.' Alleyn was smiling, intrigued, as he carefully removed the stopper from the bottle. It took just a sniff of the cork to appreciate that the bottle contained not lemonade but a clear spirit, and a very strong one at that. 'And I can guess where you're headed with this, Bix, but surely a man of the world such as Mr Kelly could tell the difference between a sip of lemonade and a sip of home-brewed spirit, sold after hours?'

'It's thirsty work, carting bodies about, what if he'd grabbed his bottle of lemonade, taken a big gulp without pausing to check—why would he, if it was his own bottle— and the stuff was so strong it knocked him out right out? And what if someone had wanted to knock him out so they could switch the bodies? What if they'd put the alcohol in his bottle for that very reason?'

Alleyn smiled, 'It's true that an awful lot of our work begins with "what if", but I usually prefer to go on something a little more substantial. Even if we were to assume that Mr Kelly usually spends his long nights sipping from a bottle of lemonade rather than strong spirit, and that someone therefore chose to tamper with his bottle in order to knock him out long enough to swap old Mr Brown's body for Matron's, as yet we have no reason for this body swap. That it happened we are sure, why it happened is the conundrum.'

'Fair point, Inspector.'

'How about you head off and wake Kelly, it's time we had a word anyway, whether he's had his coffee or no. Find out how much of this famed lemonade he drank, and more importantly who, if anyone, gave him the bottle in question. I, meanwhile, have an uncomfortable appointment with a young lady with whom I fear I am going to have to be quite stern. This is the part of my work I enjoy the least.'

'You and me both. Not that I've had a load of dealing with young ladies, mind you, but I've never enjoyed sifting through the ranks' reasons for getting themselves in the dog house. More often than not I don't reckon they know themselves, high spirits and youth, most of it. Mind you, with this lot being cooped up here in hospital, I think they're just causing trouble out of boredom half the time, no malice in it.'

'And the other half?' Alleyn asked lightly.

'A woman, usually.'

'You'd give all men a free pass, Sergeant? You don't think any of them are wicked to the core?'

Bix shrugged, ''Course there are some bad souls, Sir, one or two, we wouldn't be in this mess otherwise, the mess of the war I mean. Well all right, maybe I mean this mess tonight as well. All the same, I've got faith in the average man, you've got to in my line of work. It's the average man who'll bring us through this war, you mark my words.'

He held up the dusty bottle, jerked his thumb in the direction of the Surgery and headed off.

Alleyn watched Bix go, wishing he had the same faith in human nature. He was frustrated with the extent to which the night's events had derailed his original task at Mount Seager and irritated with those inside the cramped Transport Office. He was especially concerned about Corporal Brayling, Alleyn had felt sure the young man was trustworthy. He reached into his pocket where his fingers lingered on the comfortingly smooth wooden stem of his pipe and decided that however urgent the matter in hand, he would do better to allow himself a few moments of peace to take stock before taking his next move. The consoling plan to sit and smoke a while was dashed when Alleyn found himself in a spill of pale light and heard his name hesitantly whispered from the door.

'Chief Detective Inspector?'

Sarah Warne's voice pulled him to attention.

'Miss Warne?' he spoke quietly, neither invitation nor rejection in his manner.

'I know I risk incurring your wrath—'

'Wrath?' he interjected, 'I thought I was admirably calm with your colleagues just now.

'You were,' she agreed, 'rather in the manner of a serious headmaster explaining to his favourite pupil that he has let himself and the entire school down.'

Alleyn allowed himself a small smile, 'Did it work?'

'Oh yes, we're all suitably shamed, but at the risk of

turning your disappointment into something more fero-
cious, I really must speak with you. If I may?'

Alleyn turned into the light from the door, 'I should be
delighted to have a conversation with you, Miss Warne.'

She took a step down and as she closed the door behind
her Alleyn fancied he heard a low whistle from Maurice
Sanders, saw Rosamund's raised eyebrow, watched Glossop's
sweaty face turn a still more vivid shade of scarlet. Even
had Sarah not been backlit from the office, Alleyn felt he
couldn't be sure whether her expression was related to the
fuss that had just taken place or the more pressing matter
that had driven her to the door. Something in her open
face suggested the latter and he tried to sound as encour-
aging as possible.

'Will it help if I promise to curb any hint of ferocity?'

Despite the warmth of his delivery, she hesitated.
Whatever courage she had mustered appeared to have
deserted her and she reached for the door handle behind
her, teetering on the precipice between the revelation she
had come to offer and the relative safety of the cramped
office.

Alleyn tried again, 'Miss Warne, if I may pre-empt your
retreat—I would not, in ordinary circumstances, ever allow
my temper to get the better of me with potential witnesses.'

'Even when those witnesses necessarily include suspects?'
she asked.

'Most especially then. I far prefer to cajole confessions
from my suspects than to bludgeon truths from them.'

He spoke slowly, hoping she would be reassured and
was relieved to hear the gentle creak of the old wooden
steps as she quietly stepped down into the asphalt yard.
As his eyes once again became accustomed to the dark he

196

realized that she stood very close and that there were tears in the eyes she turned up to him. So that was the reason for her carefully controlled tone, she was afraid she might cry.

'Miss Warne?'

There was silence and he tried again.

'I fear we have not one but several concurrent mysteries tonight and the presence of one confusion is wont to obscure the truth of another. I believe there is something you want to say, Miss Warne, something you have been aching to tell me for several hours. I would very much like you to do so, not least because you are next on my list to interview.'

'I thought you'd have a search party out for Cuth Brayling.'

'I expect Corporal Brayling will turn up of his own accord soon enough,' he said, obliquely. 'I'm grateful you stepped forward before I had to come and call you. I have an uncomfortable sense of playing a role on these occasions and I'd far rather not have to pull rank.'

'But you do have rank, Inspector.'

'Yes, which is why I have no doubt that you will feel enormously relieved once you have spoken. I am a policeman, as used to hearing secrets as—' He paused, he had been about to say 'as a doctor or a priest' but neither seemed appropriate given the company she had most recently been keeping. 'As any other detective. I assure you, Miss Warne, you will not shock, or even disturb me. You may, however, find that you are able to unburden yourself, if only a little.'

Alleyn waited, aware that this was her turning point, and he hated himself for the brief moment of gratification when he heard first a sigh and then a broken held-back sob.

'Please,' he said, crooking his arm, 'come along with me to the end of the hospital drive. There is a bench and starlight enough for you to sit and speak in the safety of relative darkness and for me to listen as adroitly as I must. I will smoke my pipe and you can tell your story there.'

'Oh yes, please.' Now that she had made her mind up to tell him whatever she had been withholding, Sarah's words tumbled from her, 'I desperately need to tell you about something that has happened, but—'

'Not until we are seated, Miss Warne,' Alleyn lifted an admonishing finger. 'Let's put some distance between ourselves and this office. I feel certain you will be able to speak more freely then.'

They walked to the bench in silence and Sarah waited as Alleyn removed his pipe, refilled it slowly and meticulously with tobacco from a small leather pouch, and then carefully lit it. In the brief glow from the match she looked at him from the corner of her eye. Fine features, long nose, high brow. He gave the perfect impression of a thoughtful favourite uncle or perhaps a serious older cousin. She felt she had to trust him, she had no choice.

Alleyn took a long draw on the pipe, studied the stars, noting that since last he looked up the swirl of the Milky Way had shifted on its axis across the heavens. He waited and it was his ability to wait that drew out Sarah's words.

'My father had a pipe, I've always associated the smell of pipe smoke with long Sunday afternoons, walking in the bush or along the beach, trailing in his footsteps.'

'Were you very young when he died?' Alleyn asked gently.

'Not so very or at least I didn't feel it at the time. I'd not long had my fifteenth birthday, but it was terribly sudden and I had to become awfully grown-up, almost at once. My mother wasn't strong emotionally, she's never been strong, and my sister—well, she was much younger, just a child of nine.'

'She must have been awfully young when—?'

'Sixteen. Of course I had to come home to my poor mother when my sister became ill, and then—well, Mother couldn't bear it, she still can't.' Sarah Warne shook her head and frowned looking out into the night, 'It's terrible, isn't it, Inspector, how we can speak of these things without tearing out our hair, rending our clothes? How we can sit here with all that has gone on this evening and you can smoke your pipe, I can prattle on.'

'I daresay I've had more practice than you, and you're not really prattling, it just feels that way to you because you haven't yet reached the crux of what it is you want to say.'

'Golly,' he heard a smile in her voice, 'you're very direct, aren't you?'

'When I need to be. Go on Miss Warne.'

'I will,' she spoke resolutely, 'I promise, but I need to finish my train of thought, I feel it's connected in some way.'

This time he left a silence where she had hoped he might continue the conversation. She felt his waiting as if it were a gentle push in the small of her back.

She took a deep breath and began, 'We endure such losses, Inspector Alleyn, so much pain, and yet we carry on. I don't mean carrying on as if nothing has happened, my mother will be fractured always, I think, at the loss of my sister, her child, and yet still the heart beats. Still we breathe.'

'Still we love?' he ventured after a moment.

'Oh yes,' she replied almost bitterly, 'still we love.'

She turned to look at him and he looked back plainly, holding her gaze in the bare light.

'I won't say it for you.'

Even in the night he could tell that her smile at being caught out was as deep as her frown, 'Silly me. I was hoping you might save me by speaking the words for me. You know, don't you, Inspector?'

Alleyn's face remained impassive, and he turned from her to stare blindly towards the swollen river, still raging across the huge boulders and rocks of the deep riverbed, 'I believe I do, but you know I cannot do this for you. Come on now, be a good girl.'

When the words finally spilled out, Sarah felt dizzy and ill and unburdened all at once, 'I was so in love with Luke when we were together in London, and he with me. At least I thought so, but then when I came back—when I had to come home to my poor mother, and he was in London, and then off in the field—it all seemed so different. It wasn't that I didn't trust him, of course I did, and anyway, we weren't promised to each other, not formally, but I felt it, I felt that we were. I still do. We wrote and although the letters were infrequent, he was overseas after all, and the mail has been impossible since the war, still we wrote to each other. They were good letters, very good. Honest and kind. Then when Luke was posted here, of all places, it felt like such a hopeful omen and I thought we might just take up where we had left off. But he was so distant, very different to the Luke who had been warm and hopeful and ever so easy to be with in London. Of course that was before the war and I know he'd seen awful things, been through awful things, but as I said, we keep on, don't we? You'll think me a foolish girl, desperate to bag herself a doctor like all the other silly little VADs, but I promise it isn't that. Luke's the only one for me, always has been. And then this evening—oh, it all seems so very long ago, doesn't it? I'd given her so much, you know?'

'Rosamund?' he asked.

'Yes,' she breathed, 'So you do know?' Alleyn didn't answer and she went on, her words almost monotonous with the effort to get them out, 'I'd loaned her quite a bit when we were in London together. She was always getting into scrapes, running out of cash for rent or food, and Luke loaned her several pounds too, more than once. She owed us. She owed me. Yet she didn't once mention paying either of us back, not a suggestion of it, even though we've all been working here at Mount Seager together. Luke's people aren't wealthy, you know, and he's been sending as much as he can back to them. I'm sure she knows that's the case, yet there she was, gloating about her winnings and not a glimmer of a suggestion that the debts were even in her mind. So tonight, I mean last night, when all the VADs were squealing about her win on the drive out and then she came charging in late, with all that money, positively skiting about it, I just assumed she'd share.' She paused for breath and said, almost to herself, 'Even her win seemed unfair when Rosamund has never known one end of a horse from the other as far as I can tell, let alone how to lay a bet. Anyway, Inspector, I honestly thought she'd give us back what she owes and then Luke wouldn't feel so beleaguered, he'd go back to being the old Luke. More fool me. But she didn't say a word about her debts to either of us, not a single word. She can't possibly have forgotten. And so I—'

She paused, her mouth dry, her hands clenched in her lap.

Alleyn tried to keep his tone neutral but he couldn't quite manage it and the words that came were sharp, 'Finish your sentence, Miss Warne.'

Sarah took a deep breath and blurted it out, 'I told Luke I thought we should take her money. I knew where Matron kept the spare set of keys and I said we could just—'

'Spare set? I was told there was no spare set.'

Sarah had the grace to look shame-faced, 'Matron's been a little odd recently, Inspector, she's—sorry, she had—been worried about the hospital, lack of nursing staff, keeping the soldiers under control. It's all been awfully difficult. She told me she had forgotten her keys, left them at home two or three times, and it's a long drive all the way out here to turn right back and go home again. I suggested she bring the spare set here and hide them in her office.'

Alleyn couldn't keep the anger from his voice now, it was all he could do not to shake the foolish girl for not mentioning another set of keys hours ago. He managed to keep his hands still and asked, 'Oh, for goodness' sake, what time was this?'

'Coming up for ten o'clock, perhaps? The storm was about to break. I was still so angry with Rosamund going on about her winnings and—well, I don't know what came over me. I decided she owed us and if she wasn't going to pay up then I would force the issue. I took the keys and waited until I could talk to Luke about it.' She went quiet for a moment and added, 'I suppose I must have thought that if he agreed with me then it wouldn't be such a bad thing to do.'

'And did he?'

'He was furious. I said we could take what she owed us and then I'd put the rest back, but he was having none of it. We had a fearful row and I would have gone anywhere to get away, but then the storm broke so forcefully. Luke was saying such awful things and I realized I'd got completely the wrong end of the stick, the money wasn't it at all—I mean, I know he's not all right, of course I do, I just thought the money might help a little. It was a moment of madness that I even considered it, I know, but then there was all the fuss when Mr Glossop discovered the payroll missing, and then Matron and that awful scene with the trolley and old Will Kelly, and—well, you know the rest.'

Alleyn turned to her, 'You have been an awful idiot, Miss Warne. Not least because someone else may have known about those spare keys, someone else might well have used them to steal the payroll. Where are the keys now?'

'In the Transport Office.'

'And I suppose the argument that Glossop overheard was you suggesting to Dr Hughes that you both take the money and him refusing?'

'Luke was shocked that I'd even think of it, even though it was more or less ours.'

'It was not yours at all until Miss Farquharson gave it you.'

'That's what Luke said, he's furious with me.'

'And I'm furious with the pair of you. Between your

203

foolishness and your absurd choice not to tell me what you'd done, that you had the spare keys, you've wasted several precious hours and put me quite on the back foot. Right, get up, we're going back to the Transport Office and we're going to make some sense of this.'

He stood up and held out his hand, giving her no choice, Sarah took it meekly.

'I am sorry,' she said, 'awfully sorry. For all of it. I thought I was so clever. So much cleverer than Rosamund and her absurd affairs, but it's me who's made a fool of myself, just like her, over a man.'

'Affairs?' Alleyn asked quietly, aware that they were coming to the point of it now.

'Oh yes, Inspector Alleyn. While I was here in New Zealand, looking after my grieving mother, grieving myself, Rosamund took my place with Luke. He was posted to North Africa quite quickly and she came back to New Zealand shortly after me, so at least it can't have been anything serious, there wasn't time. I know he feels like a pig about it, but I might as well admit to you now that when I thought about taking her money I felt a moment of deep satisfaction. I felt that Rosamund owed me in more ways than one.'

'How did you know about this affair?' he asked.

Sarah's paused a moment before she said, 'Luke talks in his sleep, Inspector.' She took a sharp breath and went on, 'he cries out in horror sometimes and it frightens me.' Alleyn ached for her as she followed that admission and said, in a tone of deep resignation, 'I'm sure I'm not the first to say those words this evening.'

They walked back to the hospital buildings in silence. Alleyn heard the deep, emphatic hoot of the morepork on the useless telegraph wire as a clear signal to get on, yet he kept his pace measured and careful. Her cool hand in his felt very small and very young.

Beside him, grateful for the darkness, Sarah Warne used her free hand to brush away her tears. Dashing away her shame would take a little longer.

CHAPTER TWENTY-FOUR

Sarah walked alongside Alleyn, her eyes downcast, fearing the light of the Transport Office with every step. How could she face Luke having revealed so much? Let alone bear seeing Luke and Rosamund sitting so comfortably together, now that she could see them through the Inspector's eyes, and had seen herself through his eyes as well. She had never told Luke and Rosamund that she knew about their affair, in many ways, acknowledging it to them would be more painful than simply allowing herself to forget it had ever happened. The relief she felt at finally admitting her jealousy and shame seemed almost palpable, it must be obvious to them. She winced, realizing she was more upset about the mess of emotions that lay between Luke and Rosamund and herself, than she was about admitting she had considered taking Rosamund's money. Sarah sighed and almost smiled at the turn of events. She was so used to being thought of as the sensible one compared to Rosamund and most of the other VADs and now she had revealed herself to be as foolish as any other girl and reckless into the bargain. She acknowledged ruefully that the most painful part was that her foolishness had been a revelation to herself as well.

She was getting herself into an awful state and it was a welcome reprieve from her own thoughts when she heard Alleyn swear softly and remarkably forcefully under his breath, and felt him finally loosen his hold on her hand. She watched in surprise as he broke into a swift sprint. She could make out two men, fifty or so yards ahead of them. Alleyn's eyes must be better than hers or perhaps it was her tears blurring her night vision that meant she took longer to work out who the men were. She picked up her pace and in another ten steps she saw that Sergeant Bix had his arm very firmly on Cuthbert Brayling's shoulder and was frog-marching him towards the Transport Office. Alleyn stopped them just as they were at the steps. She wasn't close enough to hear what was said, but when she drew level they were no longer headed to the Transport Office.

'You go on ahead, Bix,' said Alleyn, 'I want a quick word with Miss Warne.'

Sarah watched Sergeant Bix march Brayling off towards the Records Office and saw that Brayling's eyes were as downcast as hers had been, although there was something about the set of his jaw that suggested anger rather than shame.

Alleyn spoke quietly and urgently, 'Go and take your place in the Transport Office. Tell no one that you have seen Brayling, most especially not his fellow soldiers. If anyone asks where Bix and I have gone, tell them we're—'

He frowned, paused, looked around and his whispered instructions came to a halt. For a very brief moment Sarah thought she saw Alleyn as perhaps his wife might see him, not the shining knight who would help them all make sense of these terrible events, but an ordinary man doing his best to cope with an extraordinary situation, made all the more difficult by the fact that he was in an unknown place with unknown people.

'How about I tell them you're with Sergeant Bix, checking Matron's office one more time? There's been so much rushing back and forwards, and no time or equipment for a proper study of the safe or the office, no one will question your choice to have another look. Might that do?'

Alleyn grasped her shoulder lightly and smiled down at her, 'Good girl. Now you go and join the rest of them, I can see you've pluck enough for the night ahead.'

As he strode off to join Bix and Brayling, Sarah smiled ruefully, if Alleyn had played her with his momentary look of need, then it had worked, not only had she come up with a solution but in doing so she had reminded herself of her own capability. Sarah knew herself to be both sensible and smart. Yes, she had made a stupid mistake—more than one, in truth—but she was not going to let it lay her low, there was much more to life than this awful night and she'd make Luke Hughes see that if it was the last thing she did.

It was a competent and calm Sarah Warne who stepped back into the Transport Office as Alleyn caught up with Bix and Brayling, humming softly to himself. He had had some practice in persuading young women that one or two foolish mistakes did not necessarily mean a life quite over, his next effort was likely to require rather more delicate handling.

*

Alleyn stepped into the Records Office, his awful sense of déjà vu undercut by the ticking of the clock on the wall. He felt his pulse race a little and checked his own watch against the clock. It was coming up for two thirty. That left them perhaps two and a half hours until twilight, and at best three hours until full daylight would not only expose the extent of the receding flood water and the damage to the bridge but, unless he could flush out the culprit or culprits who were part of the espionage chain, a far greater danger might be let loose. Alleyn had known since he took on his assignment that this night would be long and watchful, he had not expected it to be quite so busy. Aware that he was bone tired, he chose not to risk sitting down, the height advantage he held over Brayling when standing was useful. The young Māori soldier looked as strong as an ox, but Alleyn had a good head on the younger man and he knew how to use it to his advantage

He launched straight in, 'What have you to say for yourself, Corporal?'

Alleyn's first foray was met with a shrug and the detective had to suppress a smile as he saw Bix's fury. It was a mix of anger that Brayling would refuse to answer a direct question from a superior and an even deeper resentment that a New Zealand soldier was showing him up.

'Speak up, soldier,' Bix barked, and then hurriedly nodded an apology to Alleyn when the detective brought a finger to his lips and with a nod of his head to the buildings on the other side of the yard, reminded Bix of their proximity to the wards.

'Come on now, Corporal Brayling, you know as well as we do that it will only go harder for you if Sergeant Bix is forced to take this further. You've been well and truly caught in the act. It's best all round if you come clean about the nature of that act, whatever it may be. As it stands, I have no option but to assume you know something about the theft as well as the other appalling events of this evening. Worse, that you are implicated in them.'

Alleyn spoke as sharply as he dared, he had a sense that Brayling knew rather more than he was letting on and he didn't dare risk upsetting the young man, however much he was dying to shake him.

Sergeant Bix had no such qualms, 'For cripes' sake, lad, will you tell the man what you know? I'm guessing it's something to do with your people, right? Now I don't care if there's a curse or what have you on whatever information you're holding back, the Inspector needs to know what's what and there's no flamin' time to lose. You know as well as I do that your *whaea* Ina would tell you to do as you're told, so step to it.'

'Fire Ina?' Alleyn asked, confused.

'*Whaea*,' Bix spelled out the word, 'W–H–A–E–A. It's Māori for aunty, grandma, nana, what have you. An older woman everyone pays attention to—and,' he scowled at Brayling, 'everyone respects her, not just her own family. Everyone round here shuts up the minute *Whaea* Ina stands up to speak, she's a proper *kuia*.' He stopped and glared at Brayling who was looking at him from the corner of his eye, 'Don't look so surprised, Corporal. I grew up in the Bay of Plenty, we know loads of Māori up there, both the people and your lingo, and I've been round here long enough to get to know folk too, it's part of my job.' He looked back to Alleyn, 'I tell you, Inspector, that old lady would have no truck with one of their young men holding up a police investigation, that's for flamin' sure.'

Alleyn watched the young soldier's face during Bix's diatribe and it occurred to him that Brayling wasn't as sure as the sergeant seemed to be of this venerable older woman's attitude. In the Māori man's set jaw he saw a suggestion that Bix had taken his assumption too far to say she'd be on the side of the Met's finest. He was just about to say so, to soften Brayling's intransigence with a peace offering against Bix's chafing, when he heard a sigh escape from Brayling's lips. Alleyn realized that the young man was tired of holding in his secret, whatever it was. He was about to break. He heard rather than saw Bix about to start in again and put a warning hand on the sergeant's forearm. Together they watched the transformation take place. Brayling's shoulders relaxed, his chest heaved once, twice, he blinked his dark, watchful eyes and readied himself to tell what he knew.

'I told my cobbers I wasn't visiting my wife, I didn't trust them not to let on, if they'd been, well, you know—'

'Gambling? Drinking?' Alleyn offered.

Brayling shrugged, 'I can't say, Sir. I won't. But I just knew I might not get away with it if they knew where I was going.'

'So you didn't go down to the river earlier tonight?' Bix asked, pointedly.

'Ah yeah, I did that, tonight I did. But the other times we've been meeting proper, Ngaire and me. See there's a tunnel, runs from the Bridge pub to right about under here,' he gestured with his hand to the earth below, 'and further on, we've been using it to meet.'

'In the tunnel?' Alleyn frowned.

'Not in the tunnel itself. You have to go past the back of the morgue to get from the Bridge up to the hospital and I'd never get my Ngaire to meet me there, she'd reckon it was *tapu*. Sacred, Sir,' he added for Alleyn's benefit. 'Nah, we meet in the other direction.'

'The other direction?' Alleyn echoed faintly.

'That's right, not far beyond Military 3.'

'The border of wild roses?'

'Yes, Sir, the roses edge into the bush. Well, on past there, few hundred yards, there's another entrance to the tunnel.'

'Go on,' Alleyn encouraged him.

'*Pākehā* round here reckon it's all been closed up with rock falls for years now.'

'But it's not?'

'You'd need to know your way round, Sir,' Brayling said, a hint of triumph in his voice, 'and it's easily missed, but there is a way, once you're right inside the cave. It's not obvious from outside, but you can find it if you know what you're looking for.'

'And what are we looking for, Corporal?'

'There's a big old *tomo*, Sir,' Brayling answered Alleyn, adding a translation, 'a deep hole right in the ground. Our people knew about it back in the old days, before the settlers built the hospital here.'

'We don't need to know all the history, Corporal.'

''Course not, Sarge,' Brayling nodded to Bix and then continued his story for Alleyn, 'Thing is, the mouth of that cave's a good place to meet your girl, if you're worried, if you want to make sure she and the baby are ok.' He looked plaintively at Alleyn, 'That's all I wanted to do, Sir, make sure my girl was all right.'

Alleyn was doing his best to contain his anger, it wasn't Brayling's fault that he had just given them a lead they could have done with hours ago, 'You knew about this cave, Bix?'

'Yes, Sir, we all did, but I don't know anyone who thinks it's passable.'

'Is that right, Brayling? What about the fellows you're doing your damnedest not to get into trouble? Did they know there was a way in and out through the cave?'

He shook his head, 'No, I promise you that. And I don't think any of that lot over at the pub do either, they only use their end of the tunnel for extra storage. The tunnel gets lower towards the cave and they've no need to come up this far.'

Brayling glanced to Sergeant Bix and then raised his warm, open face to Alleyn's. It was with the barest hint of a defiant smile that he said, 'See, that *tomo*'s one of our people's old places. *Whaea* Ina'll have my guts for garters when she knows I've told you about it, she says we've little enough left of our own as it is.'

After extracting a promise from Brayling that he'd take Alleyn along to the cave as soon as Bix could get back from the army offices with another pair of good torches, Alleyn strode back to the Transport Office with Brayling close at his heels. He wanted to explain that he wasn't angry with the young Māori soldier for refusing to give up his mates, he fully understood the necessity for closing ranks, especially when they would be heading off to fight alongside each other any day now. His frustration was rather more to do with his concern that Brayling was too trusting of his friends and a sneaking suspicion that were the boot on the other foot, they'd not have been so careful of Brayling's reputation.

Alleyn stopped and turned to Brayling, 'I am angry with you, soldier, but not for the reasons you imagine. I can't explain just yet, but I hope you'll understand before the night is out.'

Brayling followed silently behind him and Alleyn let it go for now, if his misgivings were right the young man would work it out himself soon enough. They were just yards from the Transport Office when they heard the sound of crashing furniture.

'This really is too much,' Alleyn groaned and he raced the last few feet to the door.

CHAPTER TWENTY-FIVE

Alleyn stood at the door to the Transport Office and the small room fell silent but for the sound of Mr Glossop trying desperately to extricate himself from the far corner where he had crammed himself as far behind the desk as his ample flesh would allow and appeared to be using an intricately detailed foolscap sheaf of time logs as an ineffectual shield. To the right of Mr Glossop sat Father O'Sullivan, apparently deep in contemplation, oblivious to the brawl before him. In the centre of the crowded room Private Maurice Sanders was struggling to his knees. He looked up at the detective revealing a cut lip, while Dr Luke Hughes stood glaring over Sanders, as if daring him to rise from the floor. Alleyn noticed the doctor was nursing the grazed knuckles that had no doubt done the damage to Sanders's face. Sydney Brown looked on moodily as if the insanity of the room was exactly what he'd come to expect from these people. Against the nearside wall, Rosamund Farquharson sat bolt upright on the divan, her feet lifted from the ground and curled beneath her as if Alleyn had caught her in the act of squeamishly sighting a mouse rather than elegantly lifting her legs to allow the two young men to get on and fight. Alleyn deduced that Miss Farquharson must be in a state of shock if her uncharacteristic silence was anything to go by. Sarah Warne stood opposite Rosamund, the fighting men between them, her hands covering her face and Alleyn had a sneaking suspicion that it was hysteria rather than tears that she was hiding. When an ashen-faced Sister Comfort emerged from behind the door, and Alleyn realized he only just failed to hit her when he'd flung it open, he took a deep breath and very carefully stepped into the office, closing the door behind him.

He asked with biting calm, 'I wonder, is there anyone present who recalls that there is a war on? That there are matters of great pith and moment happening beyond this little room? Is there one of you who recalls that the petty squabbles, frustrations, insults and—yes, Mr Glossop, thefts—upsetting you all so much pale into insignificance when put alongside the very serious matters that have occurred in the past hours?'

A flurry of explanations and accusations followed, all of them talking at once, until Alleyn held up his hands for silence, 'Sister Comfort, you appear to be the least excited person here, will you please accompany me outside so we can get to the bottom of this and return to the matter in hand?'

Alleyn offered around the office a fierce glare demanding silence and compliance, and then opened the door for the senior nurse.

Outside in the slightly cooler night, Sister Comfort explained what she understood to have happened, 'Pawcett and Sanders have been bickering on and off all night, they've tried to keep it hidden, but I'm fairly certain—'

Alleyn interrupted her, nodding his head towards the

Transport Office door, 'Just what you saw for now, Sister, thank you.'

She frowned, understanding that Alleyn was right, of course they'd all be listening, she lowered her voice and continued her explanation.

'Sanders and Pawcett have been acting the lad, mates together, but there was something off between them.'

'How?'

The Sister frowned again and bit her lip with her snaggle-tooth, 'It was the tone, Inspector. Not their words as such, but they were short with each other, brusque.'

'Go on.'

'So this was on one side of the office, but then Sanders and Miss Farquharson started up as well. Private Sanders practically accused Miss Farquharson of stealing her own money so as not to have to pay off her debts. Well, once he'd said that, young Dr Hughes launched in to defend her honour, at which point Rosamund turned on the doctor himself.' She leaned in to Alleyn, peering at him over the rim of her spectacles, 'Sometimes these young ladies find that the hot water they were so keen to jump into isn't quite as welcoming once they're in, if you get my drift.'

'I do,' Alleyn remarked shortly, 'Please, go on.'

'Rather predictably, Miss Warne then leapt to the doctor's defence—how these girls think we don't know what's going on, I have no idea, I think they believe we were none of us young once.'

'That's a prerogative of the young, Sister. I've no doubt we were the same.'

'Not I,' she replied starchily and Alleyn fully believed her, 'I always had the greatest of respect for my elders. Regardless, Miss Warne's intervention prompted an altercation between the two young women. Whispered rather than shouted, Inspector. Hissed, you might say.'

'And then?' Alleyn asked.

'The entire unseemly farrago escalated into a broader fuss between Dr Hughes and Private Sanders and then grew still more frantic when that absurd Mr Glossop launched himself at the two soldiers demanding they pay attention to his concerns, instead of their love interests.'

'Go on.'

'You can imagine, neither of the young ladies were very pleased at that. It's been my observation that young women nowadays are happy to conduct their clandestine affairs with blatant indiscretion, just so long as no one ever appears to notice.'

'This forced people to notice?'

'It certainly did. I rather suspect it was this upset, real or enacted, that led to punches being thrown and the resulting bother. With no bucket of water to throw over the foolish lot of them, I retired to the safety of the corner closest to the door.'

Alleyn suppressed a smile, 'Perfectly understandable.'

Sister Comfort leaned her veiled head still closer to the detective, 'But isn't there more we ought to do?'

Alleyn held up a hand and nodded in the direction of the army offices. Sister Comfort looked down the long yard to see Sergeant Bix running towards them at a speed that belied his solid frame.

'Good Lord,' she said.

'Good man,' Alleyn said to the panting Bix who drew up short at the sight of Alleyn and Sister Comfort, a torch held tight in each hand.

Alleyn took the torches from him, he and Bix had a very

218

quick exchange of words, and the sergeant speedily took up sentry on the steps of the Transport Office, while Alleyn ushered Sister Comfort into the Records Office.

The moment the door was closed behind them, Sister Comfort turned to Alleyn. Her earlier prurience completely gone, 'It's less than three hours until dawn, Inspector, it's a terrible turn out,' she said.

'For the love of Mike,' he replied testily, 'do you think I don't know? This little lot have delayed and derailed the investigation all damn night, you might almost think some of them have done so on purpose.'

Alleyn's reply was surprisingly curt and Sister Comfort allowed herself a brief moment's satisfaction, so much had already happened this evening, she had found herself wondering if she was going quite mad in trying to remain calm while all around them were losing their heads. She was briefly relieved to realize the detective was also concerned and then even more worried. If the Inspector himself was perturbed, how was she expected to behave as if this were an everyday, an every-night occurrence? And while Matron lay—no, she would not think of it.

She bit at her lip again and frowned, 'There's not enough time.'

'It will have to be enough,' was Alleyn's grave reply, 'I haven't spent the past week cooped up in that absurd room waiting for this moment to catch our spy or spies in the act, to let it all go now simply because of an absurd chain of events, any one of which would be bad enough individually, but which collectively add up to the kind of farce that wouldn't even sell in the provinces. So, Sister,' he said, sitting down and taking out his notebook, 'Tell me everything I need to know.'

Whereupon Sister Gertrude Comfort, Chief Detective Inspector Alleyn's contact at Mount Seager, gave him chapter and verse on the three people she suspected were part of the espionage they were hoping to uncover and stop in its tracks, ideally before the midsummer sun rose across the plains.

CHAPTER TWENTY-SIX

'When I was asked to take on this work, I readily agreed, Inspector.'

'Of course.'

'I was proud that the Chair of the Hospital Board had faith in me and considered me trustworthy enough for the role.'

Alleyn nodded, recalling the Chair's words, 'Once the hospital became a military site, we had to make sure there was someone on staff we could trust. I've known the Comfort family for years, Inspector. Gertrude's nosey as hell and starchy with it, but that's all to the good, I bet there's nothing goes on out there that escapes her attention.'

Sister Comfort continued, 'But when you arrived with the suggestion that someone among the staff or patients was implicated in espionage, I couldn't believe it. I didn't want to. I've done my best, provided you with lists and rosters, given you detailed information on everyone I can think of who has anything to do with the hospital—'

'You have been enormously helpful,' he interjected.

Sister Comfort's naturally suspicious nature along with her attention to detail made her an indefatigable inside informant. Alleyn's unenviable task since his arrival had been to sift through her lists detailing the usual misdemeanours of any workplace, including staff five minutes late, misbehaving convalescent servicemen, unusually inattentive nurses, trying to decipher which were ordinary sins and which were genuine signs of potential espionage. It proved a time-consuming exercise and yet one he had found oddly soothing. He was, at least, certain that she had not missed anything. Or he had been until earlier this evening when he discovered that Sister Comfort had a secret of her own, one that had likely blinded her to the possible malfeasance of one particular suspect.

'Please, do sit down,' Alleyn offered.

'I'd really rather not, we have very little time and it is quite clear that one, if not all three of those soldiers are our suspects.'

'I agree the soldiers have been up to something,' he said, 'however, I'm not as sure as you are that they are all implicated in our current mission.'

Sister Comfort stared at Alleyn, he looked back plainly, his fine features in direct contrast to her heavy, broad face. After a moment she conceded and, taking a stiff-backed chair as her perch, she pulled her notebook from her pocket, settled her spectacles more firmly on her nose, and rattled through a concise list of patients and staff, military and civilian, and the occasions in the past twenty-four hours when eight different people had behaved in some way out of character. Five of the aberrant behaviours could be explained by illness or sheer foolishness, but she had no such excuses for Brayling, Pawcett and Sanders. Alleyn heard her out impatiently, he needed Sister Comfort on his side and perhaps this chance to demonstrate her surveillance skills would shore her up for what he was about to reveal.

'So you see,' she said, coming to the end of her oration, 'those three soldiers know something, I assure you of that.'

'There are other people in the office, Sister.'

'You cannot seriously suspect either of the girls. True, they are both foolish enough to have had their heads and more turned by the same young man—'

Alleyn raised an eyebrow and Sister Comfort gave him a genuine smile, 'I've been around impressionable young women and charming doctors for many years now, Inspector Alleyn. And as for the rest of them, Dr Hughes has, as we know, had his hands far too full to add espionage skulduggery to his case list, Will Kelly proved again tonight he's not to be trusted with a bottle and I expect even the Japanese like their spies to be sober, Sydney Brown has hardly been a regular visitor to the hospital, we had to practically force him to come and visit his grandfather, and Father O'Sullivan is—'

'A vicar.'

'Exactly so.'

Alleyn looked grave, 'Look here, I don't enjoy keeping you in the dark and happen to think you're right, but not wholly, or at least not on every point. I believe we may be looking at interlinked crimes, or attempted crimes, tonight.'

Sister Comfort sighed in exasperation, 'I wish you'd be plain in your speech, Inspector.'

'Forgive me, but I have a violent loathing for the kind of mistakes all too often made when method and routine, however tedious, are undermined by the demands of haste. There is, however, one matter I'd like you to clear up for me.' He paused and said quietly, 'It is delicate, I'm afraid.'

'Delicate?' Sister Comfort glared at Alleyn as if he had over-stepped a particularly well-defended boundary, 'I am a nurse, Inspector, dedicated to my responsibilities for over forty years. I'm well aware that my junior charges see me as a fusty old maid, likely to curl up in mortal shame were I to imagine any of the goings-on of which they are so confusingly proud, but I'm no blushing violet. My vocation means I've seen a great deal of life, death, and everything else in between. Please don't insult me by suggesting anything is too delicate for my sensibilities.'

'That's exactly the attitude I'd hoped for. In which case, I'm sure you won't mind explaining the contents of this letter to me?'

Inspector Alleyn reached into his pocket and pulled out the letter he had been keeping there for several hours. He unfolded the paper and handed it to Sister Comfort.

As she took the page she said, 'Oh, but it's Matron's handwriting.'

Looking more closely she realized it was addressed to her. She looked around, unsure, seeming to tense as if to run. Alleyn had a sense that she wanted to get out of the office, be anywhere but in that confined space with him. He looked on in quiet admiration as she steeled herself and he studied her curiously.

'I appreciate that it must be very hard to read Matron's writing at this time, but please,' Alleyn indicated the paper, 'I'd very much like to understand what I have read.'

She looked up and her broad face was ashen, 'You've read this? It's addressed to me.'

'My work requires that I must. Please, will you read it now?'

Alleyn watched as the ungainly, heavy-set woman turned

her eyes to the page in her lap. He saw her half-smile and then frown as she read on. When, at length, she came to the post-script on the second page he observed as first the tip of her nose, then her wide cheeks, and then her very ears became suffused with a deep crimson, he was not yet sure whether it was the red of shame or of rage. When she steeled herself to look up at him, he saw from her eyes that it was the former.

'I have nothing to say,' she said at last, regaining her self-control and holding the letter out to him as if it were a particularly distasteful medical specimen.

'I don't understand?' he said as he took back the letter.

Alleyn had expected one of several reactions given the contents, the most likely was grief, a viable alternative would have been fury, with perhaps bitterness or despair as other options. He had not counted on deep shame followed almost immediately by a cool and deliberate shutting down. The woman now looking up him was remarkably sure and very distant. She took off her spectacles, seemed to peer into a middle distance and then, with a small nod, put them firmly back on her nose.

'I have nothing to say, Inspector. The first part of the letter reads as if Matron knew she were to die this evening, which is absurd, giving me instructions as to the hospital routine and bills, when she was in perfect health as far as I knew. Indeed, as far as she knew. That it has today's—yesterday's—date is even more confusing.'

'And the post-script?'

'The post-script makes no sense whatsoever. I have never experienced, let alone acted upon the emotions she attributes to me. The final note reads more like the foolish ramblings of a young girl, someone more like Miss Farquharson than the woman I worked alongside and trusted as a colleague and a friend,' she hesitated, there was a moment when he thought she might break, but she drew a sharp breath and went on, 'a dear friend, for many years.'

With that Sister Comfort stood up, turned her back and left the office, closing the door quietly behind her. Alleyn had wanted to say more, but she was in too much pain and he let her go. He trusted that she would not leave the care of her hospital and her patients for long, and he rather suspected she desperately needed a quiet corner and a moment of still, dark privacy. Let her have it.

'Poor woman,' he heard himself say and then swore under his breath, there really was no time to be feeling sorry for people, no time at all. He waited a minute to give her time to get away across the yard and then he opened the office door and called quietly across to the steadfast Bix.

'Hi there, Sergeant. I think we'll need those torches now.'

CHAPTER TWENTY-SEVEN

Back in the Transport Office, Alleyn noticed a palpable sense of distress beneath the semblance of calm. Rosamund was still curled up on the divan, one arm pillowing her head, but despite her relaxed pose, her eyes were dark and watchful. Sarah Warne had successfully gathered the papers that had been knocked aside and her desk once more appeared the model of efficiency, and Dr Hughes was sitting noticeably closer to her than he had been earlier, although it was obvious that they were not easy alongside each other. Sarah was working industriously and Alleyn thought she was doing so with the kind of concentration that threatened explosive fury at the slightest interruption. Mr Glossop and Father O'Sullivan sat bolt upright on the two wooden chairs. They neither spoke nor slept, both men apparently fixated by the steadily ticking clock on the office wall, hypnotized by the passing minutes. Alleyn glanced at the clock himself and the pang of anxiety it induced made him wish he hadn't. Private Sanders and young Sydney Brown stood on either side of the window, staring through the glass out into the hospital yard. Alleyn noticed that the window also reflected the men back at themselves and wondered if they were searching their hearts or looking out for rosy-fingered dawn. Corporal Brayling stood alongside Rosamund's divan, a brooding sentinel, and Private Pawcett sat slumped against a wall, his face betraying bitterness as much as frustration.

'I'm going to have to beg your indulgence a little longer, I'm afraid,' Alleyn said as one by one they turned to look at him, Sarah Warne last of all, tearing herself away from her paperwork with great reluctance. 'I need you three soldiers immediately.'

Alleyn watched as the servicemen exchanged a look, something between resignation and concern. Whatever it indicated he felt sure he was about to hear confirmation of at least one secret. He also noticed that, as Sanders stepped away, Sydney Brown stationed himself more directly before the dark glass of the window. Alleyn had readied himself to deflect Glossop's complaint, Rosamund's sarcastic quip, the vicar's grumble, but none came. It seemed they were all as exhausted as they were concerned, perhaps the shock of the earlier fracas had broken through their personal upsets and they were beginning to take in the truth of the events of the night. He had noticed in his years on the force that it often took several hours for the reality of a crime to filter through to those under suspicion, so much energy was expended in asserting their innocence that they rarely felt the weight of the horror immediately, yet when they did, it seemed to hit them all the harder.

Alleyn asked Brayling and Bix to wait for him a moment, and he took Sanders and Pawcett into the Records Office. They stood opposite each other, Sanders fidgeting, Pawcett frowning, the older man watching, waiting.

Finally, when Sanders looked fit to explode with nerves,

Alleyn spoke. His tone left the soldiers in no doubt of the gravity of the situation, 'I'll start with you, Sanders. I have a question to ask of you and I insist on an honest answer.'

Sanders shrugged uncomfortably, ran a hand through his hair and looked up at Alleyn, his eyes wary, 'I'll do my best.'

'You'll do a damn sight better than that, you idiotic young pup. You're on a precipice right now and what happens for the rest of your life depends upon your answer.'

Sanders looked at Alleyn again, the wariness gone and in its place something much closer to shock. Clearly it was a good while since anyone had called him to account, 'Precipice? What? I don't—Sir?'

Alleyn smiled inwardly, glad to see he'd broken through the younger man's well-crafted mask of insouciance, 'I cannot say more, but a great deal rests on you telling me the truth. Unfortunately I don't have time to get the whole story from you, I shall leave that to Sergeant Bix, but I need you to tell me—and with no fuss, just simple unvarnished facts—what is the content of the messages you have been passing using the tunnel that leads to the Bridge Hotel?'

If there had been time for Alleyn to be pleased with himself, he would have enjoyed this moment enormously as Sanders turned from the cocksure, good-looking charmer who had captured Rosamund Farquharson's heart, into a penitent schoolboy, ready to tell all. To his credit, the soldier wasted no time denying the premise of the enquiry, instead he blustered a question about how Alleyn knew.

The detective smiled, 'I didn't know for certain until just this moment when you confirmed my suspicions. It's an old trick, Private, and you fell for it.'

Sanders groaned and Pawcett snarled at his mate, 'You flamin' idiot, Maurice.'

Ignoring their interchange, Alleyn went on, 'I am well aware that the boredom of convalescence or confinement is often alleviated by gambling. Miss Warne mentioned earlier that the VADs all knew Miss Farquharson intended to lay a bet on Lordly Stride, they knew she'd won long before she arrived late for work. Miss Warne also told me that Miss Farquharson was, not to put too fine a point on it, in debt to several of her friends. I wondered if perhaps someone had tipped her off about a good bet for the race meeting yesterday. Further, I understand that you and Miss Farquharson were close, which made me wonder if you weren't also engaged in some betting exploits of your own. You already admitted running a racket. What I don't know is how you came to have access to the tunnel?'

'I'll answer this, big-mouth,' Pawcett said to Sanders, who shrugged his agreement and Pawcett went on, 'No great secret. There used to be a few old sheds and a workshop at the other end of the yard, before they built the army set-up. The pub shared the stables with the hospital and some bright spark had the idea of joining it all up underground.'

Private Sanders couldn't help himself, 'Great little system they had—'

'I'm not interested in their system.'

'No, Sir, fair enough,' Sanders answered abashed.

Pawcett continued the story, 'When they knocked it all down for the new army buildings they left one of the old lean-tos. That's how we got down to the tunnel, it goes right to the pub cellar.'

'When did this start? Were you still officially in quarantine?'

Pawcett shook his head, not put off, 'We're none of us idiots, whatever you might think, we'd never have gone near the pub while we were really sick.'

Alleyn shut Pawcett down with a look that suggested that their idiocy was quite plain for all to see and then ordered Bix to get the rest of their story while he headed off with Brayling. It was a sorry-looking Sanders and a confused Pawcett that Corporal Brayling glimpsed when Alleyn opened the door wide and stepped lightly down into the yard. The sight, as Alleyn had no doubt intended, made Brayling all the more aware of his own position and he meekly took on his role as Alleyn's guide.

As he followed the Māori soldier towards the north end of the hospital grounds Alleyn wished, not for the first time in his career, that he could be in two places at once. He would very much have enjoyed sitting in the Records Office and winkling out what else Sanders had to tell. He had bigger fish to fry, however, and if he couldn't have Fox alongside him, Bix would make a fine understudy. By the time he and Brayling returned to the yard, Alleyn hoped it might take one final move to bring it all together. Not before time.

Bix, thinking it better to get the story from the two men separately, spoke first to Pawcett who refused to give any more details about their gambling efforts, and assured Bix he didn't care what happened now, he just wanted leave of the whole flamin' lot of them.

'You really have nothing else to say for yourself, soldier? Nothing in mitigation?'

'Nah,' Pawcett shook his head. 'I mean it, Sarge, I've

had it up to here. I've got nothing to say, not tonight, not tomorrow.'

'In that case you'd better return to the Transport Office.'

Bix watched from the steps as Pawcett made his way to join the others, kicking at the asphalt as he went. There was something not right with that young man, but he was damned if he knew what it was. Maurice Sanders, on the other hand, was a far easier nut to crack. His was a love story and Sergeant Bix knew enough about young servicemen to know they would always want to be thought the shining knight in matters of love, no matter how dubious their actions.

Yes, Sanders had been carrying on with Rosie Farquharson, but it wasn't the real thing at all. He had the grace to look a little shame-faced when he admitted he'd only been step-ping out with Rosamund as a way to distract himself from Sukie Johnson. They'd started an affair before the war when Sanders had been a casual labourer for one of the local farmers. Sukie Johnson was a married woman and ten years older, so they had sensibly broken it off when he'd gone away to war, vowing not to write or see each other, vowing never to be tempted again.

'Then stone the crows, but the flamin' army only went and sent me here to recuperate.'

Sanders's face suggested that he thought there had been some mystical significance to the convalescent hospital being quite so close to the woman to whom he had given his youthful heart. Even Rosamund's rather obvious charms had been unable to distract him for long and then Sukie had confided a secret in Sanders, one she'd never before told anyone.

'Her old man knocks her about, Sarge. He hits her. No one knows.'

'Not even her brother?'

'Nah, Snow Johnson's too smart for that. He smacks her where the bruises won't show.'

Bix swore then and Sanders took Bix's curse as a cue to go on.

'That's what decided me, I've got to get her out of there. I figured I needed to get some money together and fast. That's why we've been running a book, me and the lads. I know it's against the rules, but the only reason was to get a bit of a kitty going. Brayling needs a starter for him and his Ngaire, especially now the baby's due any day and I wanted to help Sukie get away to her cousins up in the Wairarapa. She'll be safe there, she can get divorced after the war and we'll be sweet.'

'And Pawcett?'

'Bob wasn't fussed about the money, he was just bored, so he volunteered to do the runs. I collected the numbers, Cuth looked after the money, and Bob took the whole lot along the tunnel and through to the pub, a few times a week. He did it through Sukie's brother Duncan. Duncan'd lay the bets when he went into town, collect whatever winnings came in, take his own cut and pass the rest back to Bob. I sorted our cut—'

'Two cuts taken before the winnings got back to those who'd put the money up front?'

Sanders frowned, flicking back the wild curl that had fallen over his forehead, 'Fair do's, Sir, we were the ones taking the risk. I'd divvy up the rest, depending on who'd won what. Tidy.'

Bix shook his head, a tidy mess, and now he knew all about it he had to decide how far up the line of command to share the story of the soldiers' transgressions, 'Tidy

233

for you, if not for those financing your little operation.'

'Ah, they were in it for the fun as much as the money.'

'That's enough excuses, Private, let's get you back to the others.'

Private Sanders stood up and followed Bix into the yard, his hands in his pockets, a deep frown cutting across his forehead, 'I do love Sukie, you know, she's a bloody good woman, nothing like the rest of them.'

'The rest of them?'

'Her old man, her brother. There wasn't anyone else who could lay the bets for us, so it had to be them. I'd thought about doing some work with the pair of them, after the war, but once Sukie told me about Snow, I couldn't even look at him without wanting to knock him out. And then I got to know Duncan better and well, let's just say that if I'd any choice in the matter, I'd have nothing to do with him.'

'How come?'

'He's always on about how the war's got nothing to do with us way down here in New Zealand, you know? Reckons we're all daft buggers for joining up, bangs on about how our dads charged off to the first war and what good did it do any of us. Sounds like a Commie half the time.'

'A Commie?' Bix asked, alert.

'Now look, I'm not saying he is one, Sarge, it's just the way they talk, you know, all that blather about how you can't trust the government, can't believe a thing you hear on the news. He's all mouth is Duncan, but most of all he thinks he's the golden boy for staying well out of it.'

'He said that to you, directly to your face?'

'No, Sir, not to me, I reckon even an oaf like Duncan

234

Blaikie would know I'd smack him one if he said that to me. He said it to Bob Pawcett. Sometimes I think he almost persuaded Bob he was right, you know? That the war wasn't worth it after all.'

'He sounds like a right piece of work.'

Sanders shrugged, 'Between her brother and her old man, Sukie's had a rough time of it. I know I've mucked up, but honest, I just couldn't see myself clearing out of here back off to Gawd knows where and not making a bit of an effort to look after her.'

They were at the door of the Transport Office and Sanders turned to his superior, 'Can I ask you something, Sarge?'

'Go ahead.'

'We can't think like that, can we? That it's all for nothing, we're just being used by the brass, the politicians and their mob, to get what they want. We can't believe they don't really care, can we, Sir?'

Bix shook his head, 'No we can't, Private. There's nothing ends a war faster than lack of morale. Too bloody right we can't think like that.'

CHAPTER TWENTY-EIGHT

Alleyn and Corporal Brayling had come to the end of the hospital yard when Brayling halted before a profusion of roses. The Inspector knew that during the day their sumptuous blooms belied their own vicious thorns and those of the barbed wire on which they grew. To their right was the staff entrance from the parking area, to their left, the last of the wards, Military 3, where the most damaged and dangerously ill of the soldiers lay, many of them no doubt awake in pain or fear.

Brayling turned to Alleyn, his finger to his lips as he slowly edged backwards through what Alleyn now saw to be a carefully disguised gap in the fence of roses. Following Brayling's guide, his head and shoulders bent low to avoid the line of brutal wire at head level, Alleyn passed through the barrier. They walked on and in less than a few hundred yards the meticulously tended hospital grounds were deftly swallowed in dense native bush. Alleyn noted again the peculiarly specific scent of the New Zealand bush, deep and loamy, a heady sense of rich damp earth even in midsummer. As the over-heated asphalt of the yard gave way to the ancient land, the air seemed brighter, the sky higher and the fantastic array of stars sharper still, tiny beams of starlight picking tracks through the bush as it closed in above them. The detective put out a hand to halt his guide and turned off his torch, Brayling followed suit. They stood together, looking up through the gathering canopy of leaves and fronds.

'You know, Brayling, the first time I saw your New Zealand night sky, I found it almost disturbing, the constellations turned about, the Milky Way rich and full, stretching over us, as if it were the roof beam, holding us up.'

'I could tell you about roof beams, Sir, the ones in our meeting houses hold us up, hold up the story of our people.'

'I've heard that and on any other day, Brayling, I should like to hear more, but not tonight, I'm afraid. I ought not to have stopped you.'

'We're almost there, Sir.'

Alleyn followed Brayling, pace for pace. Within another hundred yards the ground beneath them began to change. As Brayling quietly spoke a warning, Alleyn noticed the earth first become harder and then sharper, there was rock rather than soil beneath his shoes. Next came a slope downwards, gentle at first and then a steep incline that caused Alleyn to reach out to steady himself, grasping at the scrubby mānuka bushes lining the path into the cave itself. In the semi-darkness, their way marked only by the torchlights ahead of them, Alleyn entertained a brief idea of the descent into Hades, the Māori soldier his guide. Even as he brushed away the fleeting image, he felt a shiver, noting that the air around them was noticeably cooler. His own breath as well as his guide's sounded closer, as if the foothills had closed in. He felt his heart quicken and shook away his symptoms in frustration. He had been waiting for this moment all night, if his suspicions were right, a breakthrough was just ahead, now was not the time to allow flights of fancy, no matter how carefully Brayling was treading or how much quieter his lowered voice.

'This is where the cave opens out, the *tomo* is further in, beyond a ledge. We'll have to go round a few pools of water, they'll be deeper since the storm. The ledge itself is like a false wall, so watch out when you get inside, be careful if you climb on it.'

Brayling then took a careful step back, leaving the path ahead clear for Alleyn.

'You're not coming with me?'

The soldier frowned and his voice was gruff, 'Not if I don't have to, Sir. The thing is, you see, my people—well, I don't reckon they'd thank me for bringing you here.'

'Not even for a situation such as this and after the events of tonight? You owe me, you know, Brayling.'

'I do, Sir, and I think I could make them understand that part of it, but I'd have to tell how I've been meeting Ngaire here and then I'd be in even more trouble, breaking hospital rules, bringing her into it, as well as showing you round. I reckon they'd go crook at me, all right.'

'Whereas, if you don't escort me in, show me the cave, you don't have to admit that you brought me here?'

'Nah, that'd be like lying. I'll tell them the truth, but if I can say I wasn't the one to show it all to you, if I can say you saw it for yourself, well, they might go a bit easier on me, if you see what I mean.'

'I think I do. You're in enough trouble with the army already, you don't need to be in trouble at home as well?'

'Something like that. You go ahead and I'll follow up.'

The young soldier waited as the detective from Scotland

Yard took his first steps into the wide underground space, all the while hoping his trust wasn't about to get him a nasty smack on the back of the head.

What actually hit Alleyn was the shock of the place in which he now found himself. This wasn't his first visit to this astonishing country and Alleyn knew he hadn't seen anywhere near all of the bewildering glories that New Zealand's elemental landscape was rightly famed for, but the cave was something else entirely. He slowly shone the torch around, moving from right to left, up and down, all the while grasping for adjectives that were less idiotic than 'stupendous' or 'astounding' or 'grand'. He failed precisely because everything he saw was far more than stupendous, astounding and grand. The height of the rock as it soared above and its vaulted shape gave the cave the feel of a cathedral, deep in the earth. He stood on the edge of a rock floor that formed a roughly circular bowl, wide and low, and the floor sloped gently into an area where his torch now illuminated a series of shallow pools. As Brayling had suggested, the pools were no doubt fed by the evening's storm, separated from one another by narrow channels of rock, some of the channels still wet from the flooding earlier that night. His torchlight on the walls showed narrow runnels of water, some beginning to dry, others trickling into the pools. Where the beam hit the water, reflections bounced back and off, refracting light around the cave. In places the walls were as smooth as glass, perhaps from the years of flood water that had helped to form this phenomenon, others were jagged, with dark grey rock newly exposed, an uneven tumble of stones and scree on the ground beneath as evidence that no matter how perfectly manufactured the cavern looked, it had been carved, not by the hand of man, but by the earth on which he now stood, an earth which had never felt more living.

Beyond and above the pools Alleyn noted the ledge that Brayling had mentioned. From this distance it looked as if the ledge might be a foot wide, but no more. Looking at it from below, Alleyn felt as if he were sitting in the stalls of a particularly modern play, the set intended to suggest form rather than resemble it. To his left, stage right, the ledge was low, sloping gently upwards. It started perhaps two feet above the ground and by the time it came to stage left at the other side of the cave it had risen a good ten feet above the earth. Alleyn shone the torch on the walls above and behind the ledge. At the lower end the cave wall was solid, but as the ledge climbed, fifteen or twenty paces along, the wall behind appeared to shift backwards, as if wall and ledge separated. This was indeed what Brayling had explained, the horizontal and the vertical rock forced apart by some unseen force, leaving the fathomless chasm or *tomo* in the gap between the two. Alleyn felt it to be distinctly vertiginous, easily as unnerving as it was impressive.

Brayling must have felt Alleyn's sense of awe, for he whispered from his position at the cavern entrance, 'Sir, if you want to see something really special, you ought to turn off the torch. Wait until your eyes get used to the dark and then look up.'

'You know, don't you, soldier, that in a particular type of widely-read detective fiction, the instant I turn out the torch is the exact moment that our villain will cuff me over the head, tumble my senseless corpse into the murky pool below and make off with whatever spoils are hidden in this treasure trove?'

'No idea about that, Sir, I don't read detective books.'

'Very wise,' Alleyn answered brightly. 'In that case, I am prepared to take my chances.'

Brayling clicked off his torch and Alleyn followed suit, the retort of the soft buttons sounded surprisingly sharp in the silence. He waited a few moments as advised and then lifted his eyes to the rock walls and ceiling above. Slowly, as his eyes became accustomed to the dark, Alleyn began to make out pinpricks of light, first one, then two, then a dozen or more, followed by hundreds, perhaps thousands of small, twinkling lights. It was an underground Milky Way, the constellations all the more breathtaking for their location deep in the belly of the earth, and very alive.

'What are they? Glow-worms?'

Alleyn heard his own voice, a whisper, full of both awe and care for the delicacy of the creatures, the startling clarity of their myriad lights through the darkness.

'That's it, *pūrātoke*.' Brayling answered, coming closer.

'Is this what your people don't want others to see?'

'Have you ever been up north, Sir?'

'Yes, before the war,' Alleyn had chosen to trust Brayling to get him to the cave, but he was still aware of the need for care in his speech, this was no time to be broadcasting his movements about New Zealand to all and sundry.

'I don't know if you had much time for looking around, but you must've seen what happens when businessmen get their hands on things.'

'I have certainly seen the confusion it can cause and not just in New Zealand. There are those in my own dear mother's village who would happily build a wider road here, allow more commerce there.'

241

'Too many of our own fullas like that as well,' Brayling said darkly.

'And while it is perfectly understandable that a living needs to be made, one does sometimes wonder.'

'At the expense of what, eh, Sir?'

'Exactly, Brayling, at what expense indeed.'

Alleyn was aware of his status as a symbol of both the crown and the authority that brought the white man's understanding of property to these islands, land as a commodity rather than the living entity as explained by his friend Dr Te Pokiha. Roderick Alleyn and his brother had had it bred into them that man is but the custodian of the land, keeping it whole and good for future generations, a belief sorely tried when the brothers saw action in the Great War and tried again now. He frowned and shook his head, he was lapsing into the melodramatic, something the grandeur of New Zealand's scenery did to him on occasion. He took one more look. He would relate the scene to Troy in his next letter, she would want him to describe exactly the tones of black in the rich darkness spanning above them, the tiny twinkling lights in the cave walls and their echo in the water, encompassing in their glowing spectrum both the brilliant white of the brightest stars and the soft gold of a pale winter sun. He would no doubt fail in the attempt, but he would try anyway.

The two men stood peacefully side by side for a second more, and then Alleyn took an uncertain breath, he hated the idea of hunches but in that instant he felt something was not right, something uncanny. Brayling too, tensed beside him.

The Māori man edged ever so slightly closer and Alleyn heard the faintest whisper, 'There's someone here.'

Alleyn nodded and hoped that the pale light from the glow-worms was enough for Brayling to see the discreet movement of his head. Both men looked slowly to their left, to the darkest recess of the cave where the ledge was at its lowest. It was a spot Alleyn had noted when he tried to imprint the vision on his mind's eye for Troy. It seemed to have fewer of the little lights, presumably this was the point where the cave joined the tunnel leading beneath the hospital and on to the Bridge Hotel.

'Ready?' he whispered to Brayling.

'Āe,' the soldier replied in his own language and Alleyn felt rather than saw his companion prepare himself for action, his body tense, his legs ready to run or to leap.

Alleyn aimed the torch and clicked the switch, the cave was immediately illuminated in a fierce beam that decimated the primordial splendour of the preceding minutes, revealing brutally sharp rock and horribly deep crevices. Directly across from them, less than fifty paces distant, they saw a flash of cold white, which disappeared as someone leapt away and was gone, apparently swallowed into the earth itself.

'Hi there!' shouted Alleyn, and with the sudden acuity of a hound on the scent of a trail the two men scrambled their way across the rocks and shallow pools, doing remarkably well to avoid turning an ankle on the wet, uneven ground and found themselves beneath the section of the ledge where they had seen someone. It was of no surprise to either man that the apparition was gone and Alleyn nodded grimly when he shone the light on the empty rock ledge. Whoever it was must have inched forward from a crevice at the back of the ledge, hoping to get away before Alleyn turned on the torch. When they heard a shower of scree from the far left, Alleyn cursed in English and Brayling in Māori, and both men stumbled forward, stones and small rocks shifting underfoot, knocking them off balance and into each other. At the smack of Brayling's head against Alleyn's shoulder, the detective groaned and managed to hold onto the torch by sheer good luck, while Brayling and his own torch went down with a splash and an oath. Seconds later whoever they had seen was gone, deep into the earth.

'Hellfire, what is it with this country of yours?' Alleyn demanded as he clambered over the rocks to the now-empty spot in the centre of the ledge, 'It's as if the land itself is a trickster, determined to best us.'

Brayling followed, apologizing for stumbling and for letting his torch fall in the water, rendering it useless.

'No need for apologies, neither of us have covered ourselves in glory. Someone was here and we let them go.'

'It was someone real, wasn't it, Sir? A person?' Brayling asked anxiously, 'I mean, that wasn't a ghost, was it?'

'It most certainly was not,' Alleyn answered, shining the torch along the lower end of the ledge, looking in vain for footprints in the rock which had so recently been washed clean of dust by the deluge. 'Whoever stood here was not only alive, they were caught out and horrified to be so.'

'But not caught by us.'

'Unfortunately not,' Alleyn groaned bitterly, hoisting himself up on the ledge and turning to offer a hand to Brayling, 'Come along, Corporal, we'll take turns to check inside these crevices, no point blindly racing after someone in the dark when they know where they're going and we are as likely to trip and knock ourselves out as we are to find them. Let's take this with care and see what else there

is to find. It's a rare individual who does not leave something of themselves behind in a hasty escape.'

They explored a few moments longer, Alleyn ignoring
his own sense of unease to come quite close to the end of
the ledge where it became a bridge of rock, the cave on
one side and the apparently bottomless chasm on the other.
He felt his stomach lurch as he shone the torch down into
the dark space beneath and saw that the light went on,
touching nothing, shining on nothing. Cautiously he made
his way back to the lower end, grateful to have a good
reason to come away from the edge of the earth.

Alleyn's tone was greatly improved when his torchlight
caught on something that was neither rock nor stone just
inside another gap, 'Chin up, Brayling, we appear to have
found something after all. See there? Now, if I'm not much
mistaken that rather looks like a canvas body bag.'

Alleyn picked up the bag, shook it out, and half a dozen
or more pound notes fluttered to the cave floor as did a
tinkling metallic object. Alleyn smiled to himself as he bent
down and picked up a small key and placed it in his pocket,
'There you are.' He took a few steps forward into the dark
and shone the torch ahead along the uneven path that
presumably led to the tunnel. 'Brayling,' he called back,
'tell me about this end of the cave, will you?'

'To tell the truth, I don't know much, Sir, I know there
was a rock fall ages back, people said it shut off this end.
That's not right, you can get past, but it's tricky. Besides,
we were always scared the *tomo* had other openings as
well, not just the one off the end of the ledge.'

'And that kept you out, even as youngsters? If that's the
case then you're better behaved than our youths back
home.'

'Aw, it's not just that, Sir, the old people reckon it's *tapu* in the back of here. Sacred.'

Alleyn edged forward, the torchlight guiding his path, and spoke over his shoulder, 'Sacred because?'

'Our people, way back, they used caves as burial grounds sometimes, Sir. I've never seen any bodies in here, but, well—'

There was a pause as the soldier faltered and then Brayling heard Alleyn's voice, from a still further distance, 'I fully understand, Private. In which case I shan't ask you to accompany me any further. Do me a favour, will you? Head back to the Transport Office and tell Bix to make for the morgue right away. Will you be able to find your way without a light?'

'I'm fine, Sir.'

'Good man. Off you go.'

Alleyn waited a moment or two to be sure that Brayling was indeed hurrying away, then he knelt down and shone his torch full into the grey and very dead face of an old man.

'Mr Brown Senior, I presume.'

With an apology and a shake of his head at the indelicacy of his business, Alleyn stepped over the carefully laid-out body and proceeded as quickly as he could along the path ahead. He didn't want to keep Bix waiting in the morgue.

CHAPTER TWENTY-NINE

When Alleyn finished explaining his proposal to Sergeant Bix there was a worrying silence in the cold morgue and the detective wondered if he had been quite clear enough. Bix peered up at him, his forehead wrinkled into a forceful frown, as if trying to decipher a particularly obtuse crossword puzzle clue. Alleyn was about to elucidate further when it finally dawned on Bix that the policeman was deadly serious. The sergeant burst out laughing, his head shaking, his chest heaving with the effort.

'Are you quite well, Bix?' Alleyn asked.

'Sorry, Sir, really I am,' Bix replied, wiping his eyes with the back of his strong hand, 'I reckon I'm too flaming tired to take it in properly, only what you've just told me doesn't sound very—' he shook his head, searching for the right phrase, 'well, it just doesn't sound very Scotland Yard, if you ask me.'

'I don't think it is "very Scotland Yard" as you say, Bix,' Alleyn agreed. 'However, time is of the essence and I can think of no other way of flushing out our culprit. It may be desperation on my part and I admit we're all close to exhausted, but I simply cannot think of anything else that might, just might, do the trick.'

'Fair enough, Sir.'

'So are you with me, Sergeant?'

'Too right I am, I wouldn't miss this for the world.'

'Given I am incapable of carrying out my plans without you, I'm delighted to hear you say so.'

In the Transport Office it appeared, at first, as if little had changed in the past half hour. Sydney Brown still stared out of the window and now Sister Comfort stood alongside, her gaze turned determinedly inward. Sarah Warne was in place at her desk, a pile of completed rosters neatly in front of her. Rosamund was curled up but not sleeping on the divan, a watchful cat. Mr Glossop and Father O'Sullivan appeared to be vying for the best impression of patience on a monument on their hard wooden chairs, and Brayling, Sanders and Pawcett scrabbled to attention from their places on the floor when the detective opened the door.

Alleyn looked around the room, quickly noting the small changes that told their own story. Sarah Warne had clearly run out of paperwork, indeed of any work that might distract her from the close presence of Dr Hughes and Alleyn saw that her small frame was angled ever so slightly towards him and he to her. The thaw has begun, he thought to himself. Both Mr Glossop and Father O'Sullivan, still though they were, looked even more agitated than before, if such a thing were possible. Glossop was red-faced and sweating, while in contrast the vicar beside him appeared an alarming shade of grey, his round face drawn, his hands tight on his thighs. Sydney Brown's shoulders were stubborn as he looked briefly to Alleyn and then immediately back to the window, seemingly searching for something in his own reflection. The three soldiers stood to attention, their faces to Alleyn, but their eyes to Bix behind him.

'At ease, Cerberus,' Alleyn said.

The men stood at ease, although Alleyn saw that no one but Rosamund picked up on his joke. He and the young woman exchanged a brief nod and then, with a few interjections from Bix, some helpful and others less so, Alleyn explained the plan.

The faces that looked to the detective and the sergeant were no less aghast than Bix's had been a few minutes earlier.

'You can't seriously expect us to go along with this Inspector, it's outrageous. Unheard of, after the distressing events of the evening. I refuse to be party to such an absurd undertaking.'

Father O'Sullivan's expostulation was backed up by an even angrier Mr Glossop, 'Flippin' lunatic carry on, we all know there's a murderer and a thief on the loose and now you want us to play at dressing up!'

Mr Glossop's reaction may have been predictable, but he wasn't alone. Dr Hughes was equally perturbed, 'I must say, Inspector, it does sound a bit grisly. Are you sure there's no other way to get your evidence?'

'Get his evidence?' Glossop asked. 'He's been interrogating us all night, he's kept us locked up in here against our will—and against my better judgement I might add—and now it turns out that the great white hope of Scotland Yard appears to have no more idea of what's what than he did when this whole damn fuss started.'

249

'We know what you think, Mr Glossop,' Sister Comfort interrupted, 'you have made your views quite clear at every possible opportunity. But given none of us has any proof, nor any better suggestions, I say we go along with the Inspector in the hope that we might finally bring this ghastly night to a satisfactory conclusion, to any conclusion.'

Sarah and Luke nodded in agreement and the three soldiers shrugged a rather less certain acquiescence.

Rosamund Farquharson sat up on the divan, her feet firmly on the ground and her voice softer than Alleyn had heard until now, 'I agree with the Sister,' she smiled at Sister Comfort who looked most put out that her bête noir was taking her part. 'Even if this game of the Inspector's doesn't turn up my winnings, and I very much hope it will, I'd be hugely grateful for the chance to get out of this office. I'm sure it's doing us no good at all being squeezed in together, not to mention the air has become increasingly stuffy in the past hour or so.'

She finished speaking with a glare to Glossop, almost daring the fat man to contradict her. Despite the sharpness of her look, Alleyn couldn't help noticing that she seemed quite drawn. It was as if the effort of maintaining her devil-may-care façade throughout the night had drained her and now the real Rosamund was showing through, a much less self-assured girl and, he thought, far more attractive for it.

'What do you think, Sydney?' Alleyn asked the young man who still faced the window.

Sydney Brown turned slowly and the look he shared around the room was startlingly scornful, 'Yeah, now you're asking me. No one flippin' cares what I think. As far as you lot are concerned I'm just the kid to be told what to do, where to go, when to sit, stand, leave. No one gives a damn what I reckon.'

'I do,' Alleyn spoke calmly, 'and I'm asking you now, what do you think of my plan?'

Sydney Brown shrugged, his mouth a harsh sneer, 'Why not? I'll join in your game of cops and robbers. I guess everyone here thinks it matters more to find the blasted money than it does to find the old man's body.' Looking around the office he included the rest of them in his ire, 'I bet every damn one of you know-it-all jokers thinks you're so smart that you probably know exactly where the money is and where the old bugger's body is and where your stupid flamin' Matron is too. I reckon you think you know how to stop the damn war too, given half a chance, I reckon—'

Alleyn stepped forward and laid a calming hand on the young man's shoulder, 'We take your point, Sydney, and I sincerely apologize for any inconsideration on my part. I appreciate that this has been an especially long night for you personally, but if any memories are to be jogged by re-enacting the moments leading up to Mr Glossop's discovery of the theft, then we must all play our part.'

Sydney shrugged away the detective's hand and was about to respond when Alleyn pointed to the clock above Sarah's desk, 'Perhaps it feels as if dawn is still some time away. Given what has taken place since the sun set last night, I can imagine you feel that the night might go on forever, but I assure you, Sydney, the harsh light of morning is coming. I would very much like us to act while we have the last of the night on our side.'

The young man and the detective both looked to the

old ward clock. It was a quarter to four and Alleyn noticed that Sydney took in the time with what looked like alarm.

'Yeah, all right,' Sydney Brown conceded, throwing his much-held pillow into the corner of the room, his face still dark, his eyes lowered, 'but I'm still browned off with the whole flamin' thing and I'm only in because I want to get it over with sooner rather than later.'

'I'm sure we all would, lad,' Mr Glossop said, heaving himself to his feet, 'I'm sure we all would.'

CHAPTER THIRTY

'Now this is more like it,' Rosamund said, a broad smile illuminating her tired face.

Sarah shook her head, 'I honestly don't understand you, Rosie. Any number of awful things have happened tonight, you've been curled up on that divan for the past hour, scowling at anyone who even dared offer you a biscuit or a cup of tea, and now you're all smiles once more, as if none of it had happened. What's got into you?'

They were waiting just outside the Transport Office, ready to take up their places when Sergeant Bix gave the signal.

'Maybe I just got sick of feeling sorry for myself.'

'Oh, I think it's a bit more than that, I'm pretty sure you have a plan, don't you?'

Rosamund grinned and acceded with a nod of her head, 'You know me too well. Truth is, I've had a bit of time to think while we've all been cooped up inside, that's why I wasn't interested in tea and biscuits—well, that and my figure—and I've come up with a little plan of my own. Problem was, I'd no idea how I was going to have a chat with Maurice in private until the charming Inspector said

253

we had to take up our positions exactly the same as when Mr Glossop first started yelling his head off about the theft.'

'Why do you need a word with Sanders?'

'I'm going to tell him he can go off with Sukie Johnson or anyone else he likes for that matter, the whole flaming Marching Team if he wants, with my blessing,' Rosamund replied with a beneficent wave of her hand.

'Does he need your blessing?' Sarah asked, dubiously.

'No, but I need to give it. If Maurice feels like *I'm* letting *him* go, then I won't feel quite as much like the poor sap who's been thrown over.'

'So it's just about saving face?'

'Just? People put an awful lot of store on their pride, Sarah, you should know that,' Rosamund said, her tone suddenly serious.

Sarah felt herself blushing and hoped her friend couldn't see her flaming cheeks in the yard lit only by the dimmed lights from the wards across the way.

Luckily Rosamund had already gone on to the next thought that was cheering her up, 'On top of that, I've great faith in our Chief Detective Inspector Alleyn, even if he is a bit stand-offish. I'm pretty sure my winnings are going to turn up before we go much further.' Rosamund nudged Sarah in the ribs, 'Besides, I've an idea that young Sydney Brown might be a bit of fun for a while, if I could get him a decent haircut and teach him to stand up straight and stop glowering. I reckon he could do with someone to take his mind off the dreadful burden of inheriting his grandfather's farm.'

Sarah was shocked, 'Rosamund, you're incorrigible, his grandfather's only just died!'

'Yes,' Rosamund answered quietly, 'and I've heard a few home truths tonight. Life's terribly short, isn't it? I'm determined to make the most of my lot, whether that's taking my chances with a young man or blowing my winnings on a night on the town, I reckon now's the time to do it. We're not going to be young and lovely for long, Sarah.' Bix was indicating for them to get into place and as they parted Rosamund held Sarah's hand, whispering fiercely to her, 'And now you've got a few minutes on your own with Luke, for goodness' sake, girl, use it.'

While Rosamund was outlining her plans to Sarah, Mr Glossop, with much sighing, sweating and complaint stationed himself just inside the door of Matron's office.

He said to Bix who walked him to his position, 'I'll go along with this farce, if only to have the opportunity to point out, yet again, that your Pommie Inspector has no idea what he's playing at, none whatsoever.'

'Fair enough, Mr Glossop, if that's how you feel,' Bix answered, 'but he's probably your only hope of getting to the truth of what's gone on tonight, uncovering a murderer, finding two missing bodies and digging up your stolen payroll. So if I was you, I'd be hoping the Pommie Inspector is all he's made out to be and more. I don't fancy the conversation you'll be having with your bosses otherwise.'

'My bosses? My bosses!' Glossop expostulated. 'Stone the crows, Sergeant, they're the reason it all started going wrong. I've been telling them for weeks about the tyres and Gawd knows how many times I've warned them about the bridge. You want to look at the forms I've filled out.'

'You're right, Mr Glossop, I've enough paperwork of my own to be getting on with, thanks,' Sergeant Bix said cheerily as he went to sort out the soldiers, leaving Glossop to grumble to himself.

'Righto, let's get this straight so we can work out who was on the porch first, who second and which of you brought up the rear. Now then, Sanders, you reckon that you and Miss Farquharson were having a bit of a convo, were you?'

'Yes, Sir, we were in the Records Office.'

'All right, you take your place over with her when I give the sign. How about you, Corporal Brayling?'

'I was back in the ward, Sir. I heard the kerfuffle and came out to the porch, that's where I met Sanders with the other lads.'

Bix looked to Sanders, 'You didn't stay with Miss Farquharson? Even though it was the middle of the night and someone was yelling "thief" at the top of his lungs?'

Sanders had the grace to look a little shame-faced when he said, 'Come off it, Sarge, it wasn't that rotten of me. I knew it wouldn't look good for Rosie, if her and me were found together, I mean. As you say, it was dark and Matron had already hauled her over the coals for being late. I left her by the office and hopped back in, I was hoping to get into the ward—'

'How did you plan to do that?' Bix interrupted.

'Ah, that was me, Sergeant,' Brayling answered, 'I'd left the window unlatched for Maurice, so he could get in after he'd said goodnight to Rosie.'

Sergeant Bix shook his head, 'You really are a shower, you lot. Go on, Sanders.'

'Well, I hopped in the window, put it back on the latch, and joined the other lads who were heading out for a good gawp from the porch. And you know Rosie can look after herself, Sarge, she's a good girl.'

'Very chivalrous, I don't think,' Bix responded dryly. 'How about you, Pawcett?'

'I was just in the ward too, Sir. We'd all come in late and we've already held our hands up to having a few down at the Bridge pub. I'd been sleeping it off and woke with a jump at the yelling, so I came out with the other boys on the porch.'

'I suppose all of you lads can back up each other's stories?'

''Course we can, Sarge,' Pawcett said, putting his arms around his fellows. 'You know us, one for all and all for one, right lads?'

He looked to the two soldiers on either side of him and one by one they nodded, but Bix was still waiting, 'I want to hear it from each of you men. On your honour.'

Pawcett stood at attention and he saluted as he replied, 'We were all there, on the porch, Sergeant Bix, Sir!'

Bix turned to Brayling, 'Brayling?'

'I saw Maurice, I know that much. I was right up front, so I saw him nip across to join us. It was as he said, he left Rosie in the office, came in through the side window and then bunched up in the porch with the rest of us.'

'You didn't see Pawcett?'

Brayling looked uncomfortable, 'I wasn't looking behind me, Sarge, all the action was out in the yard.'

'Fair enough,' Bix allowed. 'How about you, Sanders?'

'Same for me, sorry, Sarge. If Bob says he was with us, then he must have been, right Bob?'

Maurice Sanders turned to face his comrade and the two men looked at each other, eye to eye.

Bob Pawcett nodded to his mate and turned to Sergeant Bix, 'On the porch? Too bloody right I was. Stuck at the back though, tried to push through and get a better look, but it was a real scrum, I'd no chance of getting up front. First bit of excitement around here for weeks and I had to give it up as a bad lot. Typical of my luck.'

Meanwhile, Alleyn escorted Sydney Brown back to the room where his grandfather had died, with Father O'Sullivan following along behind to play his part. The detective opened the door to the private room and ushered Sydney in ahead of him, with Father O'Sullivan standing watchfully at the door.

'I'm sorry to do this to you, Sydney, it's been a difficult night,' said Alleyn.

'I've had worse,' Sydney said, gruffly.

'I imagine so. Nonetheless, I'm sure this must have been very hard, being so forcefully reminded of your own losses.'

'What are you on about?' Sydney rounded on the detective, 'What losses?'

Alleyn put out a steadying hand, 'I merely meant your health and your family situation. When you explained earlier you told me you were invalided out of service and about falling out with your father. Your grandfather was the closest family you had.'

'Yeah, and I also told you that the old man didn't mean a blind thing to me. Now can we get on with it? Like I said, Matron took me off for a brew. She left me in the kitchen, they gave me the tea and brought me back to this room after

258

they'd done all their business—except obviously they didn't do it properly because they flamin' well lost the old man—and I just stopped here. They gave me a nip of Matron's whiskey in me tea too and that did me right. I'm used to kipping on the floor and I was out soundo in no time.'

Alleyn looked down at the wooden floor, 'Here?'

Sydney flung himself down on the tired floorboards, bunching up the pillow he had retrieved before they left the office and putting it behind his head. He glowered up at Alleyn, 'Like this. All right?'

Alleyn watched Sydney collapse to the ground and was surprised to feel sorry for the young man. It was on the tip of his tongue to remind him of the serviceman he had once been, but as he was about to speak he thought he heard something outside, the beginning of a bird call. These were not the birds of England, he knew he could not be sure, it might have been a nurse hurriedly turning a corner with a trolley for a sick patient, it might have been a wild creature wailing in the dark. Or it might have been the call announcing dawn. This was no time to worry about the psychological problems of young Sydney.

He turned instead to Father O'Sullivan who was wearing an oddly placatory smile, quite out of place in the circumstances, 'No need to look alarmed, Inspector,' the vicar said, 'there are loads of possums round here, pretty wild bush just a few hundred yards up the track.'

'I'm sure you're right,' Alleyn allowed, 'They do sound quite unnatural. And what were you doing at this point, Vicar?'

Father O'Sullivan looked to Sydney Brown, hunched on the floor, 'I was praying for Mr Brown's soul, of course, there is a litany, you see—'

'Of course,' Alleyn nodded, trying to hurry the vicar along, 'And then?'

'Sister Comfort was rather more brusque than necessary with the bereaved, as is her wont. I offered to go and alert Matron to this news.'

'And where did you find her?'

'In her office. We collected the paperwork and with the storm almost upon us, I escorted Matron into the porch here in Civilian 3.'

'I assume there is a protocol for an expected death, is that what you were discussing?'

'There is,' the vicar answered, looking out of the corner of his eye and lowering his voice. He edged away, drawing Alleyn with him until he was sure Sydney would not hear what he was about to say. 'The truth is, Inspector, Matron and I were not speaking of the demise of Mr Brown, nor of his grandson's grief—or apparent lack of it. We were not talking at all.'

'No?'

Looking full into Alleyn's face, Father O'Sullivan whispered quietly but plainly, 'Matron and I were in love, Inspector. That woman was the love of my life, we were discussing a future we had long dreamed of together. You may well think me, or indeed both of us, callous in the extreme for thinking of ourselves when this young man had just suffered such a loss, but it has been my experience that death often prompts a longing for life, in its most passionate form.'

Alleyn took a good long look at the vicar, 'I see. So when we spoke earlier and you told me you had left the room to fetch Matron, that wasn't the whole truth?'

'Forgive me, but you must understand how difficult this

night has been for me, I have not wanted to tell all about our love, in order to protect my dear departed Isabelle, may she rest—' Father O'Sullivan faltered suddenly and brought his hands to his face.

After a brief moment, Alleyn tried again, 'I'm very sorry to have to ask this, but where were you at this point, when you were, ah—together?'

'We were just to the side of the porch entrance to Military 1, in the shadow thrown by the porch of Civilian 3. Even with the meager light from the offices across the way we had a need to be careful. I shared a quiet moment with my beloved.'

'Very difficult for you, of course. Another question, if I may?'

The vicar sighed resignedly and nodded his assent.

'I don't understand why you and Matron chose to hide your—' Alleyn shook his head, 'I don't mean to be disrespectful, "friendship", shall we say?'

Father O'Sullivan smiled ruefully, 'Pragmatism, I'm afraid. Before the war Isabelle had a set of rooms here at the hospital. It was standard practice for the Matron to live on site, you see.'

'And since?'

'Her rooms were requisitioned for the army and she had to move into town to the nurses' home, taking the transport out to the hospital with all the others. I have my own small set-up adjacent to my church. Previously we were able to spend time together in her rooms, where we could talk and plan to our hearts' content, but since the war we have been reduced to stolen kisses in dark corners.' He shook his head and then noticed the quizzical look on Alleyn's face, 'I'm sorry, Inspector, I don't mean to compare my own

261

problems to those of the young men in active service, or those back in England suffering so terribly, but the way it has affected even everyday life, well, we are all very tired.'

'Yes, of course,' Alleyn urged him on, 'And what happened, after this stolen moment between the two of you?'

'We parted, Matron to her duties and I to see if I could be of any comfort to young Mr Brown.'

'Were you?'

'It transpired that he had no need of me at all, for he was indeed asleep, just as he said. Quite sound asleep on the floor.' He smiled as he indicated Sydney and his voice resumed its usual clarity, 'The young are startlingly robust, don't you find?'

From his place on the floor Sydney glared up at Father O'Sullivan, 'I'm robust all right, Vicar. Don't you worry about me.'

Once he had dealt with Father O'Sullivan, Alleyn had a quick word with the now wide awake Will Kelly, asking him simply to repeat his actions in going to Matron's door, knocking, and heading away again. The Irishman was keen to help, informing Alleyn that he had been a regular leading man in his village plays as a youth, 'I'll play the part as to the manner born, Sir.'

'I have no doubt about that,' Alleyn replied.

He then assigned roles to Sister Comfort and Sergeant Bix. The Sister was to speak with each of the nurses in charge of the wards, warning them that whatever they heard in the next half hour, on no account were they to allow any of their charges out onto the verandahs or the

262

porches. Further, they were to keep the patients in their beds until Alleyn himself gave notice. Sister Comfort was then to take up her vantage point, ready to come running when Mr Glossop called 'Thief!', paying particular attention to any actions that did not directly mirror what had taken place just six hours earlier. As Bix had been hard at work in his own office at the time, he would not take part in the re-enactment, but would stand sentry at the other end of the yard, between the morgue and the army offices. Both players nodded their acquiescence and Alleyn crossed the yard to call the cast to their places. The scene was set, the actors prepared. Alleyn, as director, found himself sincerely hoping that the denouement was not about to be quite as shocking for the actors as he feared it might. While they might be expecting, hoping even, to unmask a thief or a murderer, no one had yet scented the original reason for his presence at Mount Seager. He sincerely hoped it would stay that way.

CHAPTER THIRTY-ONE

At Alleyn's signal, Mr Glossop came to the door of the Surgery anteroom and looked out. Making the most of his moment in the spotlight, he ostentatiously wiped his face with his ever-present handkerchief, looking along the yard towards Matron's office. From his vantage point the yard was empty. From where Inspector Alleyn stood between the porches of Civilian 3 and Military 1, it was possible to see Dr Hughes and Sarah Warne beginning a quiet conversation inside the open door of the Transport Office, their eyes locked, their faces intent. Maurice Sanders and Rosamund Farquharson commenced their own conversation in the Records Office, equally sotto voce but with rather more animation than their matching pair. Alleyn raised his hand and, taking his signal, Sister Comfort crossed from the porch of Civilian 3 to Matron's office, turned and ducked back into the porch of Military 1. At the next signal Will Kelly, rather more enthusiastically than necessary, walked jauntily towards Matron's office, rapped forcefully on the door, called 'Anyone at home?' to no one in particular, and then trotted off back towards Civilian 3, taking his place to the side of the porch, a few yards from where Alleyn was stationed.

The Inspector spoke over his shoulder to Father O'Sullivan, 'You next, Vicar, that's your cue.'

Father O'Sullivan looked across to Matron's office and back to the detective. Even in the semi-darkness, Alleyn could see the man's face was drained of colour, 'Are you quite all right?' he asked.

'Ah, yes, of course,' Father O'Sullivan stuttered, 'I do apologize, as I explained, Matron was—'

Alleyn interrupted him calmly, 'I am asking you to do something quite difficult here, I know, but we are hoping this little performance will give us some vital information as to what must have happened to Matron as well as the matter of the theft, it's therefore terrifically important that you play your part. So if you wouldn't mind? The others are waiting.'

Father O'Sullivan sighed and nodded and shook himself in the manner of a wet dog forced back into the rain for another long walk, 'Onwards. I was making my way to Matron's office to give her the news about Mr Brown.'

The vicar carefully stepped down to the yard and began a deliberate walk across the yard to Matron's office. Alleyn watched as each one of the scenes played out simultaneously.

Rosamund stood with her arms folded, her chin tilted defiantly, 'Go off with Sukie Johnson then, why don't you? I'm just fine, Maurice, I don't need you or any other fellow to worry about me.'

Sanders looked about, 'Keep your voice down, Rosie, we're joining in for the Inspector's benefit, no need to make a scene out of it.'

'All right,' Rosamund leaned in, 'but I mean it, honest I do. If she's what you want, you should go to her. Life's too short, isn't that what all you chaps think now you've been off?'

'Seen what we've seen, done what we've done? I should flamin' well think so. And I will, just as soon as I can get away from the hospital, I'm going to get her sorted out up north before I get sent away again. Her old man knocks her about something awful, Ros.'

'That makes you the knight in shining armour?' Rosamund looked dubious. 'You'll need to practise your chivalry a bit first, won't you?'

Maurice ducked his head, 'Fair enough, girlie, I've not treated you right, I know that, but I reckon I can be a better man with her.'

'In which case you must do it, Maurice, with my blessing. Not that you need it.'

'I don't, but I'm happy to take it.'

Rosamund held out her hand and Maurice Sanders shook it. He was tempted to pull her to him, for old time's sake, but when he saw the look in her eyes he was glad he had not. It was time he gave the girl her dignity.

An altogether quieter scene was taking place in the Transport Office. Sarah Warne was speaking earnestly to Luke Hughes whose head was down, his arms dejectedly by his sides. Alleyn couldn't help but watch as Sarah spoke quietly and urgently to the young doctor. It appeared that something she said must have got through, because the doctor lifted his head, nodded and took Sarah Warne in his arms. Alleyn looked away at that point, clearly a choice had been made and it was of no relevance to the matter in hand. He allowed himself a brief smile of satisfaction nonetheless. He could sense Sister Comfort to his right in the porch of Military 1, he wondered about her attitude to the young people, if she felt the same pleasure for Sarah and Luke. He doubted it somehow, Sister Comfort did not strike him as the kind of woman to be warmed by others' happiness.

Father O'Sullivan was at the door to Matron's office, Alleyn watched him knock once, twice, and then, as he let himself into the office, a narrow band of dull light spilled into the yard and was quickly gone, the door closed behind him.

There was a moment when time seemed to stand still. Alleyn took in the couples in their respective offices, Glossop on the steps of the Surgery anteroom waiting for Father O'Sullivan to emerge with the ghostly Matron alongside him, Sister Comfort on the porch of Military 1. He had told Brayling and Pawcett to wait on the other side of the porch door just inside Military 1, ready to join their mate Sanders when all hell broke loose, albeit silently as they had all solemnly promised.

Alleyn looked about him, something felt wrong, he could sense rather than see that Mr Glossop was growing impatient at his post along the yard, could the vicar have misunderstood the instruction? Father O'Sullivan said he had gone to Matron's office, alerted the Matron to Mr Brown's death, whereupon she had collected the paperwork and left with him to return to the private room in Civilian 1. Glossop's account of what he had seen told the same story. Another moment passed and as a morepork called in the dark, Alleyn heard Will Kelly whispering his name, a surprisingly quiet and concerned whisper at that.

'What is it, Kelly?' he asked.

'Sorry to be bothering you, Sir, I know it's not in my part—'

'What do you want?' Alleyn replied, more brusquely than he intended, his eyes still directed towards Matron's office.

'It wasn't like that, Sir.'

Now Alleyn turned to the porter, 'What wasn't like what?'

'The vicar, Sir, he was putting on just now that he was all slow and painstaking, but it wasn't like that earlier. Last night he headed over to the office like he was hell-bent on getting hold of the Matron. I'd have told him she wasn't there if he'd given me the chance, could've told him I'd already knocked and there'd been no reply, but he was across the yard quick as a fox. I know we're play-acting now, but you did ask us to show how it went. Well, it wasn't the way the vicar did it just now.'

Alleyn let out a low groan and leapt across to Matron's office. As soon as Bix saw him move the sergeant came hurtling from the other end of the yard, which meant that he was just behind Alleyn and close enough to hear the detective's vehement curse as he opened the door to Matron's empty office.

Shaking his head angrily at himself, Alleyn turned to Bix, 'I've been a damn fool, Sergeant. I was so keen to preserve the crime scene for your local force, I neglected to pay proper attention to the scene itself. A stupid mistake, one I'd tear a strip off a junior officer for making and I sincerely hope we don't all pay for it. Call those three soldiers of yours and tell them to rip out this office entirely. They're not to touch the safe, I'm sure there are fingerprints a good local man can yet discover, but I want everything

268

else lifted and shifted until they find the exit the vicar used. I imagine there must be a way into the tunnels beneath this office that we have missed. Double quick.'

Bix ran off to call his soldiers to work and Alleyn took a second to berate himself, 'Very clever indeed, Roderick. Now stop feeling so damn sorry for yourself and get on with the job.'

He turned at the sound of running feet and Bix was at the door with Brayling and Sanders. Bix looked sick, while the two soldiers looked fit to bust, Brayling in particular appeared to be holding in his anger with huge difficulty, his hands formed into tight and ready fists.

'What now, Bix?' Alleyn asked.

'Private Pawcett, Sir. Nowhere to be found. Cleared out.'

Brayling spoke up first, 'We were waiting just inside the ward, Sir, like you said. Then I saw you run across the yard so I came out on the porch and I could've sworn Bob was behind me, on my oath. Only I turned round and he was gone.'

'Bastard,' muttered Sanders, underlining Bix's clear inference that Pawcett was a villain, while Brayling uttered an oath in Māori which Alleyn found both convincing and, had he been in Private Pawcett's shoes, extremely disconcerting.

Choosing to placate the men in order to ensure their co-operation rather than stoke their fury while it had no outlet, Alleyn held back his own frustration to say simply, 'Suspects do seem to be revealing themselves at a rather alarming rate. Sergeant, let's leave these good men to get on with their work, you and I must head to the morgue post haste.'

'I thought you'd want that, Sir and I've ordered the

others back into the Transport Office in the meanwhile. No word about the vicar, of course, but it won't take long for them to work it out.'

Alleyn checked his watch as they left and grimaced. The scant information from his superiors had been clear on one point only, that the dawn after midsummer night was the most likely moment of contact. What that contact might entail, whether transfer of information to the Japanese submarine sighted, lost and sighted again within the past fortnight, or something even more disturbing, and by what means, they had no way of knowing. Pawcett certainly appeared to have put himself in the frame as to whom, Alleyn sincerely hoped they might find the rascal before they were confronted with what.

'Do you know, Bix,' he said as they neared the Transport Office, 'It feels as though I've spent the last week painstakingly searching for a needle in a haystack and just as the shining eye of the needle in question shimmered into view, the entire unstable edifice has been overturned by the altogether nightmarish events of this short night. I fear the whole scene is about to come to a crashing finale. Frankly, were Bottom to emerge from the bush with a cohort of fairies and Titania fast on his tail, I wouldn't be at all surprised.'

'You what, Sir?' Bix answered, unable to contain himself this time.

Alleyn shook his head and then held up a hand for silence as he heard the unmistakable sound of an engine turning over, failing to catch, spluttering to a stop and then cranking up again, more forcefully this time, before catching into a low rumble of life.

Inside the Transport Office Mr Glossop first howled, then leapt to his feet and, pushing Sister Comfort and Dr

Hughes out of his way, let out a strangled cry, 'My van, that's my flamin' van, how bloody well dare he?'

With an agility none of those assembled would ever have suspected, and even Rosamund Farquharson knew better than to comment upon, Glossop flew down the steps like a fat wood pigeon taking flight in alarm. He jumped over the bed of the shrubs between the offices and ran straight into the long drive of the hospital. The others raced after him, Alleyn issuing stern orders for Glossop to come back, orders which Glossop utterly disregarded.

'Stop, damn you, stop!' Glossop yelled in the direction of the van, the driver impossible to see with the headlights off and dawn not yet arrived.

Picking up speed, Glossop threw himself in the way of the van, which swerved just in time to avoid knocking him clean over and, having mounted the lawn briefly, the driver then righted the van's course and continued a stalling, stop-start getaway along the driveway. Whoever was driving did not know the peculiarities of the vehicle as well as Mr Glossop, but they knew enough to drive faster than Glossop could run and, as they all watched in horror, the van picked up speed and made straight for the hospital entrance and the bridge beyond.

'Whoever's driving, they must be desperate,' Sarah Warne said. 'Even if the water level has gone down enough to get onto the bridge, those loose boards will catch any tyre, let alone a flat one.'

'There were no flat tyres,' Alleyn said darkly. 'The van was driven unevenly because the driver was in a blind panic, all four tyres were good as new.'

'But that can't be,' Glossop stuttered, 'she said, Matron said, there were no spares, she said—'

271

'No time to explain,' Alleyn shook his head and turned to Sarah Warne, 'I assume you know your transport bus better than most, Miss Warne?'

'I'll say,' said Sarah, 'it's a tricky beast at the best of times, but I think I've found my way with it.'

Alleyn held up a hand. He looked around him for a moment, taking in the fear in the faces of everyone staring at him, and made his decision. 'Take Bix with you in the bus as far and as fast as you can, after Mr Glossop's van. Hughes, you're to go with them. Whoever is driving is in a reckless state and may well be in need of medical assistance if they attempt to cross the river. I trust they will not.'

The doctor dithered for a second until Sarah took his hand and he seemed to pull himself together. They hurried off.

'And Hughes,' Alleyn called after them.

'Sir?'

'You've been out in the field, do your best to make sure they don't do anything—' he paused and Sergeant Bix thought the detective was being rather too coy with his language for such an emergency.

'Damn stupid, Sir?' Bix said, 'I'm sure the young doctor will be on top of that. Off you go, you two. Set the engine running, I'm right behind you.'

Hughes and Sarah rushed for the bus while Bix took his orders from Alleyn.

'Do whatever you must, Sergeant. I can't imagine the driver, who we must assume is Father O'Sullivan, however out of control he is, will attempt to cross the bridge, and yet that remains a distinct possibility. Use your discretion and, for God's sake, man, let's try to avoid any further alarums before dawn.'

272

Bix hared after Sarah and Dr Hughes and Alleyn turned to Sister Comfort, 'Sister, check on each of your nurses and make sure they understand they are under the strictest of orders not to leave their posts, nor their charges their beds until I say otherwise. Miss Farquharson, fetch some hot sweet tea for Mr Glossop, take him with you to the kitchen. With any luck Bix will be back in no time with the thief and Mr Glossop can breathe again. Take Mr Kelly and Sydney Brown along with you too.'

For once, Glossop was silent, stunned as he was by almost losing his life under the wheels of his own van and the fact that he could not stop thinking about the truth the detective had pointed out, that none of the tyres were flat.

Much as he might have enjoyed the moment when Glossop finally worked out exactly what that must mean, Alleyn tore himself away, leaving them with a nod, 'I'm afraid there is another matter that simply cannot wait any longer for my attention.'

Alleyn raced off leaving Rosamund Farquharson to raise an eyebrow and comment under her breath on the Inspector's elegant inscrutability even in a moment such as this, before taking Mr Glossop's arm and leading him to the kitchen.

They were almost there when the penny dropped and Mr Glossop yelped, 'No, she can't have. You mean she lied about the tyres? But why?'

Sarah reached the main entrance to the hospital driveway and took the road towards the bridge, the sound of the still-rushing water very strong now. She was driving as fast as she dared and a good deal faster than usually felt safe in the old transport.

'It must be Father O'Sullivan in Glossop's van, musn't it, Sergeant?' Dr Hughes asked Bix, 'I didn't see him when we ran out into the drive and he hasn't appeared since. How on earth did he get out of Matron's office with all of us watching the door?'

'Less speculation, Dr Hughes, let's allow Miss Warne to concentrate on driving us safely, shall we?'

Bix's response was short, his mind on the bridge ahead, the rushing water beneath. He too hoped that Father O'Sullivan was not desperate enough to attempt the crossing, but he had seen desperate men in the past and there really was no telling what awaited them when they caught up with the van, if they did.

Alleyn turned back towards the offices as Sanders and Brayling came running.

Sanders spoke first, 'Sir, we've found it, the office has an opening, heading down. It slopes right under the yard. I went a very little way along and there's what looks like an entrance into the tunnel, but it's hidden on the tunnel side, so you'd never know it was there.'

Alleyn raised an eyebrow, 'And no doubt there's a further passage that leads out to a forgotten mine beneath the mountains where the king of the faeries hoards his gold. Very well, Sanders, you're to use the entrance from the office and head along the passage to the tunnel, but stay in that section, do you hear? I don't want you to go into the tunnel itself, nor to the morgue. Take a torch and check every inch of the path.'

'What am I looking for, Sir?'

'Much as I wish you might find a beautiful fingerprint, carefully outlined in dust that has not been touched for centuries, which not only points in the direction of our culprit, but notes their name at the same time, while explaining the entire convoluted mess, I fear the time for wishing is past. Signs, Sanders, you're looking for whatever doesn't seem right.'

'With respect, Sir, none of it seems right.'

'Quite. Brayling and I will head in the other direction towards the Bridge.'

'And what are we looking for, Sir?' asked Brayling.

Alleyn frowned, 'We're looking for hieroglyphs and hoping that in finding them we will also be granted the power of translation, Corporal. Anything that looks out of place, unusual, unexpected.'

At which precise moment Rosamund Farquharson appeared, 'You're also looking for Sydney Brown, Inspector. I've been all round the houses, I've irritated the night nurses no end, not that they aren't already awfully put out about not being able to leave their posts and no one letting on a word about why and, to use the local vernacular, stone me but I can't find the little bugger anywhere.'

CHAPTER THIRTY-TWO

Sarah drove off into the dark, Dr Hughes in the passenger seat directly behind her, Bix across the aisle from him. None of them spoke as they stared out into the darkness beyond. Sarah recalled crossing the bridge not twelve hours earlier. It was a fierce river with brutally cold water fed directly from the mountains beyond the foothills, many the unsuspecting traveller caught in a whirlpool or hidden current, their breath stolen by the heart-stopping chill of the ice-cold water. Locals knew to be wary of the river, to respect it. Father O'Sullivan was a local, whatever mess he had got himself into, he must know it would be terribly dangerous now that they'd had such a dreadful storm, surely he wouldn't try to cross?

She drew the bus up to a careful halt as the road gave way to the swollen river, the bridge directly ahead. Something was on the bridge and it was not stable.

'Turn on your headlamps, Miss Warne, we need to see this, whatever it is,' Bix said.

The sudden glow of the headlamps showed clearly that not only had the bridge lost half a dozen planks, open scars giving way to rushing water beneath, but there, not halfway across, was Mr Glossop's van, peculiarly angled. It was leaning heavily on the white-painted rail, the only thing holding it in place was the left back wheel, sunk into a gaping hole where one of the planks was missing. The van rested precariously against the rail, swaying slightly, and with each deceptively gentle lurch seemed more likely to release itself from the gap and roll over into the violent river below.

Sarah was out of the driver's seat and ready to run over the remaining boards to the van when Sergeant Bix held up his hand, 'Wait.'

'We can't wait, look at the angle it's on, it'll go over any moment now,' she replied, clambering from the bus.

'I heard someone. Wait,' the sergeant demanded with the force he used to command dozens of spirited young men.

Sarah stopped, they quietly climbed from the transport bus and stood in the semi-darkness of the false dawn, the water rushing past just feet below them. There it was again, a call, a cry for help.

'I can't make it out,' Luke said. 'Is it coming from the van or from down there, along the bank?'

'Hard to tell,' answered Bix, 'the river's so loud, it's as if the sound is coming from all over the place and then not at all.' He looked from Sarah to Hughes and quickly sized them up, 'Now listen, Miss Warne, I know you're a darn sight smaller than the doctor here, but I'm not going to let you chance it. He's been out in the field, he knows what he's about. I don't mind the two of us taking a risk, but I'm not going to let you go for it as well. Dr Hughes, you get over to the van—and for Gawd's sake, take it slowly—I'll try to scramble down the bank and see if I can spot anyone along the siding.'

Sarah shot an agonized glance at Luke as he nodded his agreement, he caught it and whispered to her, 'I have to. You don't know how much I have to do this.'

'Both of you, take care,' she said, trying to hide her fear with a cool tone. 'I'll wait by the bus in case we need to transport someone back, if they're hurt.'

As she finished speaking, they heard it again, distinctly now, it was a plaintive call for help, and sounded like someone in pain.

Hughes and Bix parted, leaving Sarah to climb back into the bus, the engine ticking over just in case.

Hughes carefully made his way onto the bridge, doing his best not to look to the raging river below. He inched his way along, holding the creaking wooden rail, bending out over the churning water every time the van lurched a little more to the left.

Bix lowered himself over the edge of the bank and down towards the river's edge. It was still very high, a good three or four feet higher than usual and even in the pale light he could see the water grasping at the bank, tearing at tree roots, patches of scrub, rocks. Bix was not an elegant swimmer, but he had a strong stroke and that usually helped him to feel at ease in the water. There was nothing about the river that felt easy to him now.

Hughes reached the van and took care to hold fast to the bridge itself, rather than the swaying vehicle. Bix scoured the sides of the bank. At the very moment the two men both realized they had not heard a cry for help for several minutes, they heard, as clear as the day that was coming, Sarah's voice, high pitched but strong.

'Help, hi! Help!'

And then nothing, a dreadful silence, and next came the

horrible sound of the transport bus gears grinding, the vehicle slammed into reverse and driving off in a shower of loose shingle. Ignoring all danger, both men threw themselves back the way they had come. They arrived together, in time to see the bus rumble away.

Sarah had been sitting, heart in mouth, watching Luke edge carefully towards the van. She heard Bix call out once, twice, but no answer came. She was readying herself to run at Luke's call, to help him deal with whatever he found in the front seat of the van, an injured Father O'Sullivan or worse. She was thinking about how much she loved Luke, how strong he was now, surely he must see that about himself? He was a good man and a brave one.

Then suddenly the gloaming turned pitch black, the false dawn was swallowed by a dark blindfold pulled roughly over her eyes. She was wrenched from her seat and tumbled to the floor of the bus. She just had time to call out for help when her mouth was gagged by the same cloth, her hands pulled behind her back and tied. She was rolled along the dusty floorboards of the bus and heard scuffling, shuffling, something being hoisted into the bus and dropped down, and then the bus lurched into action and reversed, turned, drove off. Sarah was jolted and bruised against the floor and the edges of seats. She counted one, two bends, one big bump and a smaller one, a corner and another. If Father O'Sullivan was driving, and surely it must be he at the wheel, he knew his way around these roads as well as Sarah did herself. It felt almost as if they were driving in a circle and back to the hospital, which made no sense. Then the bus came to an abrupt halt and her heart sank when she recognized

Father O'Sullivan's voice now that the sound of the engine was gone. She had assumed he was talking to her and didn't understand why his frantic whispers were so quiet. When she heard the voice that answered him her blood ran cold.

CHAPTER THIRTY-THREE

After Rosamund's announcement about Sydney Brown's disappearance, Alleyn took no time at all to recalibrate his plans. Sanders was to do just as he had been instructed, Brayling was to come along with Alleyn himself to the cave, Rosamund to make sure she kept an eye on Glossop and Kelly.

'And if you can possibly ensure that no one else disappears before sunrise, Miss Farquharson, I shall be enormously grateful.'

This time they ran to the cave, Alleyn leading with a sure-footed fury that both unnerved and impressed Brayling. He was unnerved because he was still to face his superiors or his family with his transgressions, and Alleyn might yet turn out to be his only witness for the defence. He was impressed because the detective was making his way along to the caves at an enormous lick and in the dark at that. Brayling looked around him and reconsidered, it was not dark. He could see his own feet on the ground, his hands before him. It would be darker yet, briefly, and then it would be day. He didn't know why Alleyn was so fussed about dawn, but he knew it mattered. In no time they were at the mouth of the cave. Alleyn dived into the cool darkness with Brayling immediately behind, both men alert and ready.

Alleyn whispered to Brayling, 'Hopefully we can use the false dawn to our advantage. With the growing light behind us our faces will be hidden. If Sydney is inside and, as I expect, at the back of the cave, he will be more exposed. We will need to do our best to read him, and fast. Follow my lead, Brayling. I'm trusting you.'

The two men advanced into the darkness, their eyesight adjusting as they went. Without the white blanket of light from the torch, flattening rocks and crevices, the cave itself seemed more hollow, deeper, and there, right at the back of the main body of the cave, standing on the ledge where it became a bridge between the cave floor on one side and the depths of the *tomo* on the other, stood young Sydney Brown, his pale face a shock of white against the dark grey rock. He seemed to be shaking and his hands were clasped together in fear or hesitation, but he looked directly at the two of them as he spoke, his voice not only remarkably clear but also reverberating slightly, a disembodied witness, telling his truths above an abyss.

'I'll do it, if you come any closer, I'll jump.'

Alleyn held out a steadying hand to Brayling who seemed about to spring, whether to leap up and drag the young man back to safety or to run from the cave and whatever curse Sydney was about to bring upon them, Alleyn couldn't tell.

'Sydney,' Alleyn spoke gently but with determination, his careful voice firm and reassuring, 'don't be foolish, we can help you. I can help you.'

'No one can, you don't understand,' Sydney responded,

all trace of the surly young man gone, now he was just a lost boy, fearful and cold, hiding in the dark.

'I know you got yourself into a pickle of some sort, a little while back. I know you thought there was only one way out, you were told there was no way out.'

'I had no choice,' Sydney whimpered.

Alleyn wanted to shake the young man, to drag him down from the ledge and force him to see sense, make him admit that of course there had been a choice, there was always a choice to do right or to do wrong, but now was not the time.

'I know you didn't want to take on the farm, Sydney.'

'I wanted to be an engineer.'

'Yes, the farm is worth a good deal though, isn't it?'

'What's that got to do with anything?'

Standing beside Alleyn, Brayling couldn't help but agree with the tortured young man. Alleyn had said time was of the essence yet here he was discussing sale prices for farm-land, it was crazy.

Alleyn pressed on, his tone calm, rational, 'It costs to study, a fair amount I imagine, to get a good degree. Perhaps you thought you might sell the farm to do so. Perhaps you talked to your grandfather about your hopes, your plans?'

'I didn't even know my grandfather.'

'So you said, and yet here he was, leaving you this great estate.'

'Nothing great about it, half the land's run down, the stock are in an awful state, nothing's been looked after since my old man left, he didn't bloody care for it either.'

'Are those your words, Sydney, or someone else's? Someone who knows more about farming than you?'

Sydney's laugh was bitter, 'Everyone round here knows more about farming than I do. I didn't ask for it. He should have left it to my old man, that's the right thing to do, not that the lazy bugger would have thanked him for it.'

'And still your grandfather chose to leave the farm to you. It was coming your way and you'd had word that he was ill, you knew he was asking for you.'

'So what?'

Alleyn frowned, stroking his long index finger against his forehead, 'You see, Sydney, what I don't quite understand is why it took you so long to come and visit him?'

'I told you, I didn't know him from Adam, I didn't want it. I didn't fancy some deathbed scene, all playing upset with fake words and false tears.'

'I think there was more to it than that,' ventured Alleyn.

'Don't know what you're on about,' the young man mumbled.

'No?' Alleyn asked, his voice very measured. Brayling thought he could hear a warning of thin ice in the detective's tone.

Sydney shrugged but gave no answer.

'Shall I tell you what I mean? Do you want me to spell it out?' asked Alleyn.

Sydney did not respond, but he turned and stared far down into the depths behind. Alleyn and Brayling held their breath in the semi-darkness, there was no sound but the slow drip drip of rainwater seeping through the earth above them and into the pools below.

Alleyn decided this was the moment and he spoke roundly into the cool air, taking a step forward as he did so, 'You didn't come to the cave to jump into the *tomo*, Sydney, you only went to that end of the ledge when you heard us entering. You were at the other end when you heard us approaching, weren't you? Didn't you come into the cave so that you could go along the tunnel? Make your way down to the Bridge pub?'

'I—no, I don't know about no tunnel,' Sydney protested, but from the corners of his eyes he looked towards the end of the ledge, where it sloped downwards towards the tunnel entrance.

'Come, Sydney, tell the truth and shame the devil.'

Sydney laughed bitterly, 'Shame him? It's not the devil who has the shame, Inspector.'

Alleyn was thoughtful, 'No, I see that now. It must have been very difficult for you, these past few weeks, trying to work out what to do, which line you could bear to cross, how far you would allow them to push you.'

Sydney stood stock still on the ledge, as if he was waiting for Alleyn's next words, as if those words might help him decide what to do.

'They have been pushing you, haven't they? They told you that you owed them far more than you could afford, isn't that right, Sydney?'

There was an interminable silence, Alleyn could feel Brayling beside him, utterly bemused, and he wondered if perhaps he was on entirely the wrong track. He was just about to speak up again, to chance his hand, when a small whimper of agreement came from the young man on the ledge and Alleyn saw Sydney's shoulders settle a little, his body turn ever so slightly back towards the cave.

Alleyn continued, hopefully and carefully, 'I understand there has been an awful lot of gambling going on, particularly among you younger men. You were in debt to these people, weren't you? They said you had to pay up. There was no more time and they threatened you, they demanded the money now.'

285

Another murmur of agreement, another quarter-turn back in, away from staring into the gaping core of the earth.

'But when you explained that you couldn't pay, having discovered that the farm would be terribly hard to sell, and even if you could find a buyer willing to take it on in such a state it would take months before the proceeds came through, when the old man kept lingering on, week after week, at death's door but not crossing the threshold, they demanded another form of payment, didn't they?'

'I can't say, I can't.'

'You must, Sydney. It's not too late, whatever is going to happen this morning, you can still do the right thing, you can change the course. Listen to me, blackmail is a filthy crime, the very worst. The people who are black-mailing you always knew they would ask you to do this thing for them eventually. They planned it all, making you think they were happy to wait for their money and then demanding it in the few days leading up to this morning, now. They knew there was no way you would be able to repay them and they knew they would force you to repay the debt in another way. They have used you from the start.'

'Even if they did, even if you're right, it's too late.'

Alleyn ignored him and went on telling the tale, hoping he was right, a word out of line now and it could all come crashing down, 'Your grandfather was dying, you knew that and so did they, the people to whom you owe money, but the old man was dying too slowly for you to get any money from the farm. After so many requests for you to visit, you finally came out to Mount Seager, but your grandfather's request wasn't the only reason you agreed to be here tonight, was it, Sydney? Those people, the ones calling in your gambling debts, they wanted you to do something else for them, didn't they? Something they would accept as a down-payment, until you inherit the farm, until you sell it and pay them back? Something to prove they could trust you.'

There was another silence and Alleyn heard Sydney shift ever such a little. He held his breath, worried that he had gone too far. He could feel Brayling at his side, looking at him in horror, equally worried that these words would push the young man beyond sanity. Even so, Alleyn knew he had to go on. It was less than thirty minutes before dawn, he had to force the truth from Sydney somehow.

He went on, 'And that person to whom you owe your debts, they knew that you would be given time alone to grieve. They asked you to use that time to get a message from someone here at the hospital and then to pass it on just before dawn, didn't they?'

Out of the darkness there came a small, pained voice, 'Yes.'

'The message came from Private Pawcett?'

'How did you know?'

Brayling spat and Alleyn answered plainly, 'Private Pawcett has made himself rather conspicuous by his absence. Were you told to take this message to someone at the Bridge pub?'

'No, not the Bridge. They just said I was to go along the tunnel and they'd find me.'

Alleyn took a deep breath, he hated to do this, but there was no choice, it was all too close, too late. He took a step forward, 'Sydney, I'm giving you a chance. When were you to deliver this message?'

'Now, right before sunrise. He said, Pawcett said, they'd know what to do with the information, but I wasn't to give it until just now. He said if I gave it earlier then they might be tempted to use the information earlier and we'd all be sunk.'

Alleyn started, 'Were those his exact words?'

'Yes.'

With a speed that took both Sydney Brown and Brayling by surprise Alleyn leapt athletically from the edge of the narrow pool to the ledge, he advanced the half dozen steps to Sydney's position in no time at all and took hold of the young man's arm. At this end of the ledge there was less than a foot's width separating the two of them and the chasm beneath.

Alleyn spoke urgently, 'You have a choice now, Sydney, a real choice. You can come along with us, we can get through the tunnel in time for you to offer whatever password you've been told, and help us catch the culprit or culprits red-handed. I know you feel bitter about the hand life has dealt you, but I cannot believe you feel so harshly done by as to risk the lives of your fellow countrymen. Even if you genuinely care nothing for your country or for its servicemen, this is a chance to finally do something for yourself. You are in trouble, as you and I both know, or you'd not be standing here. But you didn't jump before and you haven't jumped since we came in. I don't think you want to jump, Sydney. I think you want to try again. Come with us, man, do try again.'

Alleyn waited, his mind racing. On one level he knew full well that he was taking an absurd risk, that Sydney Brown might take the chance he had rashly offered by holding onto him and pulling them both into the abyss in a moment of madness. On another level he too weighed the lives of the many against those of the few and made his own decision. Alleyn knew that he had placed himself squarely in the camp of the few and Sydney now, quite literally, had the upper hand.

Alleyn paused for a second and then, making sure that his voice was so quiet that Brayling could not hear them, he whispered, 'I know what you did, Sydney, all of it. What's done is done, but you can still try to do some good. Now, before it's too late. This is your chance to do some good in a night of terrible wickedness.'

In the seconds that followed, Alleyn found himself thinking of Troy, of the time they had already been apart, of the indeterminate time before he saw her again. He saw in his mind's eye her beautiful thin hands, her intelligent brow, her reticence, almost fear, in the face of anything emotional, anything revelatory that was not in her control. He thought too of how very foolish he had been in misreading her for so long, wasting time before being open with her. He hoped he had not misread Sydney Brown now.

'I'll tell you,' Sydney said, his voice low and dispirited.

'Good man,' declared Alleyn, his relief forcing the words out in a rush, 'Better than that, you'll help us, won't you? You'll come with us through the tunnel, go ahead a little way and then give the signal without alerting your contact in any way, and you'll allow us to catch them red-handed. Say you will, Sydney. Be a man.'

Getting down from the ledge was slower than Alleyn would have liked, the awful drop behind them was terrifying and whatever bravery had allowed Sydney to take his place on the bridge of rock had drained away with his confession, and he painstakingly edged his way towards the wider part of the ledge. It occurred to Alleyn that perhaps the greater fear was what awaited him, not only at the end of the tunnel but afterwards. The boy showed more courage than he might have expected when they finally arrived, several agonizingly slow minutes later, at the entrance to the tunnel itself.

'Torch or no?' Sydney asked.

'What were you told?'

'No torch, no light, no sound.'

'Then we shall go along with you and play out the scene exactly as you were told.'

Alleyn led the way and the three men walked forward into the tunnel, the silent darkness closing in around them.

They were nearing the point where the tunnel met the morgue when Sanders's voice, barely audible, whispered, 'Sir?'

Alleyn whispered behind to Sydney Brown and Corporal Brayling, 'Wait there a moment.' Then he walked on another few steps, turning his head to the voice, 'Sanders? Where are you?'

'To your left, Sir, I know you said I oughtn't to come into the tunnel itself, but the opening is dead peculiar and I kind of found myself here before I knew where I was.'

'It can't be helped now. What did you find?'

'Clean as a whistle, Sir, nothing to report in the pathway itself. I did as you said, followed the route from Matron's office and I've been right here ever since. It's a terrifically steep slope from Matron's office, stone me if I didn't lose my footing a few times. Right at the end, just where it levels off and before it opens into the tunnel with no warning, there's a dead sharp twist round to the right, so it's almost like you come into the tunnel from alongside it. That'll be why you didn't notice it before,' he added, sparing Alleyn's blushes.

'Very kind, Private. Do you think someone or something might have been down there all along, hidden from sight in this recess?'

'I reckon it would be dead easy to miss anything there, especially if you didn't even know it was there in the first place.'

'Wait a moment, will you? I need to give instructions to our unfortunate young man.'

He made his way back to Sydney and Brayling, 'All right, Sydney, we're almost at the way into the morgue. My guess is your contact will either be waiting there, ready to pounce, or expecting you to head on to the Bridge Hotel, where the tunnel opens into the pub's cellars. Are you sure they gave no instructions as to where you were to wait?'

'None, Sir.'

'Very well, you must go on alone. We will be close behind. You cannot undo what has been done, but you can use this opportunity to begin to make amends.'

Alleyn felt rather than saw Sydney hear the words and understand the enormity of what lay ahead. He gently held the young man's shoulder and then guided him forward. Sydney moved away into the tunnel, towards the morgue and the Bridge pub beyond.

Alleyn waited until the soft thud of Sydney's steady step was a few more feet away and then turned back to call the soldiers to action, his voice was very quiet but extremely clear, 'If my calculations are right, Sydney will be alongside the morgue in less than five minutes. I believe his contact will meet him in the morgue, there is no time to waste.'

He gave his orders with military efficiency and the two soldiers departed swiftly along the tunnel back to the cave, keen to play their part. Alleyn found himself smiling for a moment and shook his head, 'Not yet, Roderick old man, it's not time to hang out the flags just yet.'

CHAPTER THIRTY-FOUR

Much later Alleyn would remark to Troy that what happened next appeared to him exactly as preposterous and as well-choreographed as the final act of *A Midsummer Night's Dream*, when the actors all tumble in together from their night in the wood outside Athens, sweet dreams are unmasked, lovers revealed and secrets quickly shuffled out of sight, in order to pretend that all is well. Before that moment, and before Puck swept away the whole play as if in a dream, there was one final set piece to come.

While Alleyn headed on alone, Brayling and Sanders carefully let themselves into the morgue. In the quick sprint back along the tunnel, through the cave and the barrier of rose bushes, then along the yard to the morgue, their eyes became accustomed to the dawn growing lighter by the minute. The morgue, with the heavy door silently closed behind them, seemed intensely dark. They edged their way into the body of the morgue itself and waited. They could see nothing and hear nothing other than their own breath, blood rushing through their veins, pounding in their ears.

Both men had faced action, both had been scared for their lives, for the lives of comrades. This was nothing like war and yet it had a feeling of those days, a time to which they would soon return.

Peering into the darkness, their backs to the main wall, both of them facing, they hoped, towards the empty spaces reserved for dead bodies, they took careful and hushed steps forward. Walking shoulder to shoulder in the pitch black they quickly came to the empty cavities and hoisted themselves up into the first two chambers on the left-hand side of the row, their heads facing the door. They pushed back until their feet came to the solid rock behind them. When they were safely inside the cavities, they reached out and quietly pulled the thin curtains across the openings, hiding themselves from view. This was what Alleyn had told them to do and although they didn't understand the reasoning they followed his instructions to the letter. The men lay on their fronts, alert in the darkness.

Just minutes later they heard a scraping and shuffling sound coming from one of the other cavities. Sanders wished he could whisper to Brayling and Brayling wished the same, and they waited still. After a few moments the scuffling stopped and they heard the groan of exertion as whoever it was lowered themselves hands first down to the morgue floor and then stood, patting themselves down. The person in the morgue muttered something to himself, took a few steps, cursed the darkness and then they heard the flick of a lighter, once, twice, until the flint caught and a warm flame lit up the cold morgue. Brayling and Sanders each held his breath, the thin curtain just inches from their faces, now palely glowing from the light beyond. It was with huge relief that they heard the rustle of a cigarette packet, the cigarette pulled from its casing, the tap tap on the packet, each sound amplified by their tension. Then the deep inhale and satisfied exhale and the lighter clicked off. They were in darkness again, a tiny firefly light from the cigarette barely visible through the weave of the curtain fabric.

'More nerve than Ned Kelly,' Sanders thought, as he took a cautious, halting breath, 'It's all go now.'

Seconds later another sound, this time a voice whispering into the darkness. They heard young Sydney, his tone worried and fearful, coming from the tunnel behind them.

'Hullo? Anyone there? I saw a light, hullo?'

The person smoking flicked the lighter on again, took a few steps closer to the rock cavities, he was within feet of them and Brayling wondered if Sanders was having the same thought that he was. They could reach out and grab him right now, they could put an end to whatever the hell was going on right this minute. They could stop taking orders from high-falutin' blokes who told them what to do left, right and centre and they could do what was needed to be done, when it was needed. Brayling thought all of this, seething with frustration, but Inspector Alleyn had been very clear that they were to be in the morgue as back-up, ready to come if called and nothing else.

The holder of the cigarette answered, his voice lowered but clear and threatening, 'You were to give me a message, and only the message, there's no bloody time for chat. What have you got?'

Maurice Sanders's fists clenched tightly of their own accord, a vein hammering in his temple, that was Duncan Blaikie speaking. Sukie's brother who was working their book with Bob Pawcett, Duncan Blaikie who had shares

295

in a radio company in town. Snow Johnson's narrow tract of land stretched right up to join the Blaikie's old farm of rough land with huge crags, overlooking vast swathes of the plains, crags that were high enough to send a signal over many miles on a clear day—a clear midsummer day.

Sydney called out, his voice a little louder, a little less tremulous, 'The joker who gave me the message said I needed to see you face to face, make sure it was you.'

Duncan Blaikie sounded irritated. 'Damn time-wasting if you ask me, who the hell else would be waiting here for you?'

'Shall I come through?' Sydney persisted.

'I reckon you'll bloody well have to,' he answered, spitting on the floor and grinding out his cigarette as he did so.

Brayling and Sanders heard a moan as Sydney lifted himself up from the tunnel side, another scuffle as he shuffled along the rock cavity.

'Get a move on, will you?' asked Blaikie brusquely, and then, in almost the same breath he added, 'Aw, hang on, damn it. Someone's coming. Move back, let me through. Wait in the tunnel and keep your mouth shut.'

They heard Sydney push himself backwards, Blaikie take his place in the rock cavity and within moments the morgue was suddenly silent again, an empty space filled with waiting. Brayling and Sanders wondered if this was the moment that Alleyn was to make his entrance, but it was not Alleyn who opened the door, in control of himself and of the situation, it was an altogether different man, bustling, fretful and in an extraordinary hurry.

'Hurry up, for goodness' sake.'

Brayling and Sanders both recognized Father O'Sullivan's voice immediately, but the way he spoke now, abrupt, sharp, with something else in his tone, something both men had heard in superiors giving orders in the field—a genuine note of fear—sounded markedly different from the careful and considerate quality he usually sported.

'We can leave her here and get out of it, if we hurry we might still make it,' Father O'Sullivan said.

If he received a reply to his statement, neither Brayling nor Sanders heard it, but his accomplice must have agreed with the plan for there was a good deal more shuffling, mumbling as if someone was somehow prevented from speaking out and then more dragging or perhaps pushing, feet scuffling, and finally something dumped unceremoniously on the ground. The noise that followed, a muffled moan, almost a cry, sounded like someone in pain and a woman at that. At this sound, both Brayling and Sanders involuntarily tensed. Obedient to Alleyn's orders they remained silent and quite still but it took all of their training to do so and they bitterly resented the order that left them powerless to help.

They not only heard, but also felt what happened next, several sharp bangs apparently directed to the rock wall beneath the cavities where they now lay hidden, then a scraping wrenching sound as if rock were being pushed or pulled against rock, again the sound of something being moved, lifted, and then, suddenly, a fierce whisper from the vicar, 'The door, quick, in here.'

As Sanders thought to himself 'It's busier than flamin' Queen Street down here,' the door did indeed open, with no attempt at silence this time and he heard Dr Luke Hughes call out, fumbling for the gas lights, 'O'Sullivan, are you in there? Dammit man, where the hell are you? What have you done with her? Where's Sarah?'

At the mention of Sarah's name, Maurice Sanders could take no more, and evidently Brayling had the same idea, for both men pushed themselves from the rock cavities and vaulted into the chamber of the morgue. As the light Hughes had just lit grew into a substantial flame, the deep blackness of the room receded and they saw, with horror, that there was a body bag leaning against the wall, someone inside was struggling, trying to cry out. Sanders and Hughes both leapt to untie the bag, but Brayling immediately rapped both men sharply on the shoulder. His fingers to his lips, he pointed behind them. Inspector Alleyn was slowly and silently emerging from the eighth cavity, alongside the far wall, where he had settled himself before the soldiers entered the morgue, racing up through the tunnel that went under Matron's office and getting into place just ahead of Sanders and Brayling. He too had his finger to his lips, and with his other hand pointed in the direction of the fifth cavity, the one that led through to the tunnel. Sanders nodded, of course, there was still the matter of Duncan Blaikie and young Sydney Brown waiting in the tunnel.

Hughes untied the body bag and removed the gag from a furious Sarah. Eyes wide and alert with anger, she immediately understood the need for speed and silence. Alleyn then turned, took three paces and ripped back the curtain from across the fifth cavity, Sanders and Brayling reached in and grabbed the rapidly retreating Blaikie by the arms, pulling him out and into the morgue.

'What the hell? What is all this?' demanded Blaikie.

Alleyn paid no attention to the man's affronted tone, merely directing him to stand against the back wall, 'Over there, don't move. Brayling, Sanders, keep an eye on him, will you?'

The two soldiers moved closer to Blaikie, taking up guard duty on either side of him. Blaikie in return, shot them daggers from the corners of his eyes, but chose discretion as the better part of valour for the moment and held his tongue.

Alleyn turned and called through the rock tunnel, 'Sydney, come through into the morgue will you, please?'

Sydney emerged and Alleyn took him aside so that Blaikie didn't hear their exchange, 'Did you pass on your message?'

'There wasn't time. We heard the door so Blaikie told me to go back into the tunnel, then the vicar came into the morgue and there was all that banging about and—' he looked at Sarah, her face ashen, Dr Hughes alongside with an arm around her shoulders, and then he looked at the others, 'But where's the vicar flamin' well gone? How'd he get away and all of you in here?'

Bix and Hughes looked around, as did Brayling and Sanders and realized for the first time that Father O'Sullivan was nowhere to be seen.

'What the hell?' said Sanders.

'Where the blazes?' uttered Hughes.

Alleyn, having assured himself that Sarah was now safely in Hughes's care, asked them all to step well away from the rock cavities. He too had heard the thumping and wrenching sounds and thought he knew what they meant. He looked about the morgue, and finally laid his hand on a heavy piece of wood, ridged across the top, propped up alongside the main door at the top of the steep slope that led outside.

'If it's sturdy enough to hold open that heavy door, it will do the trick.'

The others edged backwards and looked on mystified as the detective crouched before the rock wall below the cavities and pulled his arm back, ready, apparently, to strike directly at the rock.

Which was when the door opened yet again and Private Bob Pawcett came running down the sloping passageway and into the morgue, 'Blaikie, where the hell are you? I've been waiting down by the pub, we've got ten minutes to get halfway up the bloody crag and unless we crack on we're never going to get up and back before Snow works out we're—'

He stopped even before he was in the morgue itself. As he tried to retrace his steps, half-turning, half-running up the incline behind, both Brayling and Sanders deserted their posts alongside Blaikie, lunged for Pawcett and brought down their comrade with a resounding crash. It was a crash that sounded a great deal louder because Alleyn took the same moment to batter the rock beneath the cavities, smacking at it with the piece of wood with all his might and what was now revealed as a façade covering a hole in the wall beneath the cavities fell away, revealing a horrified Father O'Sullivan clutching several envelopes of money and a good number of loose pound notes.

One of those notes rose up, caught in the gust of wind as the door was opened one more time and Sister Comfort was heard to say, 'For goodness' sake, Mr Glossop, will you please calm down? I've no idea where they all are, but if you will insist on checking the morgue, then we'll check the morgue together. You cannot possibly go in there unattended.'

Followed immediately by Rosamund Farquharson's more lyrical tone calling merrily, 'Only do stop your carrying on, Glossop, you've been at it for hours and I'm sure we've better things to worry about. Oh,' she said, seeing the assembled throng crammed into the morgue, 'here they all are after all.' And, as the pound note came to a stop she picked it up and examined it, turning it over to see a large red lipsticked kiss across Captain Cook's head, 'Ooh, my winnings. How lovely.'

Then there was utter bedlam. Pawcett tried to get up and Sanders roundly and quite forcibly sat on him, meanwhile Blaikie took the moment of distraction to reach up and punch out the one gas lamp that was lit, plunging the morgue back into darkness, lit only by the certain dawn beyond the door, blocked almost entirely by Mr Glossop's large and incredulous frame.

In the darkness, Father O'Sullivan himself jumped up and, dodging both Sanders and Brayling, as well as the more lumbering Blaikie, made it as far as the door, before Glossop, once again showing a surprising agility for a man of his physical stature, proved as effective at a solid rugby tackle as the two young soldiers. Sister Comfort looked on in abject horror from beyond the doorway.

'Do come in, won't you, Sister?' Alleyn called airily, 'I believe it's time to bring some order to the proceedings.'

He waited until the pandemonium had died down a little and then instructed Hughes and Rosamund to light the remaining lamps. When all were fully lit, Alleyn took in the assembled company. Sarah was flanked by Dr Hughes and Rosamund Farquharson, Sanders guarded Blaikie while Brayling stood alongside Pawcett, Bix had taken up a post beside young Sydney Brown and Mr Glossop took it upon himself to hold onto the vicar very tightly indeed.

301

'Well, here we all are,' he said brightly, rubbing his nose, 'or are we?' He looked around quizzically.

'Not quite all,' Rosamund said, 'I'm sure Will Kelly will make a well-timed appearance before the dawn fully breaks.'

'We can but hope, Miss Farquharson,' Alleyn answered with a nod. 'However I feel sure there is one other person, and not the esteemed Mr Kelly, however excellent his baritone, who must surely be eager to join us.'

He waited and saw that all but Father O'Sullivan were looking at him in confusion, while the vicar's face held nothing but growing horror.

Alleyn turned to the gap beneath the rock cavities, from whence Father O'Sullivan and the rolls of pound notes had emerged and, speaking quietly but firmly, he said, 'Your staff are waiting, Matron.'

Slowly, from a hidden recess in the rock, so far back in the shadows it was impossible to see anything, a figure in dusty white began to emerge and eventually, to the tune of Sister Comfort's gasp, Rosamund's low whistle and Mr Glossop's howl of betrayed rage, Matron—extremely corporeal and very alive—stood before them.

CHAPTER THIRTY-FIVE

As if on cue, and shouting above the hue and cry that accompanied the revelation, Will Kelly popped his head around the door and seemed to skip the several steps down the slope into the main chamber of the morgue. Without batting an eyelid, he said, 'Now there's a sight for sore eyes. Alive are you, Matron? I'm sure we'll all be very happy about that, as you will be to hear the telephone wires are working. That one in your office, Matron, has been ringing off the hook for the past five minutes. I've been all round the houses and here you lot are, huddled in together and on such a fine morning too.'

Glossop jumped up and took off like a rocket, shouting about his bosses and the other hospitals wanting their payrolls, daring anyone to touch the money the vicar was holding and rushed off to make his calls.

Seeing Sister Comfort's stricken face, the pain with which she looked upon Matron, Rosamund took pity on her. She offered her arm to Sister Comfort, 'Come along with me, will you, Sister? I imagine the Inspector has an awful lot to sort out here, we'll only be in the way. You'll be wanting to let the night staff know they're allowed to pop out now.'

she looked to Alleyn, 'That'll be all right, Inspector? There can't possibly be any more revelations to come, can there?'

Alleyn smiled gratefully at her, 'None that affect Sister Comfort, Miss Farquharson, thank you so much.'

'That's us given our marching orders.'

She led the devastated sister away, her irrepressible spirit allowing her to throw a wink to Maurice Sanders and to turn at the door with a reminder for Alleyn, 'And don't you let old Glossop take all that cash back in his van, Inspector, some of that's my winnings, remember.'

'Of course, thank you. Now, Bix,' he said turning to the sergeant, 'I shall make use of the telephone myself in a moment, to speak to my own superiors, so perhaps you can take Mr Blaikie and Private Pawcett away for now. Keep them apart, will you? I'm looking forward to speaking to both of you, just as soon as I tidy up here.'

Bix enlisted Sanders to support him in taking Duncan Blaikie and Private Pawcett away, each man to be locked in a separate office—and definitely not Matron's. As they went Pawcett suddenly became very loquacious about how he'd been running a book for his mates, that's all it was, just a book and Duncan Blaikie had been helping him with it. Blaikie, having told Pawcett to 'shut the hell up' said not a word, his jaw clamped tight shut, identifying him in Alleyn's eyes as by far the more interesting suspect of the two.

Brayling was stationed to keep an eye on Father O'Sullivan and Matron while Alleyn took Sydney Brown aside for a moment. They spoke quietly together.

'I imagine the local police will be here as soon as they get Mr Glossop's call and the bridge is passable.'

'I reckon,' Sydney responded, his face dark, his eyes on the ground.

'You'll help yourself if you can explain what led you to do this, Sydney. It will be useful for certain people to know exactly what Blaikie and Pawcett were asking you to do. If you are willing to tell them everything they ask—' Alleyn hesitated.

'If I tell your people everything I know then they might go easier on me about passing on that message for Blaikie,' Sydney snorted. 'You're trying to be kind, Inspector, and I get it, but we both know they're not going to let me off just because I was being blackmailed over some gambling debts. I didn't know what the message would be about, or what it meant, but I'm not an idiot. I know there's a war on, and since the Japs came in we've all known there's a hell of a lot more needs keeping secret.' He shook his head and looked up at Alleyn, 'Anyway, that's not going to be much help, is it? Not once you tell the police about my grandfather.'

Alleyn frowned and sighed, agreeing with the young man, 'No, it isn't.'

'You are going to tell them?'

There was both hope and defiance in Sydney's voice as he asked and Alleyn felt himself on a knife edge.

The uncertainty lasted for a moment, no more, and then he answered the young man, 'I must. His murder cannot go unpunished, no matter how old he was, how ill, or how much you believed you were forced into doing the deed. The nuance is for the court to decide, not a humble policeman.'

Sydney shrugged, 'You know we've no capital punishment here now, Inspector? They don't hang, it's life imprisonment.'

'I do know that, yes.'

'So I won't be an engineer, after all.'

Bix arrived back in the morgue and Alleyn gave his orders, 'Take Sydney and make sure he is safely stowed until the local police arrive.'

Alleyn turned back into the morgue itself. He spoke quietly and kindly, 'Miss Warne, you've been through a horrible ordeal, perhaps Dr Hughes should accompany you back to the office?'

'I'm quite well, thank you, Inspector,' Sarah shook her head, 'and given what I've been put through, I think I ought at least be allowed to hear the reason.'

Alleyn shook his head but he did not press the matter, instead he glared at the two miscreants in front of him.

'Well, Matron, you are our Juliet, returned to the world. And you made Dr Hughes here your Friar Laurence. He confided his awful secrets of battle to you and you made use of that information for your counterfeit death, providing a valuable distraction until you and Father O'Sullivan could get away with the money. You must have been waiting for the perfect circumstances for some time and jumped at your chance with the confluence of Mr Glossop's flat tyre and the storm.'

'No, no, it was not that way at all,' Father O'Sullivan protested. 'It wasn't planned. I mean, we knew Mr Glossop had the payroll, it was a regular drop-off, and yes, it seemed— well, somehow intended that the storm and he were here at the same time, but the way you say it, as if we were *waiting* for the occurrence, oh no, it was not like that at all.'

'Indeed not,' Matron answered, and Alleyn was astonished to see that both she and the vicar appeared positively affronted. 'The church is in dire need of repair, the hospital

306

in terrific debt. We wanted nothing other than to leave the vicar's church and my hospital in peace and security, for the good of all. Then last night, when all of this money arrived with Mr Glossop and the storm was about to come down, his tyre was flat—'

'Yes, the tyre. You assured him there were no spares, but that was not true?'

'It seemed, Inspector, that this was a turning point, a moment we had to take.'

'There is a tide in the affairs of men—' Alleyn began.

'Quite right,' Matron interrupted, nodding vigorously, 'we must take the current when it serves.'

'It was providence,' the vicar was certain. 'We could make arrangements to have the debts paid. Matron and I would leave, yes we might lose the respect of our respective congregations of parishioners and patients, but it would have been worth it for all of their problems would be solved, in one glorious moment,' Father O'Sullivan's quiet, thoughtful voice, seemed to suggest he actually believed his own words.

'It didn't occur to you that anyone would know where the money came from?' Sarah Warne asked.

Father O'Sullivan replied quite simply, 'The people to whom the hospital is in debt, those who will work on the church repairs, they need the work and the money. I don't imagine they would have asked.'

Alleyn was becoming increasingly exasperated, nothing seemed to make a dent in their certainty that they had done the right thing, 'But Matron, your letter to Sister Comfort, what was that for?'

Matron bristled, 'You read the letter?'

'I did.'

'It was only sensible to leave her instructions, she would have to take charge in my absence.'

'There was an unnecessarily harsh post-script.'

Matron shook her head, 'Not at all. Gertrude had a ridiculous idea of the two of us setting up a life together. There are some perversities that cannot stand.'

Alleyn raised an eyebrow, 'As perverse as allowing dear colleagues to believe you dead? As perverse as using information that this young doctor gave you in strictest confidence to enact your foolish ideas?'

Matron shook her head as if Alleyn was being particularly dense, 'I certainly never intended to play dead for my staff. You see, I brought the payroll to the morgue, I knew the under-cavity would be a useful hiding place—'

'Behind the façade?' Alleyn asked.

She hesitated, suddenly coy, 'It's for when we have too many bodies in the morgue. It happens on occasion but it's not something the staff need to know about. It might distress them.'

'And you came here via the tunnel in your office?'

'Yes, we thought it would be simple to hide the money here,' she replied, remarkably baldly.

'How did you get to the morgue, Vicar?' Alleyn asked, 'The last anyone saw, you were on your way back to Civilian 3.'

The vicar smiled, absurdly pleased with himself, 'Oh, I went along behind the wards and took the old workshop entrance to the tunnels.'

Matron took up the story again, 'Unfortunately it was at that moment that Mr Glossop started screaming the house down.'

'And so you had to hide your crime.'

'To do the right thing by the hospital, Inspector? Certainly.' Matron's voice was surprisingly clear, given the wholescale nature of her confession.

'But with such a cruel ruse?' Alleyn asked.

Matron sighed, almost exasperated, 'Our choices were made in haste, Inspector, once Mr Glossop had seen the empty safe, we knew we had to do something.'

'And quickly,' Father O'Sullivan added.

'So you did dope poor Will Kelly by adding pure alcohol in his lemonade?'

'It was simply an expedient way to ensure he didn't disturb us for a short while,' Father O'Sullivan answered.

Alleyn shook his head at the vicar's lack of contrition and continued, 'And then, Matron, you chose to take a concoction based on Dr Hughes's in-the-field anæsthetic—'

'Risking your own life!' Dr Hughes exclaimed, 'When I told you about that technique I also told you how terribly dangerous it was.' He shook his head in anger at himself, 'And of course I'd also told you that it made the patient awfully cold. You used me horribly, Matron.'

'All of this in order to usurp old Mr Brown's place on the trolley,' Alleyn went on, 'safe in the knowledge that if you were discovered, your colleagues would not think to blame you for the theft, distracted as they were by their terrible upset at your demise.'

'We had no intention of upsetting anyone,' Matron replied, 'we simply hoped that if I could replace Mr Brown on Mr Kelly's trolley then he would bring me through to the morgue out of the way of the fuss. Once I came to, we could use the tunnel to, to—'

She faltered and Alleyn stepped in, 'Make a quick getaway?'

'You make it sound so sordid,' the vicar frowned.

'It is sordid, Matron,' Dr Hughes interjected, 'Sordid and stupid and incredibly dangerous. But what really shocks me is how the two of you could have such a high idea of yourselves that you would explain away theft as worthwhile for a good cause, staging your death and causing deep pain as simply a means to an end.'

Dr Luke Hughes held out his hand to Sarah and they left the morgue, any remaining shreds of youthful idealism quite in tatters.

Bix was at the door again and Alleyn, seeing the sergeant, decided he too had heard enough for the moment. Leaving instructions to keep Matron, the vicar, and the money secured for now—all of them in separate places, if any more could be found—and then make sure the morgue was cleaned and old Mr Brown's body respectfully interred, Alleyn turned to leave.

He was just at the door when he had another thought and came back, 'One more question, why did you not simply lock the safe after the theft? Mr Glossop, and indeed anyone else who happened to be in your office, would never have known the safe was empty, you would not have been found out for many hours,' Alleyn asked.

His question elicited an unexpected response and Alleyn watched as the two people before him who had, until this moment, been quite certain in their choices, believing their behaviour understandable and almost correct, turned to simpering, youthful lovers.

'I can't say,' Matron whispered, blushing.

'Hmm, hah, then I will,' the vicar replied, his glossy face an even deeper shade of red than Matron's. 'We were happy, Inspector, hopeful and happy that we might be able to save

310

our hospital and our church and we took a moment—just a moment—to share an embrace.'

'And in that moment of silliness, I dropped the key, somewhere in the canvas bag containing the payroll,' Matron found the courage to raise her face to Alleyn's. 'Even when we transferred the notes to the body bag, we still couldn't find it.'

Alleyn's voice was cold when he said, 'You must have tossed the key into the body bag along with the notes. I found it in the bag in the cave, where you callously discarded Mr Brown's body.'

'Not at all,' Matron said, and the sure, certain woman was back, 'Mr Brown was laid out gently and carefully in the cave, just as he would have been here in the morgue. It is all the same earth, Inspector.'

Alleyn had had enough. He walked out into the dawn, a deep frown creasing his forehead. There was poor, misguided Sydney Brown facing life imprisonment for a terrible set of events that had left him believing he had no escape but to hasten the old man's imminent death so he could hand over the farm to Blaikie before dawn, to men who would continue to blackmail him about both the murder and passing on Pawcett's message. A message Pawcett could simply have delivered himself if he'd been able to get away from the ward, but Duncan Blaikie understood that tying Sydney Brown into the mess would make him forever theirs. Meanwhile, here were Matron and Father O'Sullivan, not a malicious bone in either body, dragging themselves deeper and deeper into the mire with every step, and each step to save their beloved buildings. Matron's trick of distraction

311

really had worked, all this fuss about payrolls and trolleys and the hoax of her death had entirely undermined the real matter of the night. Alleyn felt certain that Pawcett would give up some useful information and the coded message Sydney had been given would undoubtedly be of some use. He was far less sure of Blaikie, whoever he had been intending to contact would certainly know by now that something was wrong and the element of surprise was lost.

Alleyn strode off along the yard, the least he could do now was put in an urgent call to Wellington and let them know what had happened. Just as he reached the gap between the Records Office and Matron's office, the risen sun finally broke free from the long low line of cloud over in the east and the plains in front of the hospital were flooded with a fierce golden light. He turned and behind the wards he saw the foothills glowing in a clear midsummer morning, the ranges beyond lit up, the peaks shining bright. The vision was breathtaking and, unlike the bitter anger and foolish passions of the small people milling about in the foothills, unlike his own upset, it was as eternal and as untouched as the land on which he stood.

Alleyn stopped in his tracks and allowed the grandeur of the scene to touch the deep disappointment he felt in his fellow man. He whispered to himself, 'If we shadows have offended. . .'

Then he turned back towards Matron's office. There was a great deal of sweeping away to do yet, of that he was sure.

CHAPTER THIRTY-SIX

Alleyn was seated at the table in his private room when a call came at the open window. He turned to see Sergeant Bix standing outside with a tea tray, complete with teapot covered in a knitted tea cosy.

'I know you say the English don't really break for afternoon tea, Sir, but here in New Zealand we take smoko very seriously. It's gone four, none of us have slept a wink since early yesterday, I saw you barely touched a bite of the lunch they laid on for the local force—'

'Neither did you, Bix.'

'Fair go, Sir, we were both busy and I reckon you're like me, you'd rather get the work done and then have your break whenever it might come.'

'Indeed.'

'But I also think you might need a cuppa about now, it's a little way till tea and the kitchen does a very good ginger crunch, so I thought you might fancy a walk along the drive. You'll be off soon enough and it'd be a crying shame if the most you saw of Mount Seager was that little room of yours and those flamin' tunnels.'

'I couldn't agree more, Sergeant. Give me a moment and I'll be straight with you.'

Alleyn put away the papers he had been working on, making sure to lock them in the combination case and left his little room to join Bix.

Five minutes later they were seated on the bench and listening to the river beyond, now running at a far more usual pace, its pitiless flow settled into a musical backdrop for the warm afternoon. Bix had poured the tea and was pointing out bird calls as they came, tui, fantails and, 'Over there, up on the flax flowers, lovely pair of waxeyes, they'll be fighting the fantails for a feed soon enough.'

Alleyn smiled as he allowed the sun and the strong tea to warm his tired limbs. It had indeed been a long night followed by a long day, the birdsong was sweet and the sound of the river positively soothing. He might have given in to the warmth and closed his eyes for a moment, until Bix revealed his ulterior motive for the tea.

'The thing is, Sir, I don't know—well, how did you know?'

'Know what, Bix? You were with me much of the time, you saw what I saw.'

'Yes, Sir, but putting the pieces together, I mean.'

'I'm not sure I did put all that many together, I simply noted them as they revealed themselves and followed them to their logical conclusion.'

'All right, so tell me how you did that.'

Alleyn nodded his head and took a deep breath, then he began, 'There were the discrepancies in the interviews of course. Glossop was so sure he'd seen Matron and the vicar leaving her office, and yet he later admitted he'd kept his eyes tight shut against the storm. There was every chance they left separately, or that Matron did not exit through the door at all.'

'Then did you know all along that Matron wasn't dead?'

'No, not consciously. When I first chose to open the body bag on Will Kelly's trolley I had assumed it held the missing payroll. Matron's body was as much of a surprise to me as it was to everyone else. But then Hughes told me that he had a valuable knowledge of particularly effective anæsthetic. He also said Matron had been kind to him, she had listened to him when he needed a confidante.'

'And that's how you knew Matron had doped herself?'

'That's how I guessed she might have. It was entirely supposition on my part, without my usual medical experts to hand, the vials and concoctions in the morgue are just so many names on paper to me. I have come across many of them in my line of work, of course, but I'd never leap to an accusation without solid proof and that was impossible last night.'

'Especially once Matron's body had disappeared.'

'Exactly.'

'And did you always suspect the vicar?'

'Again, it was a combination of things. Unlike the rest of you he studiously spoke of Matron in the past tense. This struck me as odd at first and then, as the night progressed, it seemed positively intentional. I didn't know why he was doing it, but I knew it wasn't right. Even in our little re-enactment, as he walked across to Matron's office, there was something in his manner that was off. I honestly couldn't have said more than that though. There was one other thing, something I entirely missed.'

'Sir?'

'It was when we were preparing for the re-enactment. You were dealing with your soldiers—'

'Yes, and if I'd have been paying attention then, I'd've noticed that neither Brayling nor Sanders could swear hand on heart that Pawcett had been with them.'

'You were paying attention, Bix, your men were covering for their comrade. We make a choice to trust those we lead.'

'That's kind, Sir. Go on then.'

'While you were doing that I was with Father O'Sullivan and Sydney Brown, and I heard a most peculiar sound. The vicar assured me it was a possum, screeching in the bush. Once he disappeared and the van roared off, I realized what the sound really was. It must have been the ratcheting of the jack as Matron changed the tyre. I knew I recognized it as something more commonplace to me than one of your native birds or the invader mammals, I simply could not place it in that context. More fool me.'

'Ah, come on, no one would expect you to have picked up on that, Sir.'

'Be that as it may, once I heard the van's engine roar into life I immediately recognized the sound I had heard just minutes earlier and I knew that someone else must have been changing the tyre at that exact moment. Given the circumstances, the most likely suspect was Matron.'

'Smart, Sir, very smart.' Bix nodded and took a gulp of his tea. His next question came from a deeper place, 'And Pawcett, Sir? What do you think about him?'

'I think you can't feel responsible for the man, Sergeant.'

Bix shook his head, Alleyn had hit right at the heart of his concern, 'Ah, but I do, so your thinking I can't makes no odds. I can't for the life of me work out what'd turn a man, a soldier, and a good one by all accounts, to that. To spying.' Bix said the last word as if he were spitting.

'Nor I, but we know it has happened before and will no doubt happen again. We also know from his fellows that Pawcett was unhappy, we know from young Sydney and from Sanders's interview that Duncan Blaikie was in the perfect position to be useful for our enemies. A man with both radio interest and access to a tract of land reaching right up to the peaks is quite ideal. What we don't yet know is for whom they were working. It is to be hoped one of them has the decency to come clean. I suspect it may be Pawcett, where Duncan Blaikie seems both dangerous and persuasive, Pawcett's is a sadder case, more a matter of his boredom and disaffection with the war.'

'With respect, Sir, we've all had a gutsful of war.'

'I agree, Bix. Heartily.'

'And we don't all go and do something bloody stupid like that.'

'We don't, and I'm sure there are any number of psychology professors who would tell us it was something in Pawcett's makeup or his childhood, some sadness or perversion that sent him in one direction and his two comrades in another. The law is only interested in what he did and with whom.'

'Too right, and so it should be.'

Alleyn finished his tea and stretched out his legs, his hands behind his head. 'You were good to bring me out of my little room, Bix, I could very easily take a nap in the sun right now, a contented cat curled up on a garden wall.'

Bix peered at the detective, his face screwed up in wonder. 'What is it, Bix?'

'You, Sir, last night you were all—'

'Cold and clear?' Alleyn asked lazily.

'That's it, and now you're just—'

'Relaxed, yes. It won't last. I've learned to take my moments when I can.' Alleyn's mouth twisted into an amused smile, 'Rather like Matron and the vicar.'

'Nothing like them, Sir, they're flamin' daft as a brush, the pair of them.'

'Daft? Oh yes. But misguided I think, rather than wicked. And with the money returned, their explanations given—they told your local force about the problems with their respective buildings, you understand, not their moment of youthful exuberance—I rather feel that even Mr Glossop might consider them foolish rather than criminal, however brutal it was to so upset their friends.'

'And knocking out poor Will Kelly, don't forget.'

'Sadly, they will leave their posts under a cloud, without any of the fanfare both might have hoped for after a lifetime of service. A warning to us all, I feel.'

'I can't see you doing anything so foolhardy.'

'No?' Alleyn asked. 'There are some who would consider a lack of impetuousness a shortcoming.'

'Mrs Bix would be one of them, but not me, Sir. I like to know where I am with people. Not fond of surprises.'

Alleyn waited, Bix was not ready to finish their little chat, there was one last question bothering him, but he couldn't bring himself to ask. The detective sat up and turned to the sergeant, 'You want to ask about the murder, don't you?'

'Honest, I don't mind if—you know, if you don't want—I mean, yes. I do. How did you know? How could you know?'

'There was a moment in the night when I asked myself two questions. What else was going on, and what was I being distracted from seeing?'

Alleyn ran his hand over his face, a cloud crossed the sun and their warm spot became cooler, his moment of relaxation was gone. Murder. It always came back to murder.

The detective bit his lip, frowned and then spoke, not looking at the sergeant, 'It was a combination of things, as this work so often is. Not so much the words young Sydney said, but the way he said them. It was something to do with him choosing tonight to come out to the hospital, when he'd been asked to do so for weeks, and the timing of that visit coinciding with the information I'd been given. It was to do with his sudden anger and exhaustion. It was the way he was clearly so very frightened. Some assumed his fear was to do with a chariness about illness or death or hospitals, others that it was his anger manifesting as fear—anger at being left his grandfather's land, forced into farming, forced to give up his dreams. Then there was Will Kelly talking about the rarity of people dying at the exact opportune moment. How so often they don't die when the beloved has arrived, when the family have gathered. It is far more common that the reverse happens, many of us die alone. I know this to be true from my own experience.'

'Mine too,' Bix agreed. 'We were waiting days when my old man went, then I popped out with my mum to pick her up a bit of shopping, and when we got back, he'd only gone. She gave me an earful, as if I could've known.'

Alleyn smiled, 'I think all of those considerations played a part in giving me pause, reminding me to look more closely at what wasn't shown, listen to what wasn't said.

But it was something Sydney did show, to all of us, that finally made me quite certain that old Mr Brown had not died naturally.'

'What was that?'

'It was the way he held onto that pillow, the whole night. We all assumed it was a comfort blanket of sorts. Here was a young man, facing his first death, it was late at night, he needed the ease of a pillow. He had fallen asleep on the floor after all, hugging to himself his grandfather's pillow, sleeping at the foot of the old man's empty bed. But of course that wasn't the case. Sydney Brown held onto the pillow throughout the night because it was the murder weapon. What better way to hide a weapon than hold it to your chest for all to see?'

CHAPTER THIRTY-SEVEN

My dear Fox,

I write to you sitting on my metaphorical trunk, packed and ready to move on again. Everyone here has been sworn to secrecy and I am pleased to say I think we can trust them to keep their promise, all too many of them are mortified when they think of their mistakes, foolishness, and yes, actual crimes. Meanwhile, of course, the punishment that life exacts has taken its toll on the innocent as well as the guilty, as is so often the case. I haven't time now to give you chapter and verse about each of the players, but a few details will, I know, pique your interest for the longer letter I shall send when I am settled.

Almost everyone here at Mount Seager seems to have placed trust in someone and found it misplaced or been prepared to cross a line for love or greed. Are we really such weak fellows that all we need to stray from the path of righteousness is the lure of a charming friend when we embark on wickedness? Or are my culprits just as they claim, turned bad by an accident of opportunity rather than intent? Expedience being

the real evil. Whatever the case, the current impecu-
nious nature of both hospital and church, the presence
of the payroll cash, the vicar being called for the dying
man, Matron having received a camel's straw of a
final demand notice, created a perfect storm of oppor-
tunity, one I witnessed despite being in situ *for an*
entirely different case.

The darker case of the old man's death will follow
the course of the law, and there I can find no solace
in thinking that chance played a great part, only that
a disturbed and already alienated young man was used
in a callous and brutal way, causing him to do an
unforgiveable thing. Certainly I fear he will never
forgive himself.

As to the wider matter, you will understand I cannot
commit any of that case to paper and so your interest
must remain piqued until I am able to tell you face
to face. The fellows in charge of my work here in
New Zealand are giving out that I have been in
Auckland since my arrival, they are certain there's
more going on in the environs of Mount Seager than
we have been able to uncover so far. I must say, the
almost impressive refusal to give us any information
at all on the part of those concerned, suggests that
there is rather more going on than we guessed at,
casting a wider net than we had hoped.

Now however, I have been called up to Auckland in
actual fact. I shall journey by steamer to Wellington
where I have some meetings in parliament to share
more frankly the information I have gleaned and about
certain other matters I cannot even tell you, dear old
thing. Then by rail to Auckland all the way through the

centre of that island. I'm rather looking forward to it,
the spiral route the train takes is quite breathtaking. Of
course, I shall not speak of it to anyone, those in New
Zealand must believe the London detective has been in
Auckland since his arrival and it is to Auckland I must
go, as if I were never here. How very Puckish of me.
*   I remain yours, as ever,*
*   Alleyn.*

P.S.—do remind me to write to you of the porter
when I can. While I am not at liberty to name him,
I have no doubt you might easily conjure up the image
of a cheery older man, wiry and strong, capable of
drinking any amount of beer, to all hours, who—with
but one mouthful of spirit added to his lemonade—
becomes at first the perfect babbling fool and then a
snoring somniac, and thus facilitates the oldest of
trickster crimes, the body swap.

Alleyn blotted the notepaper and carefully folded it into
the envelope, he addressed it to Fox and set it aside. He
regretted that he was not able to give more detail, he knew
his companion in crime would have been interested in
Pawcett's choice to align himself with traitors when he had
initially joined up as enthusiastically as his friends. Fox
would have been perplexed but interested in Pawcett's
certainty that the war was an awful waste and wickedness,
and that any route to stop that waste was worth taking.
He would have professed himself unable to give a view on
the romantic entanglements of their cast, but Alleyn would
have been grateful for a confidant regarding his concern

for young Sydney Brown. No doubt Fox would have been far more phlegmatic about the young man's crime and the necessity of the harsh penalty that would surely come, and Alleyn would have welcomed his certainty.

He reached for another sheet of paper, addressed it simply 'New Zealand', added the date, and began his second letter.

'*My dear Troy*,' he wrote.

He wanted to tell her of the caves and the glow-worms, of the light just two mornings ago, when he had thought the night would never end and yet when it did end, how the brilliance of the mountain peaks at dawn had indeed soothed the savage breast. He wanted to write of the couples he had met, how their love seemed peculiar, excessive, foolish and yet he knew in his own heart that love could be all of this and very much more. There was a great deal he wanted to say to his wife. He paused and set aside his pen. He would write from Auckland.

ACKNOWLEDGMENTS AND AUTHOR'S NOTE

When I was asked to take on the task of turning the few Marsh chapters and even fewer notes into a full novel I was both daunted and delighted. It has not, in any way, been a solo effort. David Brawn and Georgie Cauthery have been generous and supportive editors, and I am grateful to the whole team at HarperCollins for their enthusiasm throughout the process. Thank you to the Ngaio Marsh Estate for trusting us to bring this piece of work to life more than seventy years after it was abandoned. Huge thanks to the Ngaio Marsh House and Heritage Trust for their kindness to me when I visited Christchurch, especially to Margaret Sweet and Lynne Holland who took me out to the land, the river and the mountains—whenua, awa, maunga—to help me set the story, and to Bruce Harding for the very useful suggestion that I re-read Frank Sargeson's short stories and Gordon Slatter's *A Gun In My Hand* to hear again the cadences and phrases of my father and his RSA mates. I have had great support as ever, from my agent Stephanie Cabot, my wife Shelley Silas, and the Fun Palaces team. I am especially grateful to Lauren Henderson/Rebecca Chance for her hugely useful insights into an early draft. I am indebted to Margaret Lewis, both for her *Ngaio Marsh* biography, and her enthusiasm for this work. Aroha nui to the Facebook team of friends and family, editors and archivists, who enthusiastically answered questions about landscape, names, te reo Māori, and the phrases our parents and grandparents actually used, as opposed to the ones we remember them using.

We have chosen to use macrons for the relevant Māori words both because it is accepted usage in Aotearoa/New Zealand and also to help the non-Māori speaker understand the pronunciation of the long vowel.

And while we're on pronunciation, the g in Ngaire—as in Ngaio—is silent.

To those of you who love Marsh and read this book with trepidation—I hope you found something to enjoy here.

To those of you who love Marsh and read it with enthusiasm—thank you, you made it an easier task to take on.

And to those of you who had never read Marsh—I hope this story leads you to many more. You have treats in store.

To Dame Ngaio Marsh herself, from a medium-sized poppy to a far taller one, thank you.

ABOUT THE AUTHORS

Dame Ngaio Marsh was born in New Zealand in 1895. Along with Agatha Christie, Margery Allingham and Dorothy Sayers she was admired as one of the original 'Queens of Crime', best known for her 32 crime novels featuring Detective Roderick Alleyn, published between 1934 and 1982, the year she died. In 1949 she had one million copies published on a single day (the 'Marsh Million'), a distinction she shared only with George Bernard Shaw, H.G. Wells and Agatha Christie. Many of her stories have theatrical settings, reflecting Ngaio Marsh's real passion, and as both actress and producer she almost single-handedly revived the New Zealand public's interest in the theatre. It was for this work that the received what she called her 'damery' in 1966.

Stella Duffy is an acclaimed novelist and theatremaker who has twice won a prestigious CWA Dagger for her short stories, and won Stonewall Writer of the Year twice and the inaugural Diva Literary Prize for Fiction in 2017. Born in London, she spent her childhood in New Zealand, has written 16 novels, and is the co-director of the Fun Palaces campaign for greater access to culture for all, and was awarded an OBE for Services to the Arts in 2016. Her website is www.stelladuffy.wordpress.com

ALSO BY STELLA DUFFY